PLACID GIRL

Praise For *Placid Girl*

"If you think this book is just about two high school chicks in a small-town rock band, then you probably think 'Jaws' is just a movie about three old dudes in a boat. After reading and destroying the edge of my seat in the process, I'll never look at a mask again without cursing Brenna Ehrlich's name."

—Ryan Kattner, Man Man

"A mixture of dynamic prose and punk rock attitude makes for a dark, realistic story that won't let the reader put the book down until the last page is turned."

—Tonya Kuper, *Anomaly*

"Ehrlich's voice is the guitar humming just before that power chord rips through the room. She's a fast and loose drum beat. She's a singer of a rousing and utterly captivating song."

—Eric Victorino, The Limousines

"A sharp, funny story about big dreams, small towns, and the bad choices you make on your way to the right one, *Placid Girl* will resonate with the aspiring rock star within you."

—Sarah McCarry, *All Our Pretty Songs*

PLACID GIRL

BRENNA EHRLICH

ALL AGES
PRESS

All Ages Press

Printed in the United States of America

First Printing, 2015

Designed by Ashley Halsey

Cover photograph of Keds by Lauren Grace Bailey

ISBN 9780692490815

All Ages Press
AllAgesPress@Gmail.com

www.tumblr.allagespress.com

For my family. And David Bowie.

ONE

"I make a really good first impression/ The rest is up to you/ If I disappoint/ It's your fault that you're blue,"

—"Not My Problem," *Masking Tape* -Haze

"I can't," I whisper through the all-encompassing suck of the venue—cigarette smoke choked with BO twisting like a wraith through the Christmas lights that festoon the wall, draped over a stuffed marlin that looks like it has never been in the sea. A tumble of kids, all trying to sit on the same (likely) bedbug-infested couch, eye me and my bandmate Sarah through the gathering indoor fog. The pathetic little throng of moshers has long since stopped throwing themselves against each other like dancing molecules and are now gaping up at us, the sad state of punk kid dental hygiene on full display. A shard of wood from my splintering drumsticks digs into my clenched palms and sweat runs down my face; my hands shake like I'm trying to execute some kind of crazy too-fast paradiddle.

"Play a fucking song!" someone bellows from the back. Then some asshole shouts for "Freebird," even though I'm like 97.88% sure that no one here even knows what that song is.

"Yeah, come on, Hallie!" Sarah twists around, her hot pink hair flying in her face, her fingers twitching above her electric guitar strings. "Let's do your song!"

Her voice is thankfully a lot less caustic than the dude's in the back, but I feel the panic prickling in the back of my throat. It's closing up. I know it is. If I open my mouth now my voice will shake all over the fucking place like some kind of spring going boi-oing! and I'll be done for. The crowd will feast upon my soul. Young 'n' tender, like veal.

"Play a fucking song!" the voice rasps again, and then the crowd starts pogoing, a faceless sea of black and denim and dyed hair and tattoos and menace, menace, menace. I can't. If I play this song I'll puke. Projectile vomit all over the audience. I guess that would be really punk rock, but probably not the kind of punk rock I want to be remembered for.

"No, Sarah, let's do the Haze cover. Next time my song. Haze cover this time," I sputter, looking up at Sarah with what I know is a kind of pathetic-little-dog pleading in my eyes. I hate myself as much as I hate little dogs.

She gives a fast little nod and a smile. "Sure, Hallie. Next time."

She turns to the microphone, "Sorry, dudes, technical difficulties in the form of a borderline panic attack, but now we're back!" she crows, lifting her arms above her head. I try not to bristle at the public mockery and hoist my sticks for the count-off.

"We interrupt our regularly scheduled block of, like, original music to bring you this fucking cover from some dude in a mask that my bandmate over here has major lady wood for." She shoots me a twisted smile. "'Placid Girl,' by Haze, the faceless—likely dickless—wonder!"

Just the sound of his name makes my cold sweat dry up and the shakes go away. A kind of warm calm mixed with a jumping-on-the-insides manic energy shakes my skeleton and I slap my sticks together three times and then swoop down to my drums, bashing out the opening notes to "Placid Girl" into the blazing fast beat.

"You'll be sorry when you're gone. You'll be sorry when the road rises up and swallows you," Sarah wails into the mic, tearing into her guitar so that it whines across the venue like a chainsaw that's gotten away from its lumberjack.

"Because the night ahead is long and all the things that you once fled never stopped following you." Her voice gets all throaty and deep and gravelly and I dance behind the kit, puzzle-piecing in clashes and beats and fills.

The crowd surges against the stage, bashing their stomachs and knees and elbows into the lip of the platform, splattering sweat onto Sarah's orange platforms as she dances across the dusty oriental carpets, digging into her guitar solo like one of the Navy guys she's always devouring in cars and on park benches. Everything in my chest feels like it's going to burst. My heart is a thousand balloons, all inflating and squealing and reaching for the sky. Pop, Pop, POP!

"And the wind, yeah it blows cold at your back as the skies roll and break and split, babe."

Massive fill from me.

"You think you know, you think you know—where the lighthouse lies, but you're lost now, babe."

Then my heart tugs and I know Sarah's does, too, because we've been playing together since grade school. I snap my wrists in the air, let them hover over the drums, then start my slow thunder roll, my slow, ominous patter of rain, my generals-and-soldiers-in-the-distance-coming-into-battle beat.

"Placid girl, placid girl. I'll tell you what—you can have me..." Sarah is barely strumming now, kneeling on the edge of the stage as the crowd huffs and puffs in the wake of their violent moshing, waiting for the next excuse to launch into another bout of socially acceptable battery.

Sarah levels her eyes at some poor slob in the front row, a pretty kind of dude who looks older than us, floppy brown hair and green eyes—wide and dreamy-looking—that match his T-shirt. He's standing next to a kid who's scribbling furiously in a notebook, the brim of his army hat low over his brow, his light brown hair hanging all down his face.

Sarah always does this—chooses some guy in the front that she thinks is hot and then sings right to him. Usually—after getting a look at her ample talents—they got a look at her other talents, if you know what I mean. Of course you do. My use of innuendo is painfully obvious. I blame my chronic virginity.

As I patter away at the hi-hat, though—slanted rain on the window sounds now—I realize that Big Eyes in the front isn't looking at Sarah, he's looking at me. And he's smiling. Sarah falters for a moment, unable to lock in his gaze because it's fixed right on my red-as-Communism face, then switches her focus to a kid with a face full of metal. Not her type at all, but he'll do in a pinch.

"Fill me up and make me whole," she croons huskily into his eyes, and I'm surprised all the metal doesn't melt off of his face in a sea of molten goo. "Wear my mask, hold me close—and we'll both be happy."

After Sarah whispers the last line, practically brushing her plump lips against the guy's pincushion ear, she slinks back toward me to a roar of applause that sounds like a million lions leaping on two million gazelles. Triumphant carnage. Sarah gives a little hip shake and the crowd screams again and I throw her a weak smile. I'm not particularly keen on the sheen of voluptuous sexuality she casts over Haze's music. Especially when she tosses it at "Placid Girl." It seems a little like sacrilege to me. But every time I bring it up she threatens to stop doing the covers all together and that, honestly, would be like someone chopping off my hands, feeding them to my mom's cat Little Edie, and telling me to keep playing drums. What's the point?

"We got one more for you!" Sarah yells, strumming on her guitar, fast and freight-train furious, riffing. "This one's an original and it's called 'Johnny's Got the Clap!'"

I'm not the biggest fan of our '50s girl group throwback numbers, so I kind of go on autopilot when Sarah shouts, "Well I met him on a Friday! And I kissed him on a Friday! And I fucked him on a Friday! Now I know-ow, Johnny's got the clap!"

I clap three times and swoop toward the drums to patter out the painfully simple rhythm.

As my hands fly over the kit I start to regret not playing my new song, "Smaller Town," and then I start to get the shakes again and take a deep breath. Sarah and I had first formed our band— My Friend's Band—after chorus auditions in fourth grade. Sarah had insisted on trying out with a Donnas track about killing some dude's girlfriend. I had vomited all over the accompanist. Needless to say, neither of us got in. After helping the janitor clean up my mess, we went over to my house, where we decided that we didn't want to sing religious standards and medleys from "Les Misérables," anyway, and we formed our own band. I opted to be the drummer—partly because of the banging on things and partly because I could sit in the back—and she wanted to sing, since when she opened her mouth to do so words actually came out in lieu of lunch.

And from that day on, she was the one who wrote the songs. I don't know what it is, but every time I sit down to write lyrics I feel like a liar. Like I don't know anything about living at all so who the hell am I to make some kind of grand statement about it that people can also dance to? I always feel like I need to get married or divorced or have a baby or die before I can create anything worth making. Or, like, maybe just kiss a dude first. "Smaller Town" is kind of about all that, but it just seems like shit next to anything and everything Haze has ever written.

I'm letting the beat lag and I perk up, swinging a stick around my fingers and drum-rolling into the end of the song. The man in the front row is still looking at me, his head cocked to the side and a lazy smile on his face. I look back down at my kit and concentrate on the end of the song. No more distractions.

"I'm gonna slap you, Johnny—it's just like the clap! But with one hand!" Sarah yells, letting her guitar fall against her hips and her hands fly into the air. The applause is less cacophonous than it was for "Placid Girl," but there's a good many people rolling around on the floor now, hopefully having fun and not bleeding from the head.

Sarah turns to me and sticks her tongue out, her bangs plastered to her forehead. "Everyone here is ugly! Let's go home!" she shouts with a grin, then fake collapses onto the stage.

I nod. I'm not really into hanging around after shows among the masses. When Sarah does manage to find someone out there in the morass whose face she wants to lick, as she so eloquently puts it, I always get stuck talking to his friend. Which would be fine if I was not the worst ever at talking to guys. And I am the worst ever. Like that whole vomiting at the choral audition thing? That's probably what would happen if I talked to male people. And the ensuing moments would likely go just as well.

Sarah grabs her amp and guitar and leaps off stage and I follow more slowly, sticking my drumsticks in the back pocket of my jeans and shading my eyes against the stage lights. The patio door at the left side of the venue slides open and the kid with the notebook and the army hat sidles outside, a cigarette in his mouth. His friend isn't with him. Little afterglow flashes like fireflies dance across my eyes and I blink.

"Hi." The voice is soft. It licks at my ear like a cat.

I jolt around and my drumsticks fly out of my pocket, careening across the stage in opposite directions. The man from the front of the crowd rolls forward like a wave and sweeps them up. I think crazily of boats and sailors and crying ladies by the sea. Then the tide comes in and I realize I'm standing there with my mouth open like a guppy. I stare at the front of his green T-shirt and try to breathe.

"Uh," I say.

"I liked the way you play," he says, his face easing into a smile as if I had not spoken—or, rather, grunted.

"Good, thanks," the words fly out of my mouth. What question am I even answering? What conversation is my mouth having that my brain isn't present for?

The man laughs softly, a sound like burbling water and jingle bells in the snow. "I mean, you feel it. I can tell that you do—especially when you were playing that 'Placid Girl' song. You're digging out something that's not right there in the words that beats below the surface like a vein, you know? Some people think the heart of the band—the singer—is the most important, but I think it's the veins, you know? The ones that take the lifeblood where it needs to go. They understand how it's all connected."

He swings my splintered sticks, black with wax, around his white, white hands. The sticks look almost obscene there. His hands look like they should be clasped together in prayer. Like a saint's.

I nod, dazzled by his words. By the recognition. Usually all I get from people is, "Whoa, dude, I didn't know a girl could play drums like that," before the guy moves on to talk to Sarah. I always felt like playing drums was something more. That it was everything in the cracks of music. The veins, like he said.

Instead of agreeing, though, or adding anything to his rumination, I just nod, eyes wide.

"You're shy, huh?" His smile is slow and warm.

I nod, slightly desperate. I'm not sure what it is about talking to guys—what freezes me up so much. Maybe it's having been friends with Sarah for almost a decade. When you're used to guys acting like you're invisible, when they actually look at you, you tend to react like a ghost that's been haunting an empty castle for too long. And then there was that whole Nick thing. That thing that I was supposed to bury like the corpse of said ghost and forget, not let sit in the attic of my mind like someone's dead mom in a horror movie.

"Well, would you like to go up on the roof and talk? I have a joint. We could, like, smoke and look at the stars." The man inclines his head to the side, his lashes casting filigreed shadows on his pale cheeks. His face looks like a damn church floor at noon.

Heartbeat in my ears—an erratic beat like drumming drunk. Hands missing the skins and ricocheting off of the metal rims.

"I, uh." I can't see Sarah anywhere. The crowd is emptying out onto the patio to smoke or onto the street below to shamble home and this man is so close I can smell his skin—all clean and soap. I stare at the fabric of his pristine T-shirt—he'd thrown on a denim jacket—and wonder how he managed to stay sweat-free through the whole performance. Meanwhile, I am covered in salt and mustiness and I can smell my own armpits.

I look up and his face is expectant. Waiting. "I... uh, have to go. My friend—she's waiting," I blurt.

I dash past the man and bash through the door to the club and into the night.

Two nervous breakdowns handily averted. Experiences of note logged, a big old zero. Drumsticks left in the hands of a stranger at a venue: A pair. A total breakeven of a night.

Outside, a kind of sideways mist of rain starts to fall, cooling my forehead and plastering my T-shirt to my back. A few smokers lurk in the shadows, exhaling little puffs of white into the humid air that curl up toward the streetlights like a cloud of ghostly moths and dandelion fluff. Otherwise, the road and sidewalk look pretty deserted. Sarah isn't among the smokers—I don't see her pink hair glowing neon bent over a light. The rain starts to fall in fat droplets, splatting on my cheeks and shoulders and I curl my arms around my sides. I consider my options. On one hand, I feel like sprinting down the street as the downpour starts, letting rivers of water snake down my back and soak my jeans and turn me into a super-fast, land-locked eel. On the other, I really want to go home and dry off, curl under my covers in warm, clean clothes and listen to the storm like a voyeur watches a couple going at it through a window.

Instinct number two wins out when I start to shiver. Most of the time I get pretty pissed at myself for not following instinct number one.

Sarah's brother Tim always picks us up after gigs, so I crane my neck to see if his car is tucked down an alley somewhere, him bent over a book while Sarah reclines shotgun, picking her nails and looking out at the rain, impatient. But all the alleys are deserted, and I don't see any headlights slashing through the fog and gloom in the distance. Besides, if Tim wasn't here yet, Sarah would be out here with me, cursing and jabbing at her phone.

My cell buzzes in my pocket a few times—service at the venue is crap and it takes a while for messages to get through after rejoining the real world—and I pull it out and squint at the glowing screen, flecked with falling rain. There's a few new "Likes" on this photo-sharing app that I like to use to take pictures of our band and the bands of others. I made my username "HazeGirl" in a fit of ill-advised fandom while tipsy on too much of my mom's pilfered prosecco. It makes me cringe now, but I can't change it.

Most of the "Likes" are from Sarah—a string of them on every picture I've posted in the last day or two. My stomach drops. This massive show of support seems a little like overkill to me—like she's trying to make up for something in advance. I click over to my texts. My entire history is basically just digital missives from Sarah—and a few from my dad—and the most recent one is no different: "Hey! Was bored and left with the guy with all the piercings. Sorry! I owe you trolley money and/or one of your shitty shows."

"Ah, no," I mutter as rivulets of water pour down my face. I blink into the downpour for a few more seconds, contemplating the 20-minute walk home, and then I sprint to the little barely covered booth on the corner where the trolley stops. Yes, the trolley. Before you get any fancy ideas about streetcars or whatever, the trolley service in my town is not half as organized as all that.

A few years back, the government or whatever decided to try to amp up our "historical value" by buying all these buses tricked out to look like old wooden trolleys—all shining wood and red paint and gleaming brass fixtures—to take corpulent tourists from one sad attraction to the other. This was all completely missing the fact that most tourists have cars and are perfectly capable of carting themselves the half mile between the salt-encrusted whaling ships bobbing in the water and the pizza restaurant that made an appearance in some shitty movie 30 years ago. Apparently the government was unable to ship the trolleys back to sender—maybe they lost the receipt?—so they became a kind of sad bus service for us locals. And, seeing as how we already live here, they decided that they didn't need to impress us or anything with such things as upkeep, so the trolleys are just these weird, hulking monsters—scratched up with obscene, anachronistic graffiti, all the fixtures dull like dead doll eyes.

As sad and pathetic as the trolleys are, however, I'm pretty happy when one pulls up right away and I can climb on, sit on one of the moldering wicker—wicker!—seats and watch my sleeping town tick by. In the fake gaslight glow, I pull out my phone to pass the time until we get to the fabled movie pizza restaurant, which squats at the base of the hill my house is on. I click through my notifications again, hoping to find something new, something I missed before. Yeah, it's a long shot, considering I only have one friend, but it's better than watching all the strip malls and underpasses undulate by like the various and sundry rings of hell.

No new texts from Sarah. No tweets or Facebook things. I click back to the photo app to look at my pictures from tonight—Sarah smiling in the empty club under the marlin before the show, me and her with our faces smashed together in front of the stage, her blue eyes bright and clashing with her hair, my black hair mingling with hers and my smile close-mouthed and not really that smiley. I look at the picture for a second, feeling irritation rise in my chest that she had just *left* me there, when I notice that there's two "Likes" there under our chins—one from Sarah and one from a user named, simply, "ZZZ."

I furrow my brow. I don't get a lot of followers on this thing—mostly because I don't grub for them, like most kids do. I mostly use it to mess around with Sarah, or take pictures of weird stuff that makes me laugh—like this woman who lives in our town who has been wearing a corset for the last 40 years. She looks like a hornet and sometimes I see her at the grocery store, buzzing around the fruit section. I feel mean taking pictures of her, but, I mean, she's wearing a corset—she must expect it, right?

Anyway, what I mean to say is that I'm not someone random people tend to follow. I click on the profile name to see if there are any clues. Immediately, I notice that "ZZZ" is less popular on this app than me, even—s/he has zero followers and s/he's only following one person. Me. There are a couple of pictures in the feed, but I can't make them out—they're mostly red and black and cast in shadow. I click on one of them and almost drop my phone. There, framed by a gold gilt mirror with a flash exploding like gunfire in the center of his bare chest, is a tall man. His thin hips jut out over the top of tight black jeans, and a blackbird tattoo adorns his right shoulder. His whole body suggests confidence and ease, but I can't see what his face projects—oh no. Because ZZZ's face is covered by a black, featureless mask. He looks just like Haze. Or, rather, his body does—and there's the mask thing.

To back up, as I'm assuming not everyone is as down with weird-shit music as I am—Haze, the guy whose song we covered at the show?—no one knows who he is. In both the "he's pretty obscure so his fanbase is pretty select" way and the "no, like, no one knows who the fuck he *is*" way. He always wears a mask—different colors, all blank. No animals. No giant eyeballs. No robots. Just always... blank. Or, I should say, "he always *wore* masks"—he's been on an indefinite hiatus for five years now. Still, I keep listening to his records and covering his songs, hoping that he'll come back. I mean, he has to come back—he's, to put it extremely lamely, my only hope. And I say this because he came from my shitty town and he got out of my shitty town and when he did he started making music that made me feel like something good could actually come out of my shitty town. Something other than decaying trolleys.

So that's why my mouth has been open for roughly five minutes and I'm nearly drooling on my phone right now. Haze. ZZZ. Whoever. The first thought that pops into my head is: "Someone is messing with me." And my money is on Sarah. Haze was—is—kind of an analog guy. I can't imagine that he would ever join a social networking app. And certainly not now—when he hasn't been playing for forever. Still, that would be a lot of effort for a cruel joke. Even on Sarah's part.

My second thought is that "ZZZ" is some kind of crazed Haze fan. It is possible. There are people out there who become so obsessed with their favorite musicians that they start dressing like them—that they would get a tattoo to match their idol's (did I mention that Haze has a tattoo of a bird on his shoulder? He does. It's adorable... is the kind of thing I would think if I were a brainless idiot). And Haze did have a pretty weird fanbase—present company included. But still—why? Why would someone create a profile and only follow *one* person? Why would he follow me—aside from the whole Haze-in-my-screen-name-thing? I'm not so vain as to think that my selfies put this dude over the edge. Also, he looks to be a real "man"—like an adult. Which could take us into some seriously creepy Lolita territory.

My heart is still drumming in my chest. I consider for a moment just putting the phone away—or blocking the guy—but curiosity takes over and instead I click on his profile and hit "follow." Immediately after doing so I toss my phone on my lap and cover my face because he can totally see me through the phone.

"Oh, Jesus, what the hell did I do?" I moan into the window, happy that I appear to be the only one on this trolley. I don't have time to get my face sufficiently smooshed into the glass before my phone chirps and hops on my lap. I give it a massive dose of side-eye, aware that I probably look insane to all the ghosts of tourists past riding with me, then scoop up the device and squint at it through one slitted eye.

There's a new notification. A private message from "ZZZ." All it says is Hi.

I poked the beast and it grunted. I click back to the pictures and scroll through—taking in the skinny chest, the broad span of shoulders. His body certainly looks like Haze's—not that I stare at pictures of his body or anything. He also just uploaded a new picture—just a second or two ago—a photo of an electric guitar against the red wall. My finger hovers over the "message back" button and I swallow down what seems like an inordinate amount of saliva.

Hi, I type back. Nice guitar. My heart sprinting through my chest, I press, "Post."

The phone pings again. Thanks. Do you want to be a drummer? I guess he had seen the copious photos of coveted drum kits in my feed that I had snapped at the music store and uploaded for later drooling-over.

I furrow my brow. Do I want to be a drummer? What else was there? I had always wanted to be one—or, at least, a musician. One of my earliest memories is of lying under the piney-smelling table in the dining room, pounding quiet rhythms into the soft carpeting and singing nonsense songs to the cats. I'm not good at anything else. Well, maybe math, but math doesn't make my body tingle and shake so much with joy that I feel like my skin is going to flay itself off.

Yes, I type back, then look at the photos again—at the man's shoulders and chest and tattoo and mask. I picture him grasping a microphone, sweat pouring down his temples as he leans over the crowd, calling out the words that I have etched into my brain from so many listenings. Could it be him? Could it be? And if it is, why is he talking to *me*? I let my finger hover over the keypad for a few seconds longer, then suck in my breath and type, Are you who I think you are?

The breath grows hard in my throat like that stuff dentists use to make models of your teeth. What if he doesn't respond? What if I scared him? What if, what if, what if? That's two legitimate concerns and one random internal blathering. Legitimate concerns are winning out.

The screen lights up again. My name is Legion for we are many.

My skin prickles. I don't know what that means, but it freaks me out a little.

The screen blinks, I'm sorry, bad joke! **ZZZ shoots back.** Maybe, possibly I am... (I don't live inside your brain as there don't appear to be any vacancies), **he writes.** But I want to talk about you. I want to know about you.

My face hurts from a sudden smile of sad, sad proportions. All of this seems like something Haze would say—at least from what I knew of him through his songs. His music always painted him out to be a brash and kind of swaggery guy, but when it came to talking about himself—who he really is—he would hide behind complicated metaphors. And masks.

My stop is rolling up so, with that same, dumbass smile spreading across my face, I rapidly type back, What do you want to know?

TWO

"Don't put all your eggs in one basketcase/ Unless you're willing to break a few,"

                —"Sterilize the Children," *Masking Tape* —Haze

When I push open the front door, soaked from my run up the hill, the light's on in the greenhouse and I can see my dad hunched over his worktable. Green light filters up toward his face, bouncing off of the leaves that his fingers linger over absently. The battered radio near his elbow—plastered with an array of butterfly stickers that signal that the device used to belong to me—blares and crackles, Dusty Springfield's voice rasping about the only boy who could ever reach her.

For a second, it feels like it's a year ago. I almost go over and sit by him—on the floor under the table where the stones are cool and moss grows between the cracks. I almost sit down and tell him about the show—about how that guy had complimented my drumming.

Almost sit down and wait for him to put his cold hand on my head and tell me some story about back when his band used to tour—maybe the one about how he got lost in Amsterdam for 48 hours and slept on the deck of a canal boat with a herd of stray cats until the boat's owner came to chase him away. But I don't. Sit down, I mean. It won't be the same. Doing that—what I would have done—would feel like visiting summer camp in the off-season. Just sad.

I want to just sneak by him upstairs and change, but I'm kind of frozen there in the doorway—transfixed by how zombied-out he's become. Dad used to want to be a musician, too. Or he was, rather. But he gave that up years ago, like he gives up on everything sooner or later. Most recently: (1) my mom, (2) me. Third failure's a charm. My mom gave up on her dreams, too—being an actress—but at least she has the tenacity to vehemently blame everyone else for it: (1) my dad, (2) me.

Dad's eyes seem unfocused, not quite taking in the fresh new life budding beneath his fingertips, the chill creeping through the room of stone and glass despite the summer heat, nor me standing in the doorway. I decide to stand there until he notices me. Only then will I say anything. It's like a game of chicken in which no one is really the winner—if I win, I score another awkward, distant conversation, if he wins, well, then, he doesn't give a shit about me, does he? I lose again, I guess. Either way, I lose.

His shoulders are all hunched and he looks really thin. I try to push it down, but a cold tendril of annoyance blooms in the center of my chest like one of Dad's flowers and I curl my fists at my sides. I just want to shake him. It's not really that often that he's home like this—he's a lawyer at a big music media company in the city and he leaves for work early and it takes him a long time to get home at night. And since this whole deal started with my mom—where she just basically sits in the living room guzzling malbec, mindlessly watching old Cary Grant movies—he's not really home that much at all. I guess most people my age would be excited about said negligence, but I don't know how to drive, so it's more of an inconvenience than anything else. Also a bummer—a huge bummer.

Dad closes his dark eyes and sighs. I do, too, but he doesn't notice, so I turn around to go, defeated. Dad one, me zero. But just as I do, my cellphone jangles in my pocket with a chorus of chirrups, rings and vibrations, and Dad finally wakes up from daydreaming amidst the flowers.

"Ah," he says, settling his face into a pleasant mask. "Hey, Miss Tambourine Girl."

My face folds into a kind of ugly smile—a smile that's almost crying—because this feels so normal. For a second I feel like it'll all be OK—a second that's long enough for the next lyrics from the Dylan song to escape in a whisper from my lips. And I wait. I wait for him to sing out the next line in his scratchy, rich tenor.

Dad's blinking at the plants again, though. The moment has passed. Dusty's lament continues, bouncing off of the stone and glass of the greenhouse—filling every corner with memories of her son of a preacher man. I wonder what it's like to know that one person—like the guy she was singing about. Someone comforting and exciting all at once. Somehow I doubt that such a person exists. Dad obviously can't be that for Mom—especially when the only thing he has been "sweet talkin'" lately is his bonsai tree.

"Mom's gonna be mad if you listen that loud this late," I say, flatly—basically just to break the silence. I wonder if he'll ask me why I'm up at— what?—one in the morning? Why I'm just getting home?

Dad gives a mirthless chuckle and pushes his black knit cap off of his forehead. He's always cold, no matter what the season, so clothes usually designated as "winter wear" are never packed away. Never stowed in cedar chests with the leftover chill from last season—with the gusts of cold air that worked their way into the folds of clothes to be released with a minty sigh months later. It's one of the quirks Mom constantly complains about.

"Your mother, she doesn't get music the way we do, huh, kid?" Dad tries to ask but really just says, the tight smile he had assumed earlier beginning to crack. My gut instantly clenches. I could have just walked by. Gone upstairs and gone to sleep. Instead, I had to be a bitch. I guess I just wanted a reaction out of him. Something other than fake affability. How could he act—so poorly—as if everything was OK? Months ago my parents had taken up residence in separate wings of the house. Dad's domain includes what was once the guest bedroom and bath and the greenhouse that juts out under my window like an overblown terrarium, its own little contained ecosystem of tamed plants and broken terra cotta pots. My mom holds court in their bedroom and the kitchen—and the living room for movie watching, of course. Our cats had even been split among the two—that's right, my parents have their own separate pets. Mom got Little Edie. Dad's cat, Big Edie, died three months ago. It would be funny if the whole thing weren't so wildly depressing.

Dad pulls off his hat and runs his hand through his thick black hair—the same black as mine but matte somehow—and reaches for a pair of gardening scissors. The plant in front of him is so perfect that it looks almost plastic, so I can't imagine what he has to prune. He seems to realize as much and puts the shears down, then reaches toward the stereo again.

"OK, I'm going upstairs now," I say with a sigh. I'm soaking wet and I want to see if ZZZ has responded. The electronic symphony my phone performed moments ago would suggest as much.

Dad frowns. "Why don't you sit with me a bit? I was about to put on some Janis. We can sing along like we used to?" Even though the words are coming out of his mouth they seem insincere somehow. Like they're an echo from a few years ago.

To be honest, I always identified with poor, tragic Janis much more than the Dustys of the world. Joplin had never felt that beautiful or desired, either. And she died young. Perhaps if I died tragically and young my family would notice me again. (Sure, it's a melodramatic thought, but I'm a teenager. Those are allowed until I'm roughly 28, right?) I indulge myself in a brief, fangirl fantasy: They'd put my picture in the paper and Haze would see it and fall in love with my black and white newsprint ghost. He would start writing songs again—this time about me—his very own "Sad-Eyed Lady of the Obits." I would become a muse, the stuff of legends like Patti Smith—only more dead. Then I remember that I might be talking to Haze and that death might not, in fact, be necessary to win his affections. I need to get upstairs and see what he said.

"So will you stay?" Dad asks, breaking me out of my mind wander. I feel my phone in my pocket and a flicker of rage in my chest. Now he wants to hang out?

Before I can come up with something less snotty to say, the word "no" flies out of my mouth, followed by the word "can't." I tighten my fingers around my phone, and before the guilt in my stomach can unfurl any further, I swing toward the door.

"Mom is going to tell you to turn it down, anyway," I say weakly, by way of some sort of explanation. "She's always complaining that she can hear it all the way on *her* side of the house." Not stopping to take in the look on Dad's face—it likely didn't give anything away, anyway—I spin out of the room and run upstairs.

My room is full of blue shadows—like ink blooming in a glass of water. I don't feel like turning the light on. Through the window I can see an eyelash of moon and the house next door cowering behind the church spire. A preacher or someone lives there. Whoever tends to the church.

A shiver undulates up my back as I watch the shadows lengthen away from the steeple, swallowing up the light in the upstairs windows of the house. A shape flashes across the pane and my heart claws at my chest—just a little. That house has always freaked me out. Not just because of the religious undertones (I'm an atheist, but I like to think I'm tolerant of other people's delusions of choice) but because there always seemed to be something strained about the place. Like it had watched and watched and watched as families trooped through and was tired of keeping all of their secrets so close. As I look now, the curtains in the upstairs windows twitch closed and the face of the house is painted black.

Suddenly tired, funeral parlor tired, I flop onto my bed and take a deep breath, staring at the pictures fluttering on the wall like bird wings when you startle a flock and they fly up and up and up. Rows and rows and rows of pictures that almost completely cover the pale pink paint that my mother and I had rolled on one spring when things were lighter. Warm-tinged cold air eddies through the window, propped open with an old building block. The rain has stopped.

Pale pink was a ridiculous choice. No one likes that shade after they're thirteen years old. No one but those guys who wear pink shorts in the summer emblazoned with lobsters—a.k.a. douchetrousers, as Sarah calls them. Not that you can see the pink, anyway, as I said. It's plastered over with the only picture of Haze I could find online—tall and wiry and dressed in black. His body all thin and muscled and tense and waiting—for something, I don't know what. I dream—guiltily, quietly, when it's dark out—of tracing his shoulders with my hands and letting my fingers wander up to cup his face. A face that's just a blur in my mind, since it's always obscured.

My fingers tingle as I dig my hand into my pocket and pull out the phone. There's another message from ZZZ: Well, how would you want people to remember you? What would you want people to say about you if you weren't in the room?

What would I want people to say about me? I know what they *would* say. Probably something along the lines of, "She's really quiet and she can play drums pretty good." Because that's all I put out there—to everyone but Sarah, that is. But I know I have, at least, the potential inside to be more than that. I know I have all these monsters tangoing inside me and I could make something wonderful if only I knew how to train them and let them go free, snapping and raging. I think of the song then—"Placid Girl." How it made me feel to play and how that feeling stood in total contrast to the word itself, "placid." How I had always thought of myself as the girl in the song—lost, while simultaneously unable to leave. I always wondered who she really was.

So I just put my fingers on the screen and start typing, not editing myself like I do when I try to write a song.

I live in a placid little town by a placid little seaside, where everyone is born and bred to wear placid little faces. I live by a placid little bridge that goes up and down, separating one side of the placid little river from the other at placid little intervals. But I am a roiling-insides girl and I feel the tide coming in and I need to escape.

Before I can agonize over how overwrought and overdone the words sound, I push "send," grab my headphones from my bedside table and mash them over my ears. I look at the phone for a second, my fingers twitching to read the message over again and criticize what I had said. To add more or apologize for sounding stupid. Instead, I put the device on airplane mode and crank The Orwells. They're singing about looking for girls at the mall. (I try to stagger my Haze listening with other bands so that I don't get tired of the one record he ever released. Not that I ever would.) I switch over to Haze now, though, because I want to hear his voice after talking to ZZZ.

There's a burst of shouting from downstairs and I push my head-phones down on my ears, blocking out the bickering that's become as omnipresent as the clanks of old pipes and creaks of stairs in our humble abode. Looks like Mom got pissed about the stereo after all. Told him.

Other kids were assured in their infancy that ghosts were non-existent by being told "the house is just settling." I know, for a fact, that there are no ghosts here—except the phantom of whatever it is my parents had. No, my house isn't "settling," it's erupting—that's what I think every time I hear those hallmark ghost soundtrack sounds: wailing, moaning, crying, clanking chains. OK, I added that last one in for fun—my parents don't truck with that S&M shit. At least I hope they don't.

I shut my eyes tight and kick my feet up on the wall above my headboard. I'm leaving marks on the part of the wall that isn't covered with pictures, but I don't care—I won't be living in this room for more than another year, anyway. I just bought this pair of Keds a week ago, but they're already scuffed and dirtied. I rubbed them in the dirt in the woods behind the house right after I got home from the mall. Yeah, it was kind of a poseury move, sure—but, come on, who wants to prance around in entirely pristine white shoes? You'd look like a church kid. Like the girl in my class who's totally obsessed with Jesus and wears T-shirts every day with biblical verses on them in all different languages. It's funny what a little dirt does for your image.

I let my eyes relax a little as the music worms its way into my earholes—one of my favorite Haze songs, "Not My Problem." I've probably listened to it a thousand times since I first discovered the band—when the guy down at the record store, Picture Disc, told me that most of the members lived near or around my town growing up and I looked at him like he had just told me that the stars were all just pieces of shiny tinfoil that I could wear in my hair.

I'm trying to figure out the drum part in the middle of the song—it's a tricky deal, not the usual single-drum-beat-pounded-out-fast fare that you find in most punk songs—so I barely notice the window sliding open next to me while I'm sprawled all over the bed. The bed dips drastically and a bright orange platform shoe lands inches from my face. I shoot up and whip off the headphones.

"What the hell, Sarah? Didn't your mother teach you how to use the door?" I sputter, dragging my dirty shoes across the bed to make room for her voluptuous frame as she heaves herself up the last rung of the ladder into my room. Her pink hair tangles into a halo of light for a moment and she looks like a sacrilegious angel as she wriggles across my bed.

Sarah flashes her crooked white teeth and leans back, hanging her feet over the edge of the bed. Sometimes she's considerate like that. Other times she'll puke all over your parents' car and just grin when you get mad.

"Didn't quite make it to that lesson, no," Sarah says, kicking off her shoes one by one and rubbing her feet with a dramatic expression of pain—like one of those theater masks that denote tragedy and comedy. "She got as far as 'If you eat it *inside* the grocery store, it's not stealing' and gave up."

I laugh and stick my hand out the window. The summer air feels all thick around my fingers and firefly-laced. Then I remember that I should be mad at her. That I should yell at her for ditching me. But she's still talking.

"Anyway, I knocked on the door, but no one answered and I texted you before but you didn't answer, so I decided to use the escape route in the opposite manner," Sarah says.

To be honest, I'm not that much for sneaking out. There's little to do in my taffy-laden, ceramic lighthouse-littered town if you don't have your own car. Sometimes Sarah and I climb down the side of the greenhouse right outside my window, though, and drink a couple of Sarah's mom's beers in the woods behind my house. Or we go for drives with one of Sarah's Navy boys. The sad-eyed boys in dress whites usually hang out at the local mall when they're stationed at the base just outside town, looking for local girls to squire them around for a week or two. Girls who remind them of sweethearts back home or mothers or porn stars. They go to the mall to shop for girls and girls go to the mall to shop for them. It's a kind of completely consensual commerce—although many of the boys are older than their local consorts, so the law probably would not agree. The first time Sarah went out with one of them she came back crowing that she was "half a virgin now." I don't really know what that means, being a full-on virgin—in all realms—but it sounds dirty. As far as I know, she's still only halfway there. Which reminds me...

"What happened to Metal Face?" I ask, pulling my hand inside and remembering that I'm still totally soaked. My dresser is all the way over *there*, though. "You *abandoned* me," I mock-moan.

Sarah tosses her hair over her shoulder and rolls her eyes. "I remembered why I hate punk boys. No money for beer," she drawls. "He asked *me* to spot him. Like, he was like, 'I have $12 in the bank until tomorrow when I get paid.' I was like, 'Dude, that's enough for, like, 12 PBRs.' Anyway, I didn't 'abandon' you; I said I owe you trolley money or a show. Fair's fair."

This was our agreement if either of us had to bolt after a show because we met a guy or something. In recent memory, though, Sarah had been the only one to take advantage. She also still owes me a shitload of trolley money.

I cross my arms. "Sure, cool."

Sarah elbows me in the ribs. "I'm sorry, OK!" she makes her eyes really wide and shiny and I try not to smile. "We can go to the shittiest of all punk shows, I promise. I'll even mosh with you." She bashes against me like we're in the pit.

This is a huge concession since Sarah says she hates moshing, so I relent a little and give a nod and smile. Every time I do force her to go in the pit with me, Sarah spends most of her time making sure enormous guys in plaid don't trample me. When some girl elbowed me in the head at the last show we went to, I had to stop her from elbowing back. She says she hates it down there—that she hates getting drenched in sweat and other people's beer—but I've seen her smiling fiercely among the swinging elbows.

"Oh, did you see that you have a new neighbor?" Sarah asks suddenly, lying down on my bed and looking up at me.

"What?" I'm genuinely puzzled. I don't really pay much attention to that kind of thing. The guy who lives next door—the preacher—called me a heathen once when I wore one of those shirts with the upside-down crosses on it. That's about the extent of our interactions.

"Yeah, lady," Sarah says. "I passed them when I was cutting through the woods—there's a big van out front." She pauses for a second and then clears her throat and looks away. "Looks like they have a kid, which is weird, because I saw something in my tarot cards the other day... about a new force coming into your life."

Sarah got really into tarot cards a few years ago—when her dad left. They never seemed to say anything about her, though—just me. Usually, they pronounced I was on the edge of death (but only when I was fixing to do something that Sarah disagreed with).

"Oh yeah?" I lean forward. "Is he attractive—like my kind of attractive?" I laugh and lean back against my headboard. I am not expecting a response in the positive—mostly because I am a horrible cynic and have pretty much resigned myself to being alone forever.

Sarah rolls her eyes. "You mean does he look like he cuts his hair with garden shears, like he stole his clothes from a homeless person and like he only showers once a week? No idea. It was really dark out. I saw him, like, sneaking in the back door on my way here—which is pretty ballsy for a preacher's kid."

"Wait, what do you mean, 'preacher'?" I was hoping from some non-Bible-suctioned neighbors.

Sarah looks at me like I'm simple. "Yes, Hallie, they're moving into the house right next to a church, so I'm guessing they'll be having something to do with that. Anyway, I seriously doubt the son of preacher is going to wind up being an Anarchy Kid—even if he does sneak out at night."

Anarchy Kids are what we call the kids who hang out downtown by Picture Disc—down an alley where there's a coffee shop, old-school video store and an Army Navy store. They usually play in bands or write zines, and every article of clothing they own has been emblazoned with the anarchy symbol. I don't know how political they really are—or how much they really know about anarchy—but they just follow their own narratives—they exist outside in a way that scares me. Needless to say, I never, ever talk to them.

"Well, maybe I'll, like, take over a fruitcake or something," I joke, twitching up the curtain to look out the window. The truck is still in the driveway, I can see through the gloom. All the lights are off now, too. The house looks like it's sleeping—or dead—all the windows dark and curtained.

"Eh, I would recommend staying away," Sarah says, her voice suddenly serious. "You know what I said before? About a force coming into your life? It's not a good one. I have a bad feeling. I had a bad feeling when I saw that kid..." She trails off, looking toward the drowsing house, cast in the shadow of the steeple.

"You always feel that way about every guy in my vicinity," I mutter, almost adding, *Especially one—until you didn't.* I'm supposed to forget about that one.

"That's because you have horrible taste," Sarah says, laughing. She's better at forgetting than me. "Luckily, you're too much of a pussy to talk to anyone. Too busy writing fan fiction or whatever about this dickwad, anyway," she jerks a thumb at my Haze photos.

"You know I would never write fan fiction. Seriously, those girls who drool all over guys in bands are repulsive. Like, don't they know they're *frightening* the dudes with all their rampant, overly public fandom? The only blog out there worth reading, and I mean *only*, is—"

"Q&A... I know," Sarah says at the same time I do, rolling her eyes. Q&A is a blog solely dedicated to tracking down info on Haze. Needless to say, I read it sometimes—and by "sometimes" I mean "every day."

Like I said, I'm not one to gush about Haze all over the Internet—not that many girls do—but I always wonder, "What would Haze think if he met me?" And I know for a stone cold fact he would turn around and book it if I wrote fan fiction. I mean, wouldn't you? And now that I'm maybe talking to him, I'm even more relieved that I never gave into my obsessive urges. I cringe again when I think of my username. Still, he wouldn't be talking to me if it freaked him out. Maybe that's how he found me in the first place—because he saw his name. I fight the urge to switch off airplane mode and see if he's responded.

I sigh. "I mean, I may be a nearly 17-year-old loser who's never kissed a dude, but I'm no mouth-frothing fangirl."

"Fine, fine." Sarah smiles, putting her arm around me and squishing me into her chest. "You're not a freak. Just a prude. Which is why I love you. You make me feel pure by proxy, which reminds me..."

"What?" I groan. I know her "I need a favor" voice well by now.

"Can I stay with you tonight? I really don't want to go home." Sarah's not looking at me, but out the window, and she looks so sad for a second that I feel bad for thinking about the thing that I wasn't supposed to be thinking about.

"Are you OK?" I ask, moving closer to her—she's kind of shivering in her damp clothes. "Did something happ—" I reach out to put my arm around her but she pulls away, grabbing my pillow and flopping down into my covers. I look at her for a second—her bright hair covering her face—then lie down next to her, giving up on changing my clothes. Instead, we curl up in all my covers like a yin-yang.

"Will you sing me the song?" Sarah asks.

I nod, "OK." I made up a nonsense song for Sarah when I was, like, thirteen. One to calm her down when she was angry or sad or just really heartbroken.

I clear my throat dramatically and sit up straight like a star pupil, "Rat bone, blouse luggage, you're a real pearl of a girl. Clamshell, holy hell an oyster brought you into the world. And all the stars at night are just crazy googly-eyes. And all the nightmares you fight are just dreams all in disguise. So sleep, sleep, sleep, sleep, sleep and don't you cry. Goodnight."

Sarah murmurs something down in the sheets and I join her. And we fall asleep, water drying on our faces like tears, the rain starting up outside again and making everything smell like memories.

THREE

"What? What don't you know?" Sarah explodes, falling back on my bedroom floor and reaching for a piece of toast oozing with butter. She crams it into her mouth and chews loudly, and for a few seconds the only sound in the room is this wet crunch, crunch, crunch and the old metal fan on my dresser, whirling and oscillating as it pushes air across our faces. I cringe, waiting for her to swallow.

"I just... All our songs are about guys with diminutive names who kind of suck..." I say slowly, fiddling with my keyboard so that the sound of an old-timey pipe organ bleats from my fingertips. Channeling my frustration into music. How artistic. I switch off the instrument before I can get too distracted by the cat sounds I programmed in as a joke last week. Little Edie stalks in, drawn by an errant "meow," and I pull her into my lap. She purrs into my ribcage and her fur sticks to my humid skin. She's getting thin. I make a mental note to feed her, since it seems my mom isn't.

"So?" Sarah says from the floor, wiping her mouth with the back of her hand. "That's our experience right now. That's what we're living. Write what you know and all. That's a thing. 'Johnny' just reflects what I know. And I know Johnny sucks."

I pick up Sarah's notebook and scan the lines scrawled on the page: "Hey Johnny, yo Johnny, don't you know I hate you Johnny? Don't you know I hate you so much?"

Usually I soften my criticism of Sarah's lyrics with some praise, but there's little here to praise. Sarah has also been extra moody all day. When I woke up, I found her sitting over my laptop, scowling. Her brow was so Neanderthal-like I didn't even bother to yell at her for touching my computer without asking. Let alone smearing it with butter.

I had reached for my phone immediately upon opening my eyes, eager to check my messages. But she had snapped at me when she saw that I was up and told me that we needed to work on new songs *now*.

A quick trip to the bathroom with my cell revealed no new messages from ZZZ, anyway, so my mood right now is about as sunny as Sarah's. I weirded him out. I knew it. This is why I keep my writing to myself.

Sarah stares at the ceiling and I sigh, trying not to get pissed at her. She's not the reason ZZZ didn't write me back. But her reluctance to listen to my criticism isn't making the rejection any easier. I have good ideas. She knows this. She's always encouraging me to actually share my songs with her. But whenever I say anything slightly negative about her stuff—well, watch your balls. Sometimes I wish I could just do everything myself—write all the songs, arrange all the music—but then I remember all my onstage mini strokes and forget about it.

"It's just... you know, maybe we should be writing some songs that don't always fail the Bechdel Test so completely," I say finally, bracing myself for the onslaught.

"The Bechdel Test?" Sarah sneers.

"Yeah, it's that test to see if, like, two women in a book or movie or whatever talk about something other than a man—"

"I know what that means, Hallie, I have the Internet," Sarah grumbles. "It's just that music *is* a failure of the Bechdel Test by principle. What else is there to sing about?"

I nudge her with my toe. "I dunno. I'm guessing, like, Kathleen Hanna and whoever might have some ideas."

Sarah rolls over on her stomach and glares at me. "Whatever. I'm not the one who's constantly making us cover songs by some dude. You get an F- on the Bechdel Test, Hallie. You fail. And if you don't like my songs, here," she shoves her notepad at me. "Write one of your own. It would probably be all about that asshole, anyway, and then you'd have a full-on panic attack on stage if you tried to sing it."

"Whoa," I say, leaning back against the bed. "What the hell, Sarah?"

Sarah covers her face with her hands. "I'm sorry, Hallie. That was bitchy..."

"Yeah, it was..." Little Edie butts her head into my chin, sensing my dismay. I pull her up so her paws are resting on my shoulders. They dance there like little mice.

"It's just... fuck... I mean, look," Sarah crawls across the floor and opens my laptop, pushing it toward me. Q&A's blog is on the screen.

"Why were you reading Q&A?" I ask, wondering what could have possibly made Sarah so upset on a blog that's mostly dedicated to theories about Haze's whereabouts.

"I got a Google alert for the band. Just read it," Sarah groans, pulling the hood of her sweater up and crossing her arms over her chest.

It's a show review post and my heart slams into an invisible wall when I notice that there's a blurry photo on top—it's a really bad snap, but Sarah's pink hair is clearly visible, all wild under the stage lights. You can barely see me, hunched over my kit in the background. My eyes skip down to the text.

"Whoa," I say, then let my eyes rove to the end. "*Whoa...*"

"Right?" Sarah bounces up onto her knees. "*Right?* What the fuck, man?"

I can't look away from the page, so I read it again, more slowly this time. It's no better the second time around:

It can be transformative, sometimes, to hear someone completely unexpected take on a song—it can create a kind of dissonance that makes your heart clench and cry, "Yes! Finally! Something new!" And you can carry that little moment around and take it out and smile at it when the rest of the music world is proving itself to be as thoroughly depressing as ever. I live for those moments. I collect them like sea glass.

Last night's performance by My Friend's Band, *however, did not produce one of those moments. When the fiery-haired lead singer Sarah Park opened her mouth to utter the first few lines of Haze's classic song "Placid Girl," slathering it with so much sexuality that it gleamed like a lubed-up sex doll, it was like a hole had been ripped in my pocket and all my gathered treasures had fallen out.*

It wasn't that she didn't have a good voice—Sky Ferreira would be jealous—it's just that nothing lurked behind it. No pain crackled the varnish. All feeling was suffocated by flash. The only flicker of truth on stage was in the hands of Hallie Reed, who tore into her drumkit like she was looking for answers there that she'd never find. She gleamed in the darkness. She burned. I recommend she join another band.

I try not to linger too much on the last few lines of the review. I try not to smile. I do, however, allow myself to feel like an asshole for wanting to.

"The Sky thing is pretty cool," I say quietly.

"I don't know pain?" Sarah growls as if I had not spoken. "What does he know? What the fuck does this asshole know about pain?"

I put my hand on her shoulder. "I know. That's all so subjective. How people perceive performances. What they want to see and what they get and how they deal with it."

"God, Hallie, why can't you just take my side?" Sarah spins around to look at me, her eyes wide.

I sit back on my heels. "I am on your side. I am. Always."

"No, you're, like, trying to protect him—that Q&A dick. Because both of you are so fucking into Haze. And, what's worse, I think you agree with him."

"I don't!"

I did. A little. Look, I'm not about to go around telling people to tamp down the sexuality or whatever. I'm not some asshole who thinks boobs will undo us all. I just agree that Sarah hides behind the shine a little too much. She has so much inside her. So much that's raw and wonderful. And I wish sometimes that it worked its way into her music. Because if it did, God, she would be ten times more intimidating and amazing than she is now. Although that thought scares me, too. And more than sometimes I feel like a bad friend.

"Then prove it," Sarah says, jabbing her finger at the screen.

"What?"

"It says here this Q&A dude is going to see some Haze cover fuckery at Picture Disc tonight. Come with me and tell him he's wrong to his face."

There is nothing in the world I would rather do less. My hands clench so hard in Little Edie's fur that she yelps. Then I think of Sarah all primed to elbow that girl in the face for me and I nod. "OK. I'm in."

"Fuck yeah!" Sarah yells, and it's the final straw for Edie—she streaks from the room.

\\\\\\\\\\

After hours more of completely fruitless songwriting—and after Sarah has layered on a sufficient mask of makeup—she bounds down the stairs ahead of me, ready for battle. I pause at the top of the staircase, looking toward Dad's room—then Mom's. Cary Grant exclaims charmingly through her open door. I guess she's decided to just forgo the living room entirely and stick to her own shadowed lair from here on out. Maybe Dad's stereo shenanigans had caused her to Little Edie-out. Who knows?

In days past, I would have had to tell someone where I was going, but tonight Dad's still at work and as I stand in the hallway, Edie stalks into Mom's room and the door starts to swing closed after her. As I watch the door travel toward the doorjamb a film-strip of images whirs through my brain: watching Mom etch red, red lipstick on thin lips, smelling like powder and roses before a date with my dad; hiding under an umbrella outside the library, our faces pressed together, smelling books and rain; crying into her all-shades-of-the-sky patchwork bedspread when I was 13 over some long-lost crush. Before the door can close, I stick my sneaker through the crack and poke my head in the room. It smells like roses and powder and she's just standing there, her fist balled up in the front of her robe and her blond hair all tangled down her back. Both of us are really, really pale. We don't tan in the summer—we just burn in spots all over our bodies like trails of slaps.

"Oh, Hallie..." she says, her eyes darting to the TV screen where Grant is running away from a plane in a suit, his tie flapping over his shoulder like a jaunty flag. "What are you up to, little one?"

Immediately I feel about seven years old, the ghost of some prim little sailor dress shrouding my limbs, my bangs all sun-tangled.

"Um, Sarah and I are going to a show... down at Picture Disc," I mutter, kicking a sneaker into a knothole and avoiding her watery blue eyes. We had never had very much in common, Mom and I—it had always been Dad and me kind of stoically trudging through life while she flitted around with a hummingbird feeder or dreamed in a lawn chair in the sunshine. Still, there had been times I had felt her blood in my veins—like when we found a blue robin's egg in an old cemetery down by the sea and glazed it for forever keeping.

Mom nods slowly, her eyes wandering to her bed and that old, blue patchwork quilt. Her hands flutter in front of her like she's folding origami cranes. It always kind of annoyed me how she did that, gestured and then left the gesture out, hanging like some kind of afterthought as the conversation wore on—a sentence abandoned at the comma. Now it tugs at me, filling me with the kind of seasick nostalgia that can hit you in the gut when you find an old concert ticket in your purse or an old coin machine ring you got down at the boardwalk on a day when you went searching for mermaids in the surf with your best friend.

That punch of nostalgia hits me now and I start to sink down on the sky-colored quilt, feeling the nubby fabric under my fingers, familiar as the topography of my hand.

Mom nods, hovering near me, not sitting down. "That's good. I'm glad you're trying, you know, with the music." Her hand wanders up into the sky and hangs there. "When I was your age, I would go to plays all the time, just sit in the darkness and try to take it all in inside me. Contain everything in some corner of my heart so that when I had my shot, it could all come pouring out—all the lights and moments and color."

She pauses, a shadow of a smile flitting across her face, her origami crane hand floating at her side.

I smile and the air in the room seems easier to breathe then. Like I'm standing on some pine-covered mountain bursting with oxygen.

"I'm glad you're trying," she says again, the hand wandering down now with the corners of her mouth. "I'm glad... because you know, I had to give it all up..." She continues and the air chokes in my lungs. "I could have been famous, I think, sometimes... I really do. But I made a decision to give it all up and love. I think that's my biggest regret."

Her eyes wander back to Cary Grant and his immaculately parted hair, forever lush and black. I blink for a second, trying to figure out how to respond to *that*. But instead I nod, barely, and turn to leave. Because I'm not really sure what makes me angrier—what she said about regrets, or that I kind of agree.

\\\\\\\\\

"So where is he? What does he look like?" Sarah's head whips from side to side as she shoulders her way through the crowd. She had stomped and swore the entire 15-minute walk here—past the ice cream shop and the bookstore and the giant section of town that burned down 10 years ago that our government hasn't gotten around to resurrecting. They'd just put up a fence with peepholes in it so that tourists could look out at the ships bobbing on the river and take pictures with their phones. One of the stores had been this miniature shop that Sarah and I used to love—we'd go in and study all the tiny chairs and tables and fake food and pretend we were gods who could shuffle the world at will. I wish the store was still there now, instead of a perch for seagulls—that we could go in and stare at the unmoving watch faces of tiny clocks and believe that we could change the world.

Inside Picture Disc, all the record racks have been pushed to the sides of the tiny shop and a bunch of kids in black hoodies, ripped denim jackets and trench coats line the walls, watching the three-piece band in the middle of room with crossed arms.

"Do you see him? I'm just looking for a dude who looks like he has a tiny dick and everyone here looks like that," Sarah cries, her hair swinging from side to side as she scans the crowd.

I shrug. I don't know what Q&A looks like. He's as secretive about his identity as Haze. My eyes linger over the record racks and I fight the urge to wander over and start browsing—to abort the mission all together. It's a mighty battle between head and soul.

Picture Disc is the only record store for miles. People around here aren't really that into music—unless it's made by auto-tuned crooners or jam bands. The guys who own Picture Disc are therefore like some kind of odd castaways on a desolate desert island—but instead of only being allowed to bring one record with them to listen to for all of eternity, they order the good stuff online from other stores and distributors in the city. I always wonder why they chose to settle down here in the first place. Probably because there's no pressure here to be the weirdest, most eclectic person in town. Just deviate slightly from the norm and you're it. I don't see the normal guys here today, though. In fact, I can't see much over all the dancing bodies.

"Hallie, are you even looking?" Sarah says, grabbing my arm. Her eyes are hooded like a snake's and she looks about ready to start slithering through the crowd, her tongue flicking out in search of her hapless prey.

"Yes," I say, glancing around the room, but my eyes keep getting caught on the three-piece act in front of me, sweating and undulating in front of a backdrop of curling, dusty posters of old rock icons: Jim Morrison with his arms spread, ready to fuck the world, Jimi Hendrix surrounded by a swirling crown of psychedelic flames, Jimmy Page and his double-necked Gibson EDS-1275. I start counting musicians named "Jim" in my head as a loud burst of feedback issues from the kicked-in speakers at the front of the stage. The band is not good. That much is apparent. Yet I still feel that sick shiver of jealousy that I get whenever I see someone else on stage doing what I can't. Making something without hanging in the background.

The bassist is throwing himself all around the room in that way that bassists do to mask the fact that they're not really contributing that much. The lead singer's glasses have fogged up from all his panting. The drummer is—oh, for fuck's sake—holding his sticks wrong, clenching them in his red fists like hammers and bashing the cymbals at irregular intervals. Through all the amateurish noise, though, I can pick out a compelling kind of tune—a harsh-edged twist on '60s rock 'n' roll laced with surprising flourishes. And the lyrics—when I can understand the words seething through the singer's gnashing teeth and flying spit—are actually really good. It's like watching really ugly people passionately make out. That's when I realize that the aforementioned shitshow is actually attempting to cover one of Haze's songs, "The Echo Train."

"Come and ride the Echo Train where all the faces are the same..." I can just make out the words through the lead singer's prominent lisp.

I swing around to look at the crowd, to find someone who looks like he—or she, I guess—might be a critic. Where is Q&A and his/her poison pen? My eyes rove over the stationary figures lining the ring of dancers, most of them with their black hoods up like ragged, evil monks. There's also a small contingent of burly Anarchy Kids in cut-offs at the front of the makeshift stage bashing into each other with guttural growls. No one looks particularly writerly.

The band crashes into the ending of the song—all at different times—and silence fills the air for a couple of seconds as the moshers all pant to their feet.

"Come the fuck on!" One of the evil monks yells by the cash register. I twist around. The monk is waving a record in the cashier's face, but the guy isn't paying attention, he's bent over a little notebook, an unlit cigarette hanging from the corner of his mouth. His brown hair falls over his face, which is shielded by the brim of a fraying Army hat. He looks vaguely familiar.

Sarah's fingers dig into my arm and I notice she's looking toward the cashier as well. "Pencil. He's got a pencil. It has to be him," she snarls, pointing.

My eyes crawl over the boy as he looks up at the band. His thin shoulders jut through the fabric of his gray cardigan—an odd sartorial choice for July. His eyes are green and on the front of his shirt is an Anarchy symbol. His nose is dusted with freckles. Q&A, in the spotted flesh. Or, at least, he could be.

"That guy!" Sarah shouts over the music, crossing her arms, releasing mine. "It has to be him, right?"

I shrug, slowly, my guts having some kind of battle. On one hand, here's this guy who's just as obsessed with Haze as I am. On the other, he hurt my friend. "Maybe," I say, finally, cringing.

"All right then," Sarah says, stomping over to the counter. A group of the monks are staring at her, my best friend with her hair streaming behind her like a pink standard in the medieval breeze. I feel proud. I feel embarrassed. I feel like disappearing.

"You!" She yells, pointing at the boy, then leaning her hands on the counter. "Q and fucking A."

"Me," he says simply. Unblinking. His voice is softer than I thought it would be. Rustle-y and quiet. There's no question there. Just affirmation. I try not to feel excited that I'm meeting him. I try to arrange my face into a mask of indignation. I try.

"You wrote that review. The one about me where you called me a lubed-up sex doll." Sarah's eyes flash and somewhere deep inside me a little voice says, *"About us—the review was about us."*

Q&A shakes his head. "No, I said your rendition of 'Placid Girl' was *like* a lubed-up sex doll. Not you. I would never say something like that about a person."

Sarah laughs. A humorless cackle. "But you would just, like, decide you know someone? You would just decide you know who I am and judge me?"

The boy shrugs, pushing his hair out of his face with the back of a freckled hand. "I wrote what I saw. When you listen to music, you don't get the backstory. You don't get someone's biography. I wrote what I saw and that's what I saw. I'm a reviewer. It's my job."

He seems unfazed by the onslaught, his face carefully composed. I try not to admire him. I've never seen someone withstand one of Sarah's rages and come away without some tears. Q&A's eyes flick over to me then, and it's like he just noticed me standing here. Typical. But what's not typical is the look that passes over his face. Recognition. And just a little smile, like a shaving of sunlight.

"Well, let me tell you something about your 'job,'" Sarah says, air quotes and all. "It sucks. It's soulless. It's a job for dead-inside assholes that can't go to a show and let go and get carried away without overanalyzing everything. It's a job for people who have forgotten how to feel."

The monks are buzzing now and the band has stopped packing up their instruments, frozen and watching as Sarah jabs her finger at Q&A, her voice hard and her eyes brimming. He's barely blinked. He just lets her yell.

"I feel!" Sarah shouts. "And it's not your 'job' to explain my feelings back to me!" Her finger shakes as a tear threatens to break through the border of her lashes and spill down her cheek. She takes one rattling breath, though, and it disappears. Her face snaps back into loveliness and she paints a sneer across her lips. The monks hold their breath and the band looks like they're playing a game of Statue. Sarah's mouth quirks up at the side.

"Besides, anyone whose 'job' it is to swing around a *pen* all the time is seriously compensating for something."

My insides put up a little cheer for Sarah—simultaneously envious that she seems to know what to say in every situation—but when I look over at Q&A he's standing there, looking totally unfazed. He looks like she just asked him how much that Ariel Pink record is instead of questioning the potency of his manhood.

The monks start howling and the band claps from the shadows. "Yeah!" They shout, leaping from the stage to slap Sarah on the back. "Yeah, man, *yeah*!"

They probably know they'll be the next ones to fall victim to Q&A's phallic pen.

Q&A blinks at us and I wonder if he's heard anything that Sarah just said. His eyes fall on me again and I stare back, kind of helplessly.

"C'mon, Hallie," Sarah growls, pulling me by the elbow toward the door. "I'm done here."

Night had fallen outside while we were being buffeted between sweating skater kids and I can hear the dying whale cry of a foghorn out on the ocean and smell the salt rolling off of the waves. A somber hoot sounds in the distance and Sarah swears—a really dirty word. "The fucking drawbridge. The fucking drawbridge is going up. We're stuck here for another 15 fucking minutes."

Oh, did I mention that our town has a completely impractical drawbridge that tourists really like taking photos of? Well, it does.

The door jingles open and I spin around, shocked to see Q&A blinking under the streetlights. He's taken his hat off and his hair snarls around his face like a thornbush, his eyes gleaming through the thicket.

"Wait..." he says, coming toward us with his hands up. It looks like he's directing traffic. Or asking the congregation to pray.

"Oh, shit, come on," Sarah rolls her eyes, stomping down the alley toward the main street. "Come *on*, Hallie!" She calls over her shoulder, not looking back.

"No, wait," he says, his hand closing on my forearm.

I throw it off, shocked, "Don't *touch* me, dude!"

His eyes widen and he puts up his hands again. "You're right. I'm sorry. I just wanted to talk to you. To—"

"Apologize for being an asshole to my friend? Is that it?" I ask, my whole body burning. I said before that I'm shit at talking to guys, but right now I'm mad. I'm mad. I'm mad at this guy for pissing off Sarah. I'm mad at Sarah for making a scene at the record store I've been shopping at since I was a kid. I'm mad at myself for letting everyone drag me all over the place in silence. I want someone to punch—metaphorically, maybe literally—and right now this guy with his Anarchy T-shirt and forest creature eyes looks pretty punch-able. I feel something coiling down there in my chest—something like you feel when you're in a car at night and it crests a big hill and doesn't slow down as it rolls down into even more darkness. A kind of wild tug right there, where the heart's supposed to be.

"Don't you think before you write?" I snarl. "Don't you consider what it would be like to be the person you've eviscerated? Existing out there, reading what you've written?"

"No, I don't," Q&A says flatly and before I can say anything else, he continues in a kind of soft monotone. "There's very few places in the world where I can say whatever I want and my blog is one of those places. Besides, I'm pretty sure I have undiagnosed Tourette's." His mouth quirks up into a half smile and I gape at him.

"That's your excuse?" I sputter.

"No, it's my outlet. Your friend seems to have no issue getting up on stage and talking about some guy's infected junk. We all have to find our places to be honest. My blog is mine." Q&A hasn't taken his eyes off my face. I look down at my shoes. I don't have that place.

"I'm Steve Q., by the way," the boy says.

"I don't care," I mutter at my Keds. There's a hoot in the distance and I can picture the rust-covered drawbridge lurching back down toward the sea. I'm starting to turn away when Steve looks at me, his eyes narrowing.

"Your eyes, they're kind of rare," he says suddenly, the words popping out of his mouth like a loose tooth.

"What?" I look up, startled.

"They're just... really orange, like a cat's eyes or a witch's or something,"

Steve stammers, looking at his feet. He's wearing a pair of heavy workman's boots without any laces. The tongues droop away from his skinny ankles.

Now that he's not behind the counter anymore, Steve seems to be standing incredibly close—I can see the stubble on his jaw glinting in the light of the ornamental streetlight that snakes out of the sidewalk. His face isn't conventionally attractive by any means; his nose is slightly long and his teeth a little crooked. But he has a freckle by the corner of his mouth that twitches up when he half-smiles—as he does now—and his eyes are framed by long, light lashes.

"That's weird. That's a weird thing to just... say," I reply, looking down at my feet, too. My Keds are getting truly filthy now.

Steve shrugs and sighs. "Undiagnosed Tourette's. I told you."

We both look at our shoes for a few seconds more, then something clatters to the ground, landing next to my toe. I swoop down and pick it up. It's a piece of blue seaglass, worn around the edges by years in the ocean, glinting rainbows incubating in its center and sending up sparks under the street light. I feel the phantom crash of waves against my back as I hold it in my hand.

"That's mine," Steve says suddenly, snatching the glass from my hand.

I blink at him. "So that 'seaglass in the pocket' thing in your review—that wasn't a metaphor?"

"My mom gave it to me. When I was five. She found it on a little dirty beach by the YMCA and told me that no matter where she was, if I looked into it she would see me." He speaks rapidly, flatly, his eyes avoiding my face.

He looks at the glass for a second and I stand there, my mouth gaping. This was not information that strangers usually offered upon first meeting.

"You're the one who likes Haze, right? In the band?" Steve asks then, looking up with that little scrap of sunlight smile on his face again, seaglass safely stowed in his pocket.

I nod. "Yeah." I think of ZZZ then and how he hasn't answered me and a kind of sick feeling spreads through my limbs.

"Why," he says, his eyes narrowing kind of.

It's not a question—it's a just a weird kind of statement. I feel heat thrumming through my chest again. This is a test. I know it. Music guys always pull this shit when they find out you're into a band. They ask you all kinds of obscure questions in hopes of tripping you up—discovering you're some kind of poseur. Reassuring themselves that they're a true fan—while you, you just want to fuck the lead singer. And while I suppose I am attracted to Haze—sure, I'm a human female—it's about more than that. It's just... I feel like if I met him I would be fully understood. I know that makes no sense and I sound insane, but I feel like he understands some corner of my heart that hasn't even started beating yet. I feel like if I ever met him I would become myself. If that makes any sense at all. "Crushes" on famous people had never been, for me, about being *with* a guy—they've always been about *being* that guy. Pretty fucked, I know. No wonder I'm single.

Steve's looking at me, his lips curling up at the side, waiting for my answer. I consider just walking away, but, instead, I take a deep breath, driven by the snapping anger in my chest and the weird desperation Haze always conjures in me. "The first time I heard Haze was in Picture Disc... like, when I was 10. The guy behind the counter, Chuck—he was playing 'Placid Girl.'"

"Like you guys played the other night," Steve says.

I wince at the memory. And Steve's review. "Yeah, something like that. Anyway, I asked what the song was—because, for some reason, when I heard that drumbeat, the one that opens the song, it just... my chest felt like it was going to split open. I didn't know why. I wanted to cry... or something. I just..." I'm not looking at Steve now. I couldn't if I wanted to. "There are just those moments in music, you know, that are perfect—that are like this little *click* in your brain. And that was one of them. And then... he started singing. And I just knew."

"What?" Steve asks—a question this time.

I keep my eyes trained just to the left of Steve, toward Picture Disc. "I don't know... It could have been the drumbeat or his voice or the words but I knew that it was possible then to just break free from your own skin, if that makes sense, to break free from what your body tells you to be and just become... something else. Some totally other shape. Some totally different person you know you are down in the blood. And I wanted that. *Want* that. So..." I stop, embarrassed. "Yeeeeah..."

For a moment all I can hear is the bleating of the foghorn—the chatter of couples as they stroll down Main Street, eating ice cream and dragging tired, sticky kids behind them. I consider just running away. Abruptly. Without looking. Just fucking booking it. And then Steve coughs. I look at him, finally.

"I want to lend you something," Steve says. He pulls his messenger bag around to the front and starts rooting around in it, pulling out a cassette tape in a battered case. He holds it out to me with that half-quirked, self-satisfied smile and a little eddy of annoyance courses through me again. *Oh good, I passed the test.* The eddy, however, disappears when I look at the tape he's given me.

"What... what is this?" I ask, my heart having a rave in my chest.

"Haze's second album." Steve says, smiling. His front tooth is a little chipped. While that would make anyone else look deranged, somehow it just makes Steve look "interesting."

"But, I thought there was only..."

"...one, right," Steve says. "This one was never released."

I look at the tape in my hands in utter disbelief. On the cover there's Haze—this time wearing a plain, white mask. The epitome of a blank face. The title is *Unmasking Tape.* I've listened to the first—and only Haze—record so many times that I know every beat, every word, every bit of strange banter. The idea that there's more is like waking up when you think you have to go to school and realizing it's Saturday—times 1,000. I want to fling myself down the street toward home immediately and put the cassette in my tape deck and just listen and listen and listen.

As I glance toward the drawbridge I notice, with a little jolt of shame, that Sarah is gone. I pat my phone in my pocket and cringe when I think of all the angry texts she's probably sent me. Instead of pulling it out and facing the emoticons, I look at Steve, cock my head to the side.

"Where did you get this?" I ask, looking down at the tape like I'm afraid he's going to take it away.

He smiles again, slightly smug. "From my cousin."

"How did your cousin get this?" I ask, my voice edging on hysteria.

He laughs and gives a little shrug. "My cousin is Alex, the bassist in the band. Actually, both of my cousins are in the band—Alex and Bethany. But Alex had the tape."

"*WHAT?*" I sound insane, but I don't care. I am standing next to someone who is like, *one degree* of separation away from Haze. There were two other members of Haze's band—Alex, who played bass, and Bethany, who played drums. Still, there are barely any photos of the whole band on the Web so all anyone really knows about the other two are their first names. They used to wear masks, too, but they weren't as careful with their identities as Haze.

Steve laughs again, a kind of rough sound, like sandpaper. "Yeah, he was visiting the last few days—he came to your show with me—and I found a few of these in his bag. I probably shouldn't have taken it, but I couldn't resist."

"He was at the show?" I ask, breathless.

"Yeah," Steve nods. "We were standing in the front row. Actually, he was as impressed with your drumming as I was." He looks down, his lashes shadowing his cheek. "Kept talking about you all the way home. Said he talked to you after the show a little, too."

Now I know why Steve looks familiar—even though I had only seen him for a moment, ducking out for a smoke. I remember the green-eyed man in the front row—the one who had accidentally taken my drumsticks. Haze's bassist liked my drumming. Haze's bassist heard me drum.

I stare at the tape for a few seconds more and then a thought flashes through my mind, bright and big like a garish neon sign. I look up, but it's like Steve can already see the question in my eyes.

"No, I don't know who Haze is—Alex won't tell me. Neither will Bethany. It's like some kind of pact or something."

I must look really disappointed—and I am, what kind of bullshit is that?—because Steve's hand hovers somewhere near my shoulder before he pulls it back, looking at his palm like it has betrayed him somehow.

The door to the shop opens then and a monk leans out. "Dude, are you gonna come in and, like, sell records or what?"

Steve flaps a hand at the monk and flashes him a "two seconds" sign. The monk rolls his eyes and jangles back inside, all carabineers and chains.

"Wait," I say, realization rolling over me. "You work here? How do you work here? I've never seen you before and I've lived here forever."

Steve shrugs. "I just moved here."

"And you're already working at Picture Disc?" I ask, grudgingly impressed. Chuck is pretty particular about his employees.

"Yeah, I mean, we used to live, like, one town over and my brother, Gabriel, he used to work here sometimes." Steve's eyes flick down to the ground and suddenly he looks really sad.

"My whole family is from around here, actually," Steve says, his face back to normal—somewhat. "My cousins' family and mine. Anyway," he shoves his hands in his pockets, his fingers poking through a hole in the wool. I think of telling him about the hole, but I can see his fingers tightly wrapped around the sliver of blue glass. "Just bring that back tomorrow, OK?"

He throws a bit more sunshine my way before ducking back into the shop and I stand there feeling, perhaps irrationally, one step closer to Haze.

FOUR

"You're just a hunk of flesh and free will/ And I would love you, love you—if you let me,"

—"I Hate You," *Masking Tape* —Haze

The house is quiet when I burst through the front door, wheezing from my run uphill. I couldn't wait for the trolley, couldn't wait one more moment to listen to the tape. I pound up the stairs in a way that always makes my mother whine about migraines, fall onto the Oriental rug on my bedroom floor, and shove the cassette into my stereo as quickly as my shaking hands will let me. My finger hovers over "Play" for a second and then I put my face down on the carpet, breathing in a smell like desert caravans and spices and cats.

A chilly sense of dread and hope cobwebs through my chest as I stare at the tape in its little cubby. What if the music sucks? Sophomore efforts usually do. The first tape was perfection—a pure, gut-searing, sad-making wonder. How could anything else live up?

For a second, I consider just taking the tape out of the stereo—giving it back to Steve and forgetting that it exists. Instead, I push "Play," vault onto my bed, and grip my pillow in my lap like a kid who's afraid of the dark.

Silence stretches on and on and I flop backward on the bed, only to pop up again as the ghostly disembodied sound of cheering fills the room—screaming, crescendoing cheering that sounds like a 1,000 girls being ripped limb from limb. That's odd. Haze never did live recordings—let alone played a room that would afford such a large crowd. I've always wondered why people scream for bands and celebrities. It seems like such an absurd response—such a weird way of showing you love, need, want someone. Maybe we scream because we've been taught since childhood that when you scream, you get what you want.

Two seconds into the recording I hear a faint count off, then the Beatles singing, "She loves you, yeah, yeah..." The vocal quality changes then—apparently Haze was starting off with a long sample, which is also out of character—and he screeches the last "yeah" at the top of his crackling voice.

The first guitar lick bursts from the boombox's speakers—a winding, rock 'n' roll throwback of a lick, like it should be issuing from a jukebox in a James Dean movie rather than a shitty old stereo. It sounds familiar. In fact, it sounds just like "I Hate You," off Haze's first tape. Could he possibly be doing some sort of remix? Is this a remix album? I still my whirling mind so that I can listen—drink it all in.

The lick doesn't stop, doesn't build and mesh with the rest of the song, bringing in drums and bass and Haze's rich voice—it spirals, it repeats, it thrums with reverb until it becomes a tangle of sound.

55

Spiders creep through my chest and across my veins—I feel the tension thrum through my body, waiting—waiting for Haze's voice to join the fray, to break apart the strange, almost monstrous web of noise—to breathe humanity and ragged pain into the notes. I clench my fists, my fingernails digging into my palms, my toes curling and arching like Little Edie's claws in her favorite Navajo blanket—and then, then it comes: the same words from the original song. The one I know in every curve of my brain.

"You're just a hunk of flesh and free will. And I would love you, love you—if you let me," Haze snarls, but it sounds like he's at the bottom of a well. It sounds like he's in a pit. It sounds like he's calling for help. The words repeat again and again—like the guitar lick—and split apart from each other, "free will" and "flesh" bouncing and volleying and lapping against and rolling over "love" and "you" and "let me." The rest of the lyrics never come—no matter how intensely my body waits for them. Words about how "you can't animate something that's dead with electricity. No buzzing generator in some dirty back shed will do it for me"—words from the original song. No, that first lyric just repeats and repeats—the words themselves becoming the embodiment of the first song as a whole, a song that originally cast Haze as a Frankenstein character who was trying to revive a deceased relationship like some kind of stitched-together monster.

That's what the new song is, really, now: a stitched-together monster, buzzing with borrowed life—but beautiful. Beautiful like licking blue flames that look like they're cold but in reality will burn, burn, burn if you touch them.

My head hums and my temples throb as I listen, each new song dissecting and flaying the original version—the songs Haze released years ago on *Masking Tape.* There is a darkness here—one I had always felt humming behind the surface as Haze's voice cracked and careened on the first tape. Now it's all there. It's on the surface. And it makes my insides clench. The back of my neck feels cold. Something in the pit of my stomach feels hot. I'm not sure whether to lie down or run away.

As Haze's voice reaches a screaming crescendo of passion—one that spirals again and again until it seems to collapse in on itself—I flop back on my bed, folding my hands over my heart, which I can feel beating through my T-shirt.

I lie like that—dazed, staring at the ceiling—as the tape whirs into static. I can't move—I'm pinned like a butterfly—but I feel like tearing my skin off all the same. I'm not sure whether I hate it or I love it. Not sure whether I'm enamored or repulsed. This music—it isn't anything I've heard before. It isn't a retread. It isn't a throwback. It's a coming apart and a coming together. It's emotion ragged and raw and screaming and it's pretty nothingness, too. It makes me want to rip it apart and put it back together again so that I can understand. Understand what makes it burn so—with a fire so cold it makes me feel like a corpse in a meat locker. Freezer burn, baby.

I drag the heels of my hands across my face and they come back black with eyeliner. I take a huge, wildly unattractive, shuddering breath and realize with a little creep-creeping of my spine that the room is now pitch dark. All the windows of the house opposite are also dark, but I think I can see a vague glow—like a spark—emanating from the one on the left on the top floor. Someone, maybe the new boy, is awake. The weak glow gives me the deep-down shivers and I remember what Sarah said before about bad changes coming into my life—then shake it off immediately. Tarot cards and whatnot are bullshit. Everyone knows that.

My phone chimes down in my sheets. Sarah. I wince, wondering what choice words she has for me for ditching her. I dig around for the cell. Putting off the inevitable only makes it worse. Like when you tape up a pipe rather than calling the plumber (which my dad has done many a time). One day all that water builds up and just blows up like a geyser.

When I retrieve my phone there are no messages from Sarah, just a single notification from the photo-sharing app. ZZZ.

I almost drop the phone, overcome by this guilty, embarrassed feeling that he somehow saw me listening to the tape. Saw me react so... viscerally to it all. Then I remember how once I had gone to call Sarah on our house's landline and when I picked up the receiver—even before I could dial—she was on the other line. We had decided to call each other at the same time. She said it was because we were so close, we had a psychic connection. I wonder if something similar could have happened with ZZZ. That scares me a little, to be honest. Now that I've heard the tape. It feels like something I shouldn't have heard without his permission first. Also, the music was... unfamiliar somehow. Strange. A little off. I shake my head. Of course it's unfamiliar—it's new. Or at least a new version of the old.

My fingers tingling, I click on the message icon and try not to read every word on the screen at once—not to skip to the end. Little Edie slinks into my lap and I barely notice:

Hello Hallie,

I'm sorry I've taken a little bit to write back to you. I guess I was just very struck by what you said—because I understand. Because I know exactly how you feel and I wanted to be able to come back to you with advice of some sort.

I thought and I thought and looked at the stars and the moon and smoked a joint and thought some more and this is what I came up with: Even when you leave your town, Hallie, I'm guessing you will always be that "roiling-insides" girl. At least I hope you will be. I hope you will never be satisfied, because that's when you stop making. Moving. When you stop trying.

Now tell me, Placid Girl, what will come of all that boiling inside you? What will you make with all that desire?

- ZZZ

All of my insides melt and congeal on the floor. The weirdness of *Unmasking Tape* retreats into the background.

I feel like he's been spying on my brain—that somehow he got the key and has been shifting through all the filing folders in my head. My soul feels a little closer to the atoms of the air somehow then—like it's reaching out toward something and that something is him. Someone out there in the abyss who can understand me, know me—despite how much I hide. I want to understand him, too—I think—after listening to that tape. It feels like jumping into ice-cold water, but I do. I'm scared to, but I do.

Little Edie, bored of my statue act—I'm sitting frozen, my eyes locked on the phone—stalks off, waving her tail in the air like a chiding finger. I stretch out my legs, now cat-free, and tap "Reply." My finger hovers over the keypad for a second, and then I swoop in:

Hello Haze, I type, then delete the second word. He never told me his name. I have a pretty good feeling this is Haze—who else could it be?—but I don't want to scare him away. Hello… ZZZ… what should I call you? I type slowly. Maybe if I ask more directly he'll tell me. Since you apparently know my name. How do you know my name anyway?

The letters spelling out "Hallie" had snagged my attention on the first read, but I'm guessing he has an explanation. The Internet does hold a myriad of wonders.

To be honest, when I think about what I need to make, I feel this huge bubble growing in my chest and pushing all my organs together along with this surge of adrenaline that races through my spine like too much caffeine mixed with roller-coasters mixed with crack. Or what I imagine crack to be like. And then… it all drops off into nothingness and my hands freeze and my mind dies and I am paralyzed, looking at the page like it's a dead star. Like everything I write will suck.

I want to write songs, I guess. I mean, I do. I just don't feel ready to do it.

How do you do it? How do you let go enough to do what you do? Assuming that you are who I think you are? How do you rip it all out of you and stand there holding your heart in your hands?

Hallie

I wonder how quickly he will respond. Last time, it had taken him days. To take my mind off of the upcoming reply—impossible!— I put Haze's cassette into this little device that turns tapes into MP3s that my dad gave me for my last birthday and listen to it again as it transfers over. The music jitters through my veins as I think of Haze—of the man who might be reading my words somewhere out there and thinking about me.

My phone pings again. He's faster this time:

Placid Girl,
You can call me ZZZ — that works well for me. I know your
name because I looked up your band ☺

Oh, fuck it, he used an emoticon.

Are emoticons weird? They're weird, right? OK, that's the end of
that.

Relief is tangible.

You've asked a pretty expansive question that I'm going to
have to think a little bit about, but right now I would suggest not
finding out if crack is how you imagine and to just sit down and
write. Like automatic writing. You know it? When you just let the
spirits write through you. I think that might work for you. I think
you have a lot of spirits down deep inside, am I right?

Now, for that bit of advice I want one thing in return…

-ZZZ

I furrow my brow. What? I type. The response comes seconds later:

A photo of you… You don't have to smile. I would just like a picture of you that you took for me and me alone. One without your pink-haired friend in it.

-ZZZ

I glance in the mirror across from my bed—my hair hangs all limp around my face and my skin looks extra pale from all the staying inside I've been doing. Maybe I could slap some more eyeliner on? A little bit of lipstick? But then I think of Haze and how raw he is on the new record. How... unpretty. He would probably like me better with all my flesh and freckles. All my flyaways and hollows under my eyes. I turn on the camera on my phone and flip the view so that I can see myself in the little screen—a girl with a face full of dark shadows. A girl with witchy eyes, according to Steve. I try for a half-smile, but as I start to snap something falls heavily on my bed. Something much larger than Little Edie. I whirl around.

"Hi," Sarah says gruffly, clambering onto my bed in a skin-tight red romper. "Fancy meeting you here." Her eyes flick to my phone. "Were you about to take a *selfie*?"

I toss the phone on my bed and cross my arms, mortified. "No, selfies are disgusting. No, of course not," I stammer, pushing the phone under the pillow in case ZZZ says anything else. I know I should probably tell Sarah about him, but that whole Nick thing—oops, I mean "Thing I Cannot Mention"—makes me not want to share.

"Don't let me stop you," Sarah says, stretching out on my bed.

"So, I was going to freeze you out for a day or two but then I got bored so I decided to come over and give you a chance to kiss my feet and apologize and bake me muffins."

She flings a backpack onto the floor that I try not to look at. There are obviously other motivations for her coming over—for the second night in a row. Her mom's probably doing badly again.

I'm still distracted by ZZZ and the whole exchange so it takes me a second, replete with blinking, to figure out what she's talking about.

She glares at me. "*Apologize*, Hallie. You fraternized with the enemy."

"Steve?"

"Whatever the hell his name is. Sure, Steve. You fraternized with him." She scowls.

"That makes it sound like we went to a kegger and paddled each other's asses or something," I say, laughing.

"I don't want to know about your kinky misadventures, Hallie, I want an apology." She crosses her arms and pouts.

I sigh, leaning my head against the wall, dangerously close to Haze's crotch in one of my many pictures. I should tell her what Steve told me. I should tell her about the tape. But I don't really want to mar my ZZZ euphoria with a fight right now. So I decide to lie.

"I didn't 'fraternize.' I told him the fuck off. You didn't give me a chance back in the record store, so I got my shots in after you took off," I say, pounding a fist into my palm. It feels like a fake gesture even to me.

"What, really?" Sarah asks, looking shocked—and delighted. "What did you say?"

"Oh, just... uh, some stuff. And there was swearing, lots of swearing," I say, looking absently toward my phone. I'm worried that if I don't answer soon ZZZ will think I'm over it. Over him.

Sarah laughs, throwing back her head so that it knocks lightly against the headboard. "I can't even picture that! You, going off on some dude? No frame of reference for that. I wish I had seen it."

"Me too," I say, inching my hand under my pillow to get my phone. No new messages.

"Well, I'm glad you didn't, like, make friends with that *asshole* or anything," Sarah says. "I was really pissed at you so I went on some site called Adult Friend Finder to find your replacement, but it turned out to be some creepy hookup site." She kicks off her shoes and pulls my blanket over herself with a little contented sigh. "Fuck, I'm glad we're not so old that we need to go online to find dates. That just sounds depressing as shit. I believe in pheromones, dude," she slaps her chest. "You can't fall in love with pixels. There's no juice in pixels."

"Gross." I glance at my phone again. I feel the same stirrings now in my chest that I did when I had crushes on boys in school. That same kind of pattering in my stomach. That same feeling of winning some massive reward when they acknowledged me some-how. But times a million.

"I read something once, though," I say slowly, trying not to sound too interested in the topic of online love, "some study where they put a bunch of people in a pitch dark room and had them talk to each other—without seeing anyone's face. They also put people in a bright room and did the same thing as, like, a control. Anyway, I guess the people in the dark room formed really close relationships because they didn't have to worry about what they looked like or what the other people looked like. They could be themselves. I guess some of the people even, like, hooked up and stuff."

"So... ugly people got some action in the dark?" Sarah says slowly, then gives a little bark of laughter and rolls her eyes. "Jesus, I wonder what happened when they finally turned the light on. Regret City!"

I look down at the phone in my hand and frown slightly, then tighten my fingers until the casing crackles.

"Not everything is about looks," I almost snarl.

"*Some* things are," Sarah says, yawning. "But we're pretty, so we don't have to worry about any of that. Plus..." she kicks me softly with her foot. "... we have each other. We'll always have someone to watch out for creepers in the dark."

Sarah stretches elaborately. "Turn out the light. I'm tired."

I lean over to switch it off, then bounce off the bed. I'll take the photo in the hallway and send it before sleep smothers us.

"Hey, Hallie?" Sarah says sleepily from the blackness.

"Yeah," I say, half in the room and half out.

"Thanks—for telling off that dickface for me." She yawns again. "I've had... a really, really bad week..." Her eyes are just hollows in the dark.

I close the door, feeling like shit for lying to Sarah but also stupidly excited about ZZZ, and flick on the hallway light. I want to be as close to lights-on Hallie as possible. I flick on the camera again and let my eyes slide over the lens as I snap the photo. Done. One take only.

There I am on the screen. Pale and dark-haired and in-the-flesh me. I send ZZZ the photo, my fingers flying, pushing "Send" before I realize I should have asked for a photo in return. Resolving to do so tomorrow, though, I turn out the light, darkness descending over my eyes like a mask with no eyeholes.

FIVE

"I feel empty/ I feel empty/ Please, please fill me up,"
—"Nada," *Masking Tape*—Haze

Sarah is still asleep when I slide out of bed and into my jeans at 11 a.m. The girl could sleep all day if you let her. I decide to let her. Steve will be waiting for his tape, and I don't want to have explain why I'm going to Picture Disc—two days in a row—to a newly risen Sarah. Talking to Steve made me feel closer to Haze, somehow. Because Alex and Bethany are his cousins or he's also a fan, I don't know. But I want to feel that closeness again. And maybe he has some information that could help me figure out once and for all if ZZZ is who he says he seems to be.

I look down at Sarah clutching my pillow, Little Edie curled into her side, her face soft and relaxed. She looks really young asleep. I wish she would look like that all the time, but then she wouldn't be Sarah. Sarah is her hardness and her edges and her scars. Like a rock all tossed by the sea. She would also kill me if I ever compared her to a rock tossed by the sea.

I drag a T-shirt over my head and shove my phone in my pocket. ZZZ hasn't answered me yet. Maybe he had fallen asleep. At least I hope he had—not took one look at my face and took all his words back.

I pad down the stairs as softly as I can, but Dad is sitting in the greenhouse with his headphones on, oblivious, wearing an old, ripped Cramps shirt and humming softly—an atonal, buzzing sound that bounces off the stone floor and nips at my ears like a black fly. Mom's door is shut tight.

When I get outside into the sunshine—the fresh-cut grass and garden hose spray of summer—my shoulders relax and I start pounding out the beat to one of Haze's new/old songs on my thighs as I shamble down the hill toward town, skipping out of the way of cars and bicyclists. I had only listened to the tape twice before Sarah came over, but I think I can probably figure out a song or two from memory. Sure, the lyrics had been the same—but the beat, the part that came most naturally to me, had been warped somehow. It was more erratic. More complicated. The edges of the cassette case dig into my thigh and I wrap my hand around its outline. I want to keep it. Sure, I have the music, but I want the physical object that Haze had held. A deranged part of me wants to smell it to see if I can pick up his scent. The part of me capable of feeling shame sneers at that other part of me and pushes it down like a snapping dog.

When I reach Picture Disc and push open the door, a couple of Anarchy Kids look up from where they're browsing in the new punk section and then promptly go back to pawing through the vinyl. Steve, sitting behind the counter, doesn't even bother to look up.

He's far too engrossed in reading a zine titled *They Live!—But Just Barely: Zombie Mom & Dad*. He's wearing an old baseball cap—black, no particular team represented—slightly askew, and his mess of curly hair flips over the collar of a long, trench coat-like military jacket.

Suddenly, as if he can feel my eyes roving all over him, he looks up. Surprise lights up his eyes, but his lips only half-quirk up into a smile. It's like the expression has wandered half into the room—but hasn't yet decided to stay.

"Hey," he says, putting the zine on the counter and kicking up his feet on top of it. "That was fast. Did you listen to the tape?"

I think back to my room, listening to Haze's voice broken and echoing, his words split and flayed, notes and beats and sounds overlapping into nothing and something all at once. I shiver, kind of. Then I think of ZZZ's message and my mouth twitches.

"Well?" Steve is looking at me weird. Probably because I had just shivered and twitched. Now I'm just staring vacantly. Quickly, I nod, my ability to speak sorely gone due to embarrassment.

"It was..."

Steve nods, "I know. Not the same, right? But also still kind of... amplified. Scary but wonderful."

"Yes," I say quickly, embarrassment retreating. He gets it. He understands, too. "It was... Yes. What you said."

Steve Q.'s smile officially enters the room and sits down. Suddenly he looks a lot more open. A lot less like an Anarchy Kid who had bashed my best friend and more like a boy I can talk to.

"That's why I'm here actually," I say, digging my hands into my pockets. "I want to know more about him. About Haze. Like, everything you know. I mean, I know a lot, but, obviously, your cousins and whatever..."

Steve Q.'s face falls a little and he takes his feet off the counter and leans forward in his chair. "Well, to be honest, I told you all I know yesterday. Alex and B know all about him, but, like I said, they won't share any of that info with me."

"Was he... did he go online much? Like did he use social networks?" I ask, feeling a little silly. What am I expecting him to say, "Why yes, he's well-known for contacting young girls via photo-sharing apps"? The vague creepiness of that statement is not lost on me. Haze is at least 10 years older than me, which I know should weird me out—and it does, kind of—but it's *Haze.* Or at least I think it is. If he's talking to me, he must have a reason. He must see something in me.

"No," Steve Q. shakes his head. "Nope. No Twitter. No Facebook. No nothing. He had a website, sure, where he dropped songs, but that's offline now. He's kind of like an analog ghost. Pretty rad, really. I, for one, think the Internet will be our ultimate undoing—you know, trapping our collective consciousness and taking over the world and all that. Also, there's all those lists with puppies and cats," he deadpans, then cracks a smile, tossing his hair out of his eyes.

"Oh," I say, disappointed.

"Any reason you ask?" Steve Q. looks at me and tilts his head.

"I dunno," I say. "I was just thinking if he had a Twitter or something, there'd be some clues in there. You know, to who he really is." I sound like a dipshit. Steve knows about as much about Haze as I do, it seems. Despite having cousins in the band.

"Trust me, if he had given up some nugget of info via the Internet, I'd be all up on that," Steve says. "Social networks are seriously not my thing, but I'd be willing to make an exception in this case."

For a brief, wild moment I'm tempted to take out my phone and show the photofeed to Steve Q. Show him the string of messages. At least then I'd have someone to talk to about all this. Someone who understands Haze. Maybe he could even help me figure out why this notoriously reclusive guy might be talking to me. But a darker part of myself—the selfish part—doesn't want to share.

Steve takes his feet off the counter and kind of scans the room. The Anarchy Kids aren't listening—they're too busy fighting about whether or not Black Flag is lame. He gives me a quick appraising look and then kind of smiles at his feet before looking up at me again.

"There *is* a way that you can find out about Haze, you know. If you're willing to travel," he arches his eyebrows and leans toward me.

"How?" I instinctively lean forward too, so that our faces are so close together that I can smell the cigarette smoke and mint gum on his breath.

"Haze is playing a show in the city this week. His first in five years. It's a super secret underground thing—Alex told me about it when he was here—but since you dig the tape and you're a fan, I think it's OK to tell you."

"What? I don't fucking believe you!" I half-shout. The Anarchy Kids all look up for a second and I lower my voice, my heart hammering away at some phantom nails in my chest. A show. A chance to see Haze in the flesh. A chance to talk to him, see him—and my mind clamps down after that, unwilling (and perhaps too scared) to let me imagine further.

Steve smiles. "Alex told me, so you're getting it from the source."

"Are you going?" I ask, slightly breathless, simultaneously trying to figure out how I can go, too. My dad might be seriously stratosphered-out, but he would probably not let me go to the city by myself. Sarah seems like my only option. She might not be into Haze, but she's definitely into getting out of town.

"Hell yes I'm going. I kind of need to..." Steve's face darkens for a moment and he looks lost, and then he smiles. Then, as if he suddenly notices how close our faces are, his eyes wander all over until they lock on mine. He smiles wider.

"What?" I say, feeling oddly light-headed.

"I think we're neighbors," he says, still kind of smiling close to my face.

"What?" Then I remember Sarah telling me about the Anarchy Kid moving in next door. I feel extremely idiotic for not putting it together until now.

"I saw your friend climbing a ladder last night at the house across from mine. So I'm guessing it's either you or her that lives next door. I'm hoping it's you," Steve says, still extremely close.

"You were watching my house?" I say, furrowing my brow.

Steve laughs and leans back, finally. "I was looking out my window. Your friend has pink hair. She's hard to miss even when she's not climbing a ladder." He narrows his eyes a little. "Don't your parents notice?"

"What?" I'm still a little thrown that Steve lives next door to me, making him a preacher's son. He doesn't look like a preacher's son with his wild eyes and cracked tooth. Also I really want to get back to talking about the Haze show.

"Children—climbing up ladders into bedroom windows?" Steve deadpans.

I laugh. "My parents don't notice much of anything—unless it's a glass of wine or a bonsai tree."

Steve pushes his hands into the pockets of his tight jeans. "I'm not sure I get the bonsai tree part, but I'm really jealous. I wish my dad didn't notice me. We don't even have a ladder."

"What? Why?"

"So I don't do what your friend did last night," Steve replies, his face stony. "I get where he's coming from, but it definitely makes painting things and rescuing cats from trees way harder." His expression is stony, but something ripples in the back there, like a desert hiding behind a mirage.

I open my mouth to say something else, but Steve cuts in. "So this show..."

"Yes, please tell me about it," I interrupt, my brain buzzing again at the prospect of seeing Haze.

"I'll tell you about it tonight," Steve says, like he's a cat swimming in a pool of cream.

"What's tonight?" I ask, getting a little annoyed. Why can't he just tell me now? My fingernails itch with the need to know.

"There's a party tonight—at Machineworks by the water. You should come. I mean, if you want to," Steve says. "I can give you all the details on the show there. My friend Randy is driving me up to the city in his van in a few days." He looks a little nervous.

"Yes, yes, I will 100% be there," I say, and he looks down at the counter and smiles and smiles. I realize, somewhere in the dimness of my brain, that a guy just asked me to hang out with him, but the thought of Haze existing out there, a show on the horizon, pushes that potentially terrifying realization down, down, down. I'm going to see him play. I smile, too, and Steve smiles wider.

When I get home the kitchen is all lit up even though it's day-time and I can see my mom sitting at the table in her nightgown through the window—one too many buttons undone. Any levity I had gleaned down at Picture Disc takes a major nosedive. She looks like a reflection. I stare through the window for a few seconds, unable to move.

She's got an open book sitting in front of her, and her hair is tied really tightly back from her face. I can almost see the skin of her skull peeking through. I can feel the gravel crunching as I shift from foot to foot, not wanting to go inside. Not wanting to talk to anyone. I don't like seeing my parents acting like this. They're supposed to be the ones in control of their emotions or whatever. They're supposed to keep it together. And it makes me mad—maybe unfairly—when they don't. It feels like the world shifts just a little when that happens and I'm not sure how to right it. Yeah, I guess that sounds pretty dramatic, but it's how it feels. Like a stage set being ripped down and revealed to be just paper and glue.

The summer air is thick in my lungs—the kind of air you can only breathe in halfway before it threatens to choke you. I can see the hyacinths from where they wave next to the porch and a line from something I once read filters through my mind: "They call me the hyacinth girl..." then something about a hyacinth garden and wet leaves. The forest heaves a big sigh behind me.

Just an hour ago I was excited—about the prospect of meeting Haze, about the show. Now, standing out in the summer sunshine, scared of the flesh-and-bone ghosts that haunt my house, I feel like I could easily melt into the heat, take a great, big deep sigh and float into the branches and become part of the atmosphere. Or smash my phone on the gravel and wander into the woods. Wander until I reach the highway and just keep walking, walking in the middle of the road where humans aren't supposed to be. It's funny that there are those places—places where we can't go. Like in the road and on airfields during takeoff. On sloping roofs and airplane wings. It's funny because we made all those places, but we can't stay there.

The future feels like that. When I try to imagine what it will be like, all I can picture is me, standing in the middle of a field, spinning around and around with my arms out. I've got a mental block. Like when you try to think what's beyond space and your brain just stops. Maybe I should ask Sarah to ask her tarot cards for me, but they would probably just say I'm going to get hit by a bus.

I start walking down the driveway, away from the front door. I know I should go inside the normal way, but fuck it, I don't want to. My mom in her ill-fitting nightgown. My dad with his blank stare. It's all just a major fucking bummer. Just for the hell of it I start running, my Keds flipping gravel up toward my ass. Crazily, I canter off into the grass and start doing cartwheels, my hands coming up all wet. One more cartwheel and I collapse in the grass, opening my mouth into a soundless yell. I will not cry. I will not fucking cry.

The grass pricks my bare arms and I feel the hot earth pouring its strength into all my limbs as I breathe heavily, not used to the exertion of running. My pocket vibrates. My breathing quickens. Bordering on desperation I jam my hand into my pocket.

I like this. I like how you hide everything in your eyes. It's nice. You require effort to get to know, I can tell. I'm pretty willing to expend that effort if that's cool with you?

ZZZ

The sky wheels above me blue and clear and dusted with sugar drift clouds and I spread my fingers in the grass, rooting them into the sun-scorched blades. I sit up then, shaking off the dirt and grass cuttings, and if I hadn't been sure before that I would be going to that show come hell or proverbial high water, I'm sure now.

I tap back a message as quickly as I can so that I don't lose my nerve: That's definitely cool with me. Maybe I could get to know you better, too? Maybe you could also send me a photo?

Then my phone rings. I shriek and drop it on the grass before realizing that Sarah's name is flashing across the screen.

"Hello?" I stammer.

"Hi. Are you going to lie on the grass out there all day or are we going to do something?" she asks. I look up and see her leaning out my window, her hair streaming down like Rapunzel.

I look up at her and grin, flipping her my middle finger and scrambling to my feet. "Yeah, we're gonna do something. I'm cashing in all my trolley money tonight. We're going to a party."

SIX

"I can't fight this feeling, this desert island feeling/ The rocks and stones and volleyballs are all I have to play with,"
                    —"Desert Island Feeling," *Masking Tape* —Haze

"Tell me again who invited you to this party?" Sarah asks, kicking her feet up on the splintering bench of the trolley, her tight jeans hugging her hips and her racer-back T gaping in all the right places. I look down at my jean jacket and sigh. She had told me I looked frumpy when I left the house—ever so helpful—but I had declined to put on the tight black tank she had suggested. My tent of denim might be cozy, but it definitely hugs me in none of those aforementioned right places.

I shrug. "I heard some kids talking about it in town. Sounded fun." I still haven't worked out how I'm going to deal with Sarah once she sees Steve or hears about my plan to sneak out of town for Haze's show. But I also know that I can't go without her. Sure, that may sound lame and cowardly, but I need my best friend when it comes to shit like this.

She's the one who, when I was freaking out before our first show ever, took me outside and presented me with a tub of water balloons and told me to chuck them all against the wall before we went on stage. She said each exploding elastic body was equivalent to one bored-looking audience member. I still sometimes picture exploding water balloons when I get nervous—their contents splashing across the pimply faces of scowling hipsters with no room in their pockets for their hands.

Also, she's the one with access to a car. So there's that.

"Fine," Sarah says, dragging out the "i" into a kind of lilting song and tapping her rings against the window. "I hope there's beer."

Giving a noncommittal shrug—there's always beer—I crack open the old-fashioned window and stick my fingers out into the rushing air. We're rolling past strip malls and grocery stores—still lit up even though it's dark outside. I always thought that was a waste—illuminating all these deserted places, sending all this light into the atmosphere that does nothing but confuse birds and wildlife and whatever. After the whole school shooting thing started to get really bad, they started leaving the light in the gym on all night as some kind of twisted security measure. They even left it on during school dances, rendering everyone even more awkward now that they had to undulate to Top 40 bullshit under the bright, bright fluorescents.

The trolley jolts a little now as it rolls over the drawbridge—dormant at this time of night—and speeds through the gauntlet of darkened windows downtown. A couple of housing developments later and we're stopping outside a dark warehouse crouching next to the river. At one point the town was going to turn the place into a prison for delinquent boys, but everyone protested and came to town hall meetings and everything, and it just remained abandoned. It was a blight on the community this way, but a building filled to the brim with wild kids—real wild kids, not "Anarchy" kids—would be a bigger blight for sure. I used to imagine them all breaking free one day, spilling into the streets all muscles and emotional scar tissue, and wreaking havoc on everyone's flower beds—looting the tourist stores and gnashing their taffy-gummed teeth in the wrinkled faces of the local garden club.

I suppress a wily memory before it can loom too large—that Nick used to work here—and, instead, wonder what it was like when Haze was growing up. I want to ask him, but when I pull out my phone and check my messages for the 500th time today ZZZ has not yet answered my request for a photo. Maybe I'm fooling myself thinking that he's Haze, but I just have this feeling... this feeling that something out there in the wildness has reached a tentacle out and wrapped it around my wrist, fixing to pull me into the abyss.

When we climb out of the trolley—Sarah in even taller platforms, this time made of red vinyl to match her purse—the humming night air is full of noise that's pretty close to what I imagine a jailbreak sounding like,

"I repeat, I hope there's beer," Sarah mutters, then swings her hips toward the entrance.

Inside the warehouse there's a huge throng of kids crowded around a keg (see? beer) and a card table laden with bottles of alcohol. A few kids are off to the side spraying letters and tags onto a bunch of sheets taped to the wall. The band hasn't yet finished setting up their gear, so old-school punk blares from a sound system manned by a pimply kid wearing huge headphones, staring down at his laptop in intense concentration. In the center of the room, there's a makeshift skate ramp that looks like a serious death trap—the sides are all uneven and the wood is splintered. There are a few guys crowded around the ramp, taking turns doing tricks. Steve Q. is standing with a lanky older guy in a knit cap. He's traded his work boots for a pair of sneakers that look like tires. This time he's not wearing a bulky cardigan or a trench coat. Instead he has on a tight blue T-shirt.

"What the *fuck* is that pants ferret doing here?" Sarah appears behind me with two cups of beer that she almost drops on the floor—and all over me.

"What?" I wheel around, cringing, waiting for the deluge. "Pants ferret?"

Sarah's cup is already half empty. She shoves one at me, her eyes locked on Steve. She's practically shaking. "Yes—like he's got something creepy and crawly in his pants with a nasty, nasty bite," she snarls. "Please don't tell me that asshole is the one who told you about this party, Hallie."

"Um." I take a huge swig of beer and look down into the foamy depths as Steve spots me, his face breaking into a huge grin as he lopes over.

"Hey, Hallie! Guess what? Alex is here! Somewhere..." he says, still grinning as he looks around the room, then seems to notice Sarah. "And um..." The smile evaporates.

"Already forgot my name, dude?" Sarah snaps. "What kind of 'journalist' are you, anyway?"

Steve looks from her to me, awkward, blinking. Sarah just stares at me, her eyes burning into my forehead like a bullet through a zombie's brain.

Finally, I let out a very eloquent strangled "Gah!" and grab Sarah by the elbow, dragging her into the shadows where a couple grunts and grabs at each other's orifices. Surreptitiously, I flash Steve a "hold on" sign and he nods, looking relieved.

"What the hell, Hallie?" Sarah wails. "I thought you said you told that dude off! For *me*! You guys seem like fucking best friends or something! 'Hi Hallie,'" she mimics, making Steve's reedy voice extra high-pitched, "Guess whaaa-aat?!" She crosses her eyes.

I sigh. "I did, Sarah." And that's not wholly a lie. I had started to, after all. "But then he told me about this show. This *Haze* show. There's going to be a *Haze show*, Sarah!" I grab her shoulders as the words tumble out, exciting me anew. I talk faster and faster so that she can't cut me off. "We don't need to stay, I promise. I just need to find out about this show and then we can get out of here. Then..." I say cautiously. "Maybe we can go to the show? Together? Roadtrip? It's in the city. You like the city."

"Yay," Sarah deadpans. Then she rolls her eyes, her face softening slightly. Probably because she can tell I'm so excited. "But why are we here? Why do we have to talk to that dick?"

"His cousins are in the band," I say, excitement practically frothing out of my mouth. I remember him saying Alex is here, but I don't see him. I'm pretty sure I would recognize the smiley man in green who had accidentally taken my drumsticks. "It's a secret show and he said he would tell me about it tonight if I came here."

Sarah laughs a little. "Wow, you must have had your very first orgasm when he told you that. How do you know he's not full of shit?"

"He gave me a new tape," I babble. "It's weird and different and kind of out-there, but it's definitely Haze. It has to be."

"And you were going to tell me about this *when*?" Sarah's face falls a little and guilt tugs at my guts.

"Um, tonight? After a few beers?" I say, a sad attempt at humor. She doesn't bite, just looks at her shiny toes. "Besides, you were so pissed at him about the review and so bummed about... other things. I figured the first word I should mention should be 'road-trip'—instead of, you know, 'pants ferret.'"

Sarah cracks a smile then. "That's two words."

"So are you in?" I ask, grabbing her hand and squeezing.

"We can leave *right after* you talk to scabies boy over there?"

I nod.

"OK, fine, but *I'm* not talking to him." She pouts.

"Naturally."

The couple next to us starts groaning heavily, like beasts, cooing odd nicknames—one that sounds like "bitch bear"—and we clutch each other, laughing.

Steve eyes Sarah warily as we cut through the crowd back to him and his hatted friend, who has wandered over with two beers. He weaves in and out of my sightline and it seems to take longer to cross the room now that it's more full. Everything smells like smoke and BO. My pocket chimes and I almost stop in my tracks, digging into its depths. I like your jacket. You look cute.

I freeze, my eyes leaping all around the room. My blood goes chilled like it did when I was listening to the new tape and I feel like my fucking head might explode. He's here. ZZZ is here. My mind seizes on the words but doesn't really understand. How can he be here? Why is he here? What does he want? And who the hell *is he*, really? I whip my head around, searching for whoever sent the message, but nearly all of the faces populating the warehouse are lit up by the blue-light glow of their phones. I type back, quickly, watching to see if anyone responds when I send the message. Thanks! How did you know that? Tapping, texting, chiming, flashing, I never realized how little our generation look up from their phones until now. There's no way to tell if my message has been received by that guy over there with the black leather jacket and mullet or that dude over there with bleached blond hair and a mini mustache. They're all looking down—laughing, scowling, reacting. My pulse is pounding like a drum fill gone off the rails.

I'm at this party. But I'm not any of those guys standing near you.

I look up again, my eyes trying to take in everyone at once. Then I find myself staring into the blackness of the recording booth in the back. The venue does recordings of all of its shows. That's how it stays off the cops' radar when it comes to noise complaints. As far as I know, there's no liquor license—which makes the bar highly suspect. A little voice in my mind chimes, *That's where Nick worked.*

I squint, trying to see past the reflective window into the gloom, but all I can spot is a dark shape that could be a person or a chair. I shift to the side to avoid some girl barreling through the crowd, tears pouring down her face, and smack right into a wall of navy blue. My beer goes flying, the liquid turning the dark blue even darker.

"Ah," Steve's voice comes from above me and I look up. The front of his shirt is adorned with a spreading stain. My beer.

"Oh, no, I'm sorry... I spilled all over you," I groan, still looking toward the booth, searching for the telltale glow of a phone.

Steve laughs. "It's fine. Most of my stuff is pretty stained, anyway. Now this shirt just blends in with the rest," he pauses. "Which is not information I should readily be offering up to pretty girls..."

I nod, dumbly, still craning to see into the booth. My phone lights up in my hand again. **ZZZ:** Why are you talking to that kid? Should I be jealous?

A crowd of Anarchy kids floods by, blocking the booth from view and Sarah's voice snags at my ears. I turn around. She's talking, animatedly, to Steve's friend.

"Oh, yeah, my friend Hallie and I are in a band, but I don't know if that's what I really want to do, though. I think I want to be a psychic." She cocks her head to the side and smiles.

The hatted boy blinks, "A what?"

"A psychic. Like someone who tells the future?"

Why is Sarah talking to that dude? He's 100% not her type. She must be bored. And when Sarah's bored, I know first-hand, she fucks with people. I cringe inwardly, and probably outwardly, judging by the weird look Steve gives me. I still can't see the booth. I wheel back toward Sarah and Steve and his friend.

"You can tell the future?" the guy asks Sarah's boobs.

Sarah nods slowly, a wicked smile spreading across her face. "Give me your hand."

The guy's dumbfounded face breaks into a lazy smile and he extends his dirty palm to Sarah. A flash of disgust erupts across her face, but she smiles and takes his hand.

"Let's see," Sarah says, tracing a finger along the inside of his palm. The guy groans a little. A creepy, pleasure-filled groan. "Your lifeline is a little erratic..."

"Is that good?" hat boy purrs, now staring, unabashedly, at

Sarah's cleavage. He's old, I notice now. Probably in his late 20s.

"Maybe," Sarah says. "I'm guessing that you're really into juicing —that I can tell from the livid orange stain on your shirt— and that you likely read a lot of things on the Internet about sustaining a healthy lifestyle. Simultaneously, however, you snort copious amounts of cocaine and ingest hallucinogenic mushrooms like they're popcorn, going on weeklong trips that find you lost, muttering, and naked in the woods behind your parents' house, where you still live. Still, cockroach-like, you will live on while your friends slowly die from overdose after overdose, until you reach the ripe old age of 40, at which point you will discover that you spent the better part of your youth in a juice- and drug-fueled haze. You will then go into a major spiral of shame and sadness, brought about by the fact that you have zero marketable skills and that, due to your rapidly expanding gut, young girls have no urge to fuck you anymore. At which point, you will off yourself in your childhood room, next to the broken toys and broken dreams. So, yeah, erratic is probably bad in this case." Sarah smiles.

The guy looks back blankly, blinking. "You're kidding right? You're, like, fucking with me?"

"No, that's exactly what I will NOT be doing anytime soon, you creepy old perv," Sarah spits. "What the fuck is your problem, dude? Hitting on fucking teenagers? What are you, like, 30?"

The guy blinks at her for a second, then scowls. "I know you."

"I seriously doubt that." Sarah tosses her hair over her shoulder.

"You're the bitch who got Nick fired," he slurs.

My body seizes up. He had said the name. The name that shouldn't be said.

Sarah's eyes flash toward me and I see Steve reach for the guy's arm from the corner of my eye.

"Dude, Randy, maybe you should just leave her alone," he murmurs.

"Ah, fuck her!" Randy explodes, dropping his beer in frustration. The foam splashes toward my Keds and I dance back a little. He's obviously a lot farther ahead of the rest of us when it comes to intoxication.

"This little slut got with Nick! Got him fucking fired! On *purpose!* Stupid little fucking cunt!" Randy roars, balling his now-empty fists at his sides.

Before I can think. Before I can figure out what he meant by "on purpose." Before I can even blink, Randy is on the floor, blood gushing out of his nose, a stunned expression on his face.

"*Mother*fucker!" Sarah roars, cradling her hand to her chest. She glares down at Randy, her fist raised in the air. "I am NOT a fucking slut, you fucking piece of shit! I am NOT a fucking cunt, you fucking dick! You fucking asshole! You fucking—"

I never do find out what colorful expletive Sarah has lined up next, though, because just then sirens pierce through the teeming warehouse and the cops burst through the door.

\\\\\\\\\

There's a lot of blood pouring out of Randy's nose, squirting from between his fingers and pooling on the floor. Bright spots start to dance like drunken bees in front of my eyes as I watch it meet his pooled beer like a ghastly tie-dyed art project. The spots only increase in number when I feel an iron fist close around my upper arm. A face swims into a view—a surprisingly young face belonging to a police officer. He's not looking at me, though, but at Steve. Sarah struggles in his other hand.

"Gabriel Quilty..." the cop says slowly, staring at Steve. "You don't look a day over 20."

Steve's face suddenly goes really pale. "I'm not Gabriel. I'm Steve."

The cop laughs and almost lets go of my arm—almost. "Little Steve Quilty? Oh man, you've grown up, kid! Just exactly like your brother." He pauses and looks around the room at all the chaos surrounding us. "In more ways than one."

Another cop materializes from the shadows, swinging a pair of handcuffs and looking at his watch. He runs his hand over his jowls and yawns elaborately. "Stop socializing, Joe, and let's bring these kids in. My wife was supposed to be taping a game on the DVR and I'd like to watch at least the first half before I pass out."

Joe gives Steve a kind of half smile, like "What are ya gonna do?" and starts dragging us toward the door. It seems like the rest of the kids were able to beat a retreat that was hasty while we were all preoccupied by the punching. There's only the four of us left.

The other cop grabs Sarah's arm and prods Randy—who is still lying in a pool of beer and blood—with his foot. "Get up, asshole," he grunts.

"Wait, how do you know my brother?" Steve interjects, his voice a little strangled. The other cop ignores him, but Joe pauses and smiles, his eyes all faraway.

"We went to high school together in Mapleville," he says. "He was always getting in trouble, too, you know? Real badass of a kid. Whatever happened to him? Your dad was always so wrecked when the cops had to drag him home."

Steve's face contorts into a kind of twisted smile before he can cover it with a deep-set frown. "Yeah, my dad... he was wrecked." Something rings a little sarcastic about the statement. I notice he doesn't answer the cop's first question. "I'm guessing he would be even more wrecked you know, though, if you brought his other son in. He's so fragile these days..."

The other cop narrows his eyes. "You say your name is Steven Quilty?"

Steve's smile falters for just a second. "Yes, sir."

"I've got a buddy over in Mapleville," the cop says, the game apparently forgotten for now. "You used to live there?"

Steve pulls his grin tighter. He looks almost manic. "Yes, sir. Just moved."

"I know this kid, Joe," the cop says, jerking his thumb at Steve. "My buddy Tom works over in Mapleville. Weird kid. Homeschooled. Would have a record a mile long if he were an adult. Snot-nosed little vandal, this one. I heard his pop had to leave his parish because someone—and I swear to Christ it was this one—painted a massive ding-dong on the church bell."

"I'm glad you caught the subtlety of the pun," Steve says softly.

"What did you say, you little shit?" the cop hisses, grabbing Steve by the shirtfront.

Steve gives a ghost of a shrug.

"You're not getting away with that kind of shit in this town, kid," the cop says, dragging Steve and Randy toward the warehouse door. "Grab those other kids and let's get the fuck going. And I hope to God that my wife figured out how to use that DVR."

Joe gives Sarah and me a kind of apologetic look and I feel almost sorry for him—I mean, I would if he weren't dragging us off to our town's shitty little one-cell jail. The shock of the whole thing hasn't really sunk in for me. Unlike Steve, apparently, I've never been arrested. The worst I've done is litter. Also, my mind keeps swimming back to Nick, even though it's not supposed to. But, then, he had just been violently reasserted back into our lives—and Sarah keeps giving me these little sneaking glances to see if I'm mad at her. If I might be thinking about the whole Nick mess again. To placate her, I turn and give her a little thumbs-up. She exhales and shoots me a battered-looking smile. I'm the best, most understanding friend there ever was.

Nick had been the only guy to ever talk to me first—instead of Sarah. After we played shows at Machineworks, he would always come up to me with two beers and we'd go outside, sit on the steps and sip them while he smoked weed and squinted at the sky. He was older than me—maybe in his early 20s—but he always said I was easy to talk to. And talk to me he did—about his band and unpaid bills and his girlfriend who had died who he thought he might love forever. He never tried to touch me or anything, but I liked looking at his renaissance-painting profile surrounded by a sky full of stars, his lips moving and moving with words just for me.

Until, that is, one night he never came up to me with two beers and an offer to go outside and smoke. I looked for him everywhere and then me and his boss, Ed, found him at the same time—in the bathroom, half-dressed with Sarah. Or, rather, they spilled out of the bathroom like one of them had leaned on the door handle mid-grope. They landed at our feet, all sweaty and tangled.

Ed promised not to call the police if Nick never came back again. And I never saw him again, either. He didn't even look at me as he walked past me into the night, pulling on his shirt and zipping his pants. I wanted to be mad at Sarah, but she was fucked up before we even got on stage. She had drunk a massive amount of her mother's vodka before we left. So her mom wouldn't drink it herself, she told me later. She said she didn't even remember what happened with Nick and I shouldn't either. But neither option seemed realistic to me. Forgetting is impossible—what you've done and said are always there, ripples expanding and expanding.

SEVEN

"You're too pretty/ I'm too pretty/ We're too pretty to be nice,"
—"Nice 'n' Vacant," *Masking Tape* —Haze

There are about 100 bricks in the wall. I've counted them a few times and each time I've come out with 100. Sarah pokes me in the arm. "What time do you think it is?" she asks for the thousandth time.

I shrug. I'm still thinking about Nick, to be honest, even though I'm not supposed to. And ZZZ. The cops took my phone before I could answer him. They took all our stuff. Or at least that's what I thought. When I look over at Steve he has that piece of sea glass out again and he's turning it over in his hands, his skinny shoulders tenting the back of his T-shirt. I want to ask him about the show, but it seems inappropriate at this juncture.

It's just the three of us now. Randy's mother came for him a little while ago, silently leading him out of the police station, her face white and pinched. I felt really bad for her—bailing out some 26-year-old loser of a son. I bet she still does his laundry. I bet she separates his whites and folds them and leaves them on his bed—which she also makes. Apparently, Randy isn't pressing charges, which is good news for Sarah. The bad news is that neither her mother nor Tim picked up the phone when she called. The landline was just straight-up dead.

Steve tips his head back against the wall and mutters something, his hair hanging down into his face.

"What?" I ask, a little over-eagerly, thinking irrationally that he's said something about Haze.

"I need to leave tonight," Steve says, and looks up, his face wan and his eyes shining a little. It looks like he might cry. This mildly horrifies me.

"Didn't you call your dad? Or Alex?" I ask. He seems really upset. I mean, I'm pretty upset right now—about Nick and not answering ZZZ and just generally being in a jail cell—but I'm not about to shed tears. "Isn't he coming? If you want, I can ask my dad to bring you home, too. He's taking Sarah," I gesture toward Sarah, who gives Steve a kind of sneery smile. If that's a thing.

"*They* called him," Steve inclines his head toward the cops. "He's coming—my dad. I dunno where Alex went." He shudders a little. "But I mean I have to *leave*, leave. I need to get out of here. And I doubt Randy will take me now."

My mind clicks two and two together. Randy. The one with the van. The one Sarah punched. Two and two equals one big zero.

I look around the police station. Neither of the cops seems to be paying much attention. Joe snores lightly at his desk and the other scrolls angrily through his phone, perhaps looking for the score of tonight's game. I'm not even sure if we were *really* arrested, you know? Like in the way real criminals are. It doesn't quite seem protocol to let some other kid's parent take Sarah home. Maybe they just decided the whole "scared straight" thing isn't worth the effort.

"Why do you hang out with that asshole, anyway?" I ask.

Steve snorts, his fingers wrapping more tightly around the seaglass. "I don't hang out with him, really. Gabriel... my brother, used to." He goes quiet for a second and stares at the wall. I wonder what he means by "used to." I'm starting to get the sense that something happened to him. Something not-so-good.

He shakes his head. "Anyway, I don't think he's taking me now. And frankly, after that shitshow, I'm glad." His face falls momentarily, and then he looks at me like I might secretly be Santa Claus. "Do you have a car?" he asks, his eyes shining. "You're going, right? To see Haze?"

"Um, I think... we're going," I say, gesturing toward Sarah, who's picking her nails, bored.

"Oh," Steve says, his face brightening.

"Operative word 'we,'" Sarah says, gesturing between her and me, barely looking up from her nails.

Steve's face crumples and he nods a little, pulling himself together.

I turn toward Sarah, creating a little wall with my body. "Maybe we could... take him with us? There's room in Tim's car, right?"

On the way over here, Sarah had whispered in my ear that she was down for the show. That she would steal Tim's car—I didn't ask how—and that we would leave tomorrow night. I'm supposed to tell Dad that I'm staying at Sarah's for a few days. I doubt he'll care. I was confused a bit by her willingness to split, but then remembered the backpack and how she hadn't stayed at her own place for the last few days. I figured she would explain it to me when she was ready. I wondered somewhere deep in my gut if I should ask. If I was a bad person for not asking already.

Sarah's eyes get hard. "No, absolutely not. He's not coming with us. That's what buses are for."

"But he's..." I start, but Steve's voice cuts through the echoing silence of the cell.

"Please?"

"What did you say?" Sarah says, whirling toward the miserable-looking Anarchy Kid.

"I said, please. This is my only way out. I never thought I'd find one and now here one is and I want it. It's my way out." His voice sounds small and husk-like.

"Of what?" Sarah snaps.

"Of my house." Steve isn't looking at anyone. He's just staring at his feet, picking at the edges of his sneakers.

"So you're running away?" Sarah asks. If I'm not mistaken, she sounds a little impressed.

"Not exactly. I'm turning eighteen really soon. I don't really need to run away. I can leave if I want—in a few months. It's just... this is my way out. My way that doesn't involve being broke and homeless and a loser and dying in a fucking gutter." He pauses and Sarah and I stare at him, waiting.

"Care to elaborate?" Sarah coaxes, not entirely unkindly.

His face lightens a little and he looks down at his hands, at the sea glass. "This magazine contacted me the other day—because of my blog. They said they liked my writing, admired my dedication to Haze—said they'd heard about the show, too. When I told them Alex and B were my cousins, well, they got really excited—said if I can get this story about Haze, who he really is..." Steve says, his eyes flicking to me, "... if I can find out, they said they'd give me a job. Not an awesome job or anything, but something. Something that pays. That lets me do what I want. And I can leave. The right way."

"What happens if you stay?" Sarah asks.

"Nothing good," Steve says with a grim shake of the head. "My dad throws me out of the house, or I go to seminary school."

"That doesn't sound too bad," Sarah snaps. "At least you get to go to college. At least he's paying."

Steve laughs. "Yeah, he's paying all right. To own me forever. My dad is not... shall we say, the most pious of men outside of the church." Steve pauses for a second and then slowly slides up the corner of his shirt. There's a huge dark bruise yellowing on his ribs. I suck in my breath and look toward Sarah, who's staring at the bruise. Sarah's father left a few years ago. By law, he isn't allowed to return.

"Besides," Steve says, his voice taking on new power, a harder kind of edge. "I'm the one who knows where the show is. You need me."

Sarah closes her eyes, takes a deep breath and lets out a long sigh, and when she opens her eyes, the sullen anger that had radiated out of them moments before is replaced by her familiar ferocity. I hold my breath and so does Steve.

"Fine. You can come. But you're not riding shotgun."

\\\\\\\\

The air suffocates me as soon as I walk outside, even though it's probably getting on three in the morning. It's one of those wet blanket nights that threaten to smother you in your sleep. Dad's car is icy cold when I get inside, though, and I lean my sweltering forehead against the window and sigh. He doesn't say anything. Just turns on the radio—loud, loud, loud. All the shuttered-up shops and swaying phantom trees blur by in blacks and blues, and then Dad is pulling into Sarah's driveway.

"Thanks for the ride, Mr. Reed," Sarah says and Dad barely nods. Sarah turns to me and mouths, "One hour." She could have spoken at a normal volume, though. Dad's blasting The Doors, vaguely nodding along as Jim Morrison wails. I try to ignore the ominous undertones of the song and focus on what's set to go down later tonight—or this morning, rather. *This isn't the end; this is the beginning.*

I nod and tap my phone, whispering, "Text me." Then I scroll through my messages to see if ZZZ has said anything else. Nothing, just that last question, still left unanswered. I want to answer now, but I don't want Dad to see. Although it's highly unlikely he would ask about it if he did.

We had left before Steve's dad arrived, having exchanged numbers and sketched out a quick plan to meet up later that night after Sarah swiped Tim's keys. Although Steve still looked pretty miserable before we left, some of his cockiness seemed to return; as we were leaving, he gave me a weird crooked smile.

Now, sitting in the dark car with Dad and The Doors, the bruise on Steve's ribs flashes through my head and I shiver in the AC. Steve doesn't really strike me as the son of a preacher man—he seems wholly uninterested in the divine, possessing myriad sins. But I guess that's actually what you would expect, right? Isn't that what kids are meant to do? The opposite of what our parents tell us? I don't know. Up until tonight I pretty much did what they asked of me. I even got along with them most of the time—or my dad, really—a concept that's totally embarrassing to my high school compatriots. Obviously, though, that feeling of camaraderie has been fading for a while now. And I miss him. It feels like he and I live on opposite sides of a big piece of glass. I can see him moving and I know that he's talking, feeling, being, but I can't reach him and he can't reach me. I really wonder if he'll notice when I'm gone. If he'll worry. Or will he just squint through the glass and see the same vagueness there and carry on living?

Steve's father will definitely notice that he's missing. The thought comes unbidden, accompanied by a flash of Steve's terrified, strangely attractive face. My stomach gets all squirmy when I think of the bruise again, painting his ribcage an ugly shade of maroon and yellow.

The music cuts out suddenly and I notice that we're parked in front of my silent house. Dad still hasn't said anything. He hasn't spoken at all during the entire car ride. He hasn't even sung along to the radio, which seems almost a physical impossibility for a man who has memorized basically the entire rock catalogue.

Weirder—and almost worse—he hasn't yelled at me. He hasn't even looked disappointed. He's just like some kind of auto-driving robot programmed to go "home." Sure, he's never been that forceful of a man, but, then, he's never had a reason to be. Still, this silence is straight-up eerie. It sat down between us like a ghost when I first got in the car and now it's brushing its icy fingers all up and down my spine.

Dad still hasn't cut the engine. It purrs like a drowsing cat. The radio is still on, really low, and I can hear Kurt Cobain muttering about finding his friends in his head. Dad takes off his glasses that he uses for driving and rubs them on his faded shirt, then looks at me–kind of. More to the left of me than at me.

"You're grounded, you know," he says. "I've never had to do that... It's weird. It's... disappointing."

Something stabs at my sternum. I'm not sure if it's relief that he's paying attention–or pain. Or anger. Disappointing? I'll show him disappointing. Someone get me a mirror.

"So why don't you..." It seems hard to get the words out, like he's speaking while falling asleep. "Just... just go inside."

A sick wave of nostalgia floods through me. When I was a kid, my dad and I had a name for that feeling–the "mossy feeling." A kind of gross, damp feeling of missing something–something you're not sure you've even lost yet. Something you didn't even know how to look for. I feel mossy now. Way mossy. I want to hug my dad around the middle like a kid and breathe in his smell–plants and cedar and old cotton T-shirts washed too many times.

"Dad, I..." I reach toward him, awkward, waiting for him to turn toward me. To hug me. To something. I was just in a fucking jail cell, after all. Instead, he's just kind of looking toward the house. Mom's window is dark. The shades are drawn. Her car isn't in the driveway. She's probably at my aunt's house–her sister's. A few times a month she visits and ends up staying the night, wandering in the next afternoon blinking like a mole that has been flushed from its hole.

"You know," Dad shakes his head and looks at me, not really see-ing me. Looks past me. The ghost leans its head on my shoulder. "If I could go back to my younger self and tell him something, you know what I would say?" He doesn't wait for me to respond. "I would tell him: You can't force someone to love you. You just can't. You can't make someone want you."

I blink at him and he starts crying.

I open my mouth, reach out my hand, but I don't know what to say. I can feel the pain radiating off him—it's like sitting close to a roaring fire, seeing how near you can inch until your face starts burning. Dad doesn't look familiar anymore. Nothing does. It's like I'm in some dream version of my real life and it's all melting around me. This must be what dropping acid is like.

"I need you to go inside now," Dad says slowly, tears dripping onto the steering wheel. "You're grounded."

"But..." I begin, feeling utterly alone, the idea of entering that big, cold divided house suddenly too much to endure.

"We'll talk about it in the morning," Dad says, exhaustion edging into his voice.

I nod, dumbly, and—my fingers fumbling and numb—I open the car door and get out. I wait for Dad to follow, but he drives away instead. Fear clenches around my guts. Who does that? Who just drives away at three in the morning? Who leaves their daughter standing in the dark like that? Ghost Dad, that's who. I turn toward home, everything hurting, somehow—a real, physical pain. I feel like the house is just crouched and waiting. It looks dark, the house— cold and stoic, offering up none of its secrets. The windows suck in darkness like sightless eyes and the locked doors are like sewn-up mouths. It's like a tomb, a charnel house.

Steve's house across the way is dark too, but I swear I can see a flicker of light dancing in what I think is his window and I remember what we're going to do in a few hours. I turn resolutely toward my house. Not daring to open the front door, lest a dark shadow find its way in, I go around to the back and climb up the ladder propped up outside my window. I tumble onto my bed and lie back, staring at the ceiling, my heart throbbing painfully in my chest.

Sarah will be here soon. I cling to that fact, thinking of the black asphalt of the nighttime road unfurling in front of me—the miles stretching between me and my parents, toward Haze. I try not to think about Dad. About his taillights disappearing into the night. *"Disappointing."*

I blink up at the fading glow of the fluorescent plastic stars stuck on the ceiling, brighter now that the room is cast in almost absolute blackness. A flash of light issues from inside my purse accompanied by a muffled "ping!" I sit up, rooting around in my bag. Dragging my cell from my purse at last, I squint at the sudden brightness of the screen. **ZZZ:** Are you OK?

My face breaks into a smile and I almost start crying because someone cares. Someone wants to know how I am. Someone sees me. I tap back: Yes, are you? Did you get out before the cops got there?

I hid. I'm OK, though. I was more worried about you.

I look at my clock. It's getting on 3:30 a.m. now. You're up late.

I'm usually up late, but tonight that reason was you. You're OK, right? You're not with that boy or anything?

I grin, despite everything churning inside. He was worried about me—*and* jealous.

No, he's a just a—the word "friend" seems a bit of a stretch. And

I can't say "He's your bandmates' cousin," since ZZZ hasn't actually owned up to being Haze. God, it's hard to communicate with someone when you know so little. No, I finally type, I don't even really know him. Speaking of, tell me something about you.

Darkness swims into the room as the screen goes black, my eyes adjusting to the gloom as I wait for a response.

I fucking hate cilantro.

I blink. The phone pings again.

Just kidding. Tell you something about me... I like secret places. Hideouts and all that. I have a few, but what I really want is a tree house in a forest—one that reaches into the sky and the other trees, the kind that are so woven together it seems you can walk on them. I want to live in a tree house or something, but that's not really possible with what I do.

I smile, thinking of a platform high above oaks and birches, soft wind brushing my face with its fingers—ZZZ's soft fingers.

What do you do? I type back, still feeling the phantom chilled warmth of fall in my dark room.

No, your turn.

Something about me? I pause, my finger hovering over the screen. Sometimes, in my dreams, I look in the mirror. I always see the real me. I look in the mirror across from my bed now, but all I can see is darkness.

I wish I saw myself as clearly as you do. OK, my turn…

For an hour, I sit in the darkness, trading bright embers of my life with ZZZ. I built a castle in the woods out of scrap metal and old tires when I was six. He saw a coyote once in the woods when he was ten and howled and howled but it never came back. I tucked notes to future generations into the knotholes in our house. He dreamt of the Dalai Lama once—they sat on a high mountain, drinking mossy green tea. The messages ping into the darkness like sparks from a campfire until the clock inches closer to the time Sarah's supposed to come collect me.

We're both supposed to leave notes for our parents—and Sarah has to write one for her brother (his including some kind of blackmail so he doesn't rat her out for taking the car). I write mine now—fast—telling Dad I'm at Sarah's for the weekend (I know it's a flimsy barrier of safety since I'm grounded, but whatever).

I have to go to sleep now, I type, sorry to break the connection. Tell me something else in the morning.

Sweet dreams, Placid Girl… But before I go, just… listen to me on this: That pink-haired girl isn't good for you. Your friendship with her worries me. She almost got you hurt tonight.

It's the second time in as many days that someone has said that—in some form or another. Steve said it in the review and now ZZZ. Two lines of invisible soldiers start to line up in my chest then—one waving a bright pink flag, like Sarah's hair, the other one emblazoned with Zs. Just as they start to charge a light flashes two times at my window. Hurriedly, I shove a pile of clothes into my backpack.

When I drop to the ground, Sarah is smiling, tapping a flashlight against her hip.

"My mom and Tim were passed out when I got home," Sarah says over her shoulder. "The phone wasn't working, either. Guess Mom forgot to pay the bill again." Sarah laughs, and my insides relax—just a little. Neither Steve nor ZZZ know Sarah. She seems like... a handful on the surface, sure, but once they get to know her... that is, if I ever meet ZZZ and if he is who I think he is, he'll meet her and get to know her.

We dash toward Tim's car in the pitch black and climb in, start rolling down the driveway. Dad's car is still gone. I peek at the string of messages on my phone and my chest floods with warmth again, pushing out all the other no-good feelings. *Sweet dreams...*

"I can't believe we're doing this," I say, my face relaxing into a smile. The road thrums under our wheels and headlights flick by. We're supposed to park close to Steve's house, but far enough away that his dad won't see. Excitement bubbles up inside me at the thought that soon—very soon—we'll be in the city. A city that I had only been to before with school groups and my family, under watchful eyes and constant supervision.

"Me neither," Sarah sighs, propping her head on her hand with a slight yawn. "The things I do for you." She shakes her head.

I look at her and smile. "You're pretty much the best friend ever, you know that right?" My heart bursts with warmness for Sarah now—ZZZ's words almost forgotten. This will be an adventure that we'll always share—one that we can take down and smile at when we're old and gray and wasting away on front porches or by the fireplace.

She's silent for a few seconds, and I watch her profile, black against the landscape as it slips by.

"Remember how..." she says slowly, almost sing-song. "Remember how you used to make me do math when I was mad?"

I laugh, pulling a sneaker up onto the car seat and fiddling with my shoelaces. "Oh, yeah."

"When I was mad at my mom or someone at school or Tim, you used to make me do, like, addition and multiplication and whatever." She flicks on the windshield wipers and turns them off again, toys with the high-beams. "Like, that one time when Mom grounded me for no reason. You know, when she was dating that guy, Bill, and he yelled at me when I wouldn't stop singing Nirvana songs into his face while he was watching football."

"To be fair, it was that song about where bad people go when they die..." I say, laughing, but not really. Sarah's mom dated the worst people. Not violent guys or anything—just losers. The kind that don't pay taxes and steal from their girlfriends. It always made me nervous going over to Sarah's house when one of them was there.

"Ha," Sarah says, rather than laughs. "Anyway, you remember you made me do math? I wanted to trash Bill's car and you said..."

"Minus one if this will get you grounded for longer..."

"Right," Sarah turns to me and I can see her eyes glittering in the dark. "Plus one if it will make you feel better. Minus two if it will make Mom even closer to Bill and less likely to break up with him. Math... anyway," she takes a deep breath. "That always made me feel better. It made it easier for me to breathe and think things through."

"Good," I say, nodding, not really sure what she's getting at. Maybe she has a new problem. Maybe it's something to do with her mom and why she'd been staying over so much. Maybe I had been neglecting her. The thought makes my stomach drop with shame. I open my mouth to say something—I don't know what yet—but she keeps talking.

"And, you know, I think maybe you should do it now, the math..." she says slowly. I start to nod and then she finishes her sentence, "For yourself..."

"For what?" If I had hackles they would be raised. I know my voice sounds a little hard, and I clear my throat. "I mean, why?"

"I don't know... if this is a good idea... You know, Mercury is in retrograde, which means it's a terrible time to make decisions, and that guy... I don't think he's good news," Sarah says softly.

I don't say anything, just stare ahead into darkness. I can't go home now. I can't go home now just because Sarah has one of her "feelings." Fuck Mercury.

"So, maybe, minus one for that pants ferret... Because, for one thing, everything in that review was total BS..." Sarah says and laughs, nervously. I notice she's slowed down. She's been circling the block over and over, I realize.

"Of course, but the review has nothing to do with anything," I half-yell, my blood simmering and my heart fluttering around like a dying butterfly. *It's all BS except for the part about my drumming,* I think somewhere in the corner of my brain, but I don't say it out loud. I wonder briefly why I don't say it out loud. "Sarah, I need this," I say finally, the words thick and pounding in my throat. "That's plus a million. That's plus everything. I need this."

Neither of us says anything as we circle the block again, past all the slumbering homes, and finally stop a bit down the street from Steve's house, lurking under the shadow of the church. My nails dig into my thighs and I realize I'm not breathing.

Sarah puts the car in park and sighs, putting her head down on the steering wheel. "And it's worth all the minuses, though? I've had my share of minuses, Hallie, and they're not always fun. Is this going to be worth all the negative numbers?"

I think of ZZZ again. Of Haze. I think of years of wondering if I was right about him—if he has the key to something deep inside myself that I have yet to even begin to know about to unlock. "It's worth all the minuses," I say, with a firm nod—one Sarah returns in the gloom.

"OK, but don't say I didn't warn you..." she says with a sigh.

\\\\\\\\\

"It's been forever," Sarah grumbles, knocking her head lightly against the car window in frustration. "Is he coming or not?"

I look at my phone again. It's dark—like the windows all throughout town.

"I haven't heard from him," I say, "Let's give it another five minutes."

"Why don't you *call* him?" Sarah whines.

"I don't wanna bother him, Sarah. I'm sure he's just... packing," I finish lamely. The truth is, I'm starting to worry that he's going to bail. I can feel the rising panic that accompanies the idea of just going home and forgetting about the concert.

"Jesus, Hallie, it's super *hella* late and we're running away from home to go to some random ass show—I think we're past the whole 'gender norms dictating who calls whom' thing," Sarah cries. "Please, I beg of you, call Anarchy Douche and let's *go!*"

I sigh and look at my phone again. I wish I could send ZZZ another message, but he's probably sleeping by now. I miss talking to him all of a sudden and it's such a weird thought–a thought that seems so bizarre to have about someone I've just met–that I blush, rather furiously.

Suddenly, Sarah gives a strangled roar and lurches toward me, grabbing the phone from my hand. "Fine," she snaps. "I'll do it, then." Scrolling through "Contacts" and pressing "call," Sarah throws the already-ringing phone into my lap before I can so much as yell "fuck!" ZZZ's words about Sarah echo in my head again as I look down at the phone and up at Sarah's livid face. Did everything really have to be on her schedule? Did we always have to do things by her rules? *She almost made you stay home,* a little voice says in my head, tinny and nasty.

"Hello," a muffled voice comes from my lap.

"H-hello," I pant, shooting Sarah a scowl as I retrieve the phone and press it to my cheek. "Steve?"

"You called me." Steve sounds tired and far on the phone, even though he's only a few hundred feet away.

"I'm sorry?" Irritation starts to bubble up in my chest. Why does he sound so relaxed? And why the hell isn't he down here with us already?

"You said 'hello' in a questioning tone, as if I were the one calling you," Steve says in an antagonizingly calm voice.

"Whatever," I spit, more venomously than I planned. "Where are you? We've been sitting out here for fifteen minutes."

"Locked in my room." There's that annoyingly calm voice again, but something pulsates under it. Something dark.

"WHAT?" I yell, my heart starting to speed up its quest to distribute blood throughout my body.

"I said—"

"I know what you said, dude, but what the hell? I mean... What the hell?"

"What's going on?" Sarah asks, looking slightly disturbed and more than a little amused. "Can he not come? What a shame..."

I put my finger to my lips and glare at Sarah. "What do you mean you're locked in your room?"

"My father was not very happy about the whole me-getting-arrested-thing, so he locked me in my room. My room only locks from the outside, so I'm stuck," Steve says, matter-of-factly.

"That's horrible." My hand flies to my mouth like I'm some kind of damsel in distress and I take it down—quickly—as Sarah is looking at me like she might vomit all over Tim's car any minute now.

"I know," Steve says. "What if the house catches fire?" His voice is so even, so bereft of emotion that I wonder if he might be joking.

"Just go home, Hallie." He sounds tired. "My father wins. He always wins. I'm stuck. I can't get out of here. I'm done. I should just accept my fate and go to seminary."

"No!" I cry, surprising myself with the firmness of my voice. "We're getting you out of there. You said the door is locked from the outside?"

"Yeah..." Steve says slowly.

"Is your dad asleep?"

"Yeah..."

"Does he keep a spare key under a ceramic bird on the porch like parents in movies do?"

"A duck, yeah, why?"

"I'm coming in," I say, hanging up the phone before he can respond. I spin around to face Sarah. "Steve is lock—"

"Yeah, I heard," Sarah says, looking at me with wide eyes. "But are you sure about this? Breaking and entering–I'm pretty sure that's one of those illegal things..."

"Yeah. I'm sure," I say, setting my mouth into a firm line. Somewhere deep inside, a voice has started whispering to me–the one that tells me to run across streets when the light says "Walk" and there are no cars are around and screams at me to study for math tests that are two weeks away–hissing that this whole thing is a *bad idea*. I close my eyes and push it back down deep inside. That voice has been chatty enough for the last 16 years–now it's time for another voice, one that sounds suspiciously like Haze's, to take over. And that voice, with its ragged roughness, is telling me to sneak into that house and spring the preacher's Anarchist son from his cage. And, yes, that is not a sentence I have ever imagined any of my inner or outer voices ever uttering.

Yes, ZZZ–or Haze... or whoever–doesn't want me to get hurt, get in trouble. But his kindness radiates through his messages. He wouldn't want me to abandon Steve, either. He also wouldn't want me to miss out on a chance to meet him.

"I don't think this is a good idea," Sarah says interrupting the battle of my multiple personalities, her mouth in a thin line. "I think we should just go back to your place. This just doesn't seem worth the trouble."

"Jesus, Sarah," I half-shout, exasperation bubbling over. "His dad locked him in his room and who the hell knows what else. Can't you just get over the fact that he didn't like your music for two seconds and think about someone other than yourself?"

Sarah gapes at me, her face slack. And then sad. And then tight.

"Is this about before... about Nick?" she asks stiffly and I groan.

"No," I say, equally stiffly. "This is about right now. This is about this particular moment in time. This is about helping Steve," *and meeting Haze,* my brain hisses, *you're not the martyr you seem.* "Now please, just stay in the car and wait for me. I need you out here and ready to drive." I sound like I'm in a bad movie about bank robbers, but I don't care.

I put my hand on the door handle and Sarah looks at me, angry, but perhaps a little ashamed. "Fine," she says with a heavy sigh. "If you see the preacher, just start talking backward. They hate that."

That's about the closest Sarah gets to "I was wrong."

I start across the lawn toward the dark house, the looming spire of the church casting it into even deeper shadow. It seems as if every archangel in the heavens is looking down at me, pointing their fingers and muttering about the abyss.

The key is right where Steve said it would be, under an impossibly cheerful-looking ceramic duck that I can picture neither Steve nor his father purchasing. Maybe it came with the house. I always wondered about that practice—hiding keys in nearly plain sight after installing expensive alarm systems. Sometimes the most effective way in is the easiest.

The foyer smells like beeswax and old coats. There's no light anywhere in the house, and all I can hear are the creaks and groans of old wood.

The stairs are covered in heavy shag, so my footfalls are nearly silent. Steve's room is to the right of the landing. There's a crack of light under the doorframe—like that cast from a flashlight—and a lock, the kind that locks automatically when you close the door. I can't imagine what kind of person installs something like that on their kid's door. And I don't really want to.

Holding my breath, I reach toward the lock, expecting the

preacher to come bursting from his room at any moment, wielding a fiery sword and yelling about Beelzebub or something. When nothing happens, I twist the knob, silently swing open the door, and dart into the room.

"Don't shut the door!" Steve hisses from his bed, his face cast in gloomy contrast by the flashlight in his hand.

I realize that I had been instinctively swinging the door closed and snatch it back with a sharp intake of breath. That was close. The last thing I need is for Steve's scary-ass father to find me—locked in his son's bedroom. Even with my limited knowledge of all things holy, I know that that must be one of the big sins.

"What are you *doing* here?" Steve says, frantically gesturing for me to come closer.

His bed is littered with music zines and he has traded his jeans—I notice with a weird thrill that I immediately quell—for black boxer briefs. Seeing my eyes wandering, Steve looks embarrassed, then smirks and scoops up his jeans from the bedroom floor. I look away as he wriggles into them, hopping and undulating until they slide over his hips. So that's how they get into jeans that skinny.

There's a brief clearing of the throat and I realize that Steve is now fully clothed and looking at me expectantly.

"What...?" I ask, shifting from foot to foot.

"I asked what you're doing here?" Steve says, his face suddenly serious. "I told you, it's done. We're not going."

I cross my arms. "Why not? I'm here, the door's open, you're wearing pants. What's stopping us?"

Steve sits down on the end of his bed and puts his head in his hands. "It's just... it's just too *much*. Running away? Fuck, that's heavy, man. Running away never got anyone anywhere..." He's rubbing that sea glass again, and I wonder how much its smoothness has to do with his hands, rather than the actual sea.

"Well, I'm game," I say, walking closer to him. "And I bet you've got a lot more experience with this type of stuff than me."

Steve shakes his head. "No, I've never run away. My brother, Gabriel—he was the one who did shit like that. Reckless shit. Or, he did shit like that once, I guess. You only really need to run away once if you're good at it. He ended up sucking pretty hard."

I don't know what to say, so I move closer to him and sit next to him on the bed. "Where is he now? Your brother?"

Steve looks at the sea glass again, digging into its depths with his eyes, kind of. "Dead. Two out of four of us are dead now." He gestures around the house, limply. "My mom and Gabriel were driving—or, Gabriel was driving—and he crashed and she died and my dad nearly killed Gabriel afterward. And then he left. And then, I guess, he died, too—a few years later."

I don't ask "how" because it seems like an insensitive thing to do but Steve answers me anyway.

"Dad won't tell me how. He just said it was bad. He said Gabriel was a loser. He wouldn't even let me go to the funeral. If there was one."

I sit, mute.

Steve sighs and puts his hands on his face. "Gabriel. Fuck it. He's why I don't want to leave and why I have to leave and why... I'm scared."

I don't really know anyone who has died. My grandmother died when I was five but that's it. My parents didn't let me come to the funeral, but I remember my mom coming home from the cemetery with a scrap of black fabric pinned to her dress, smelling like strange perfume. Then it just seemed like my grandmother disappeared. I missed her, sure, but there was no finality. No wrenching loss. I can't even begin to come close to understanding what Steve has had ripped away from him.

So I sit quietly, examining the zines and notebooks scattered on the coverlet. One of them is scrawled all over with the same tag. Squinting, I can just make out the letters: "Q&A."

"You're a good writer, you know," I say, fingering one of the notebooks.

"Even though I trashed your friend?" Steve asks, with a ghost of a smile.

"At least you did it with fancy words," I say softly, instantly feeling guilty—like I'm siding with Steve. Still, it seems possible that I can respect and even like both of them—my best friend and this strange boy—without feeling like a total traitor. Even if Sarah doesn't understand. "If you can talk to him—Haze—if you can get this story... I just know that things will be good."

My phone buzzes in my pocket and my heart clenches. *ZZZ*, my mind screams in that same voice it was babbling in before—the ragged one. And immediately I feel ashamed. I hold the keys—potentially—to Steve's freedom in my pocket and I haven't even told him.

Steve looks up, a sad smile on his face, which is cast in the light of the flashlight for the first time since I came into the room. My hand flies to my mouth and I stifle a cry. An angry red bruise blossoms near his eye, barely concealed by his curling hair.

"What—what *happened*?" I say, my voice strangled as my hand flutters around his cheek like some kind of nervous bird looking to land. Finally, my palm falls awkwardly on his knee and I pat it, weirdly. A sick feeling surges through my chest and I want to hit something—and to hold Steve close to me and make sure nothing bad ever happens to him again. The feeling disturbs me. I clamp down on it and desperately try to shove it away, but it keeps boomeranging back.

I try to take my fingers away from their perch on his knee but Steve's hand closes over my hand and his eyes lock on my eyes, his breath getting shallow. He moves slightly closer. A phantom string tugs from the center of my chest, seemingly connected to a similar location on Steve's. I stare at the freckle at the corner of his mouth. Dear God in heaven that may or may not exist whose house I'm almost certainly desecrating, is Steve about to kiss me?

My phone chooses that moment, of course, to chime again and I take the opportunity to tear my eyes away from Steve's. I cough and reach into my pocket, ignoring his questioning gaze. No new messages from Haze. Just two texts from Sarah.

There's another light on in the house! Get out now!

I just saw someone walking around. Seriously, dude, get the FUCK OUT!

A door closes in the hallway and Steve spins to face me, his eyes wide.

"My dad," he gasps. "My door. He'll know." Steve grabs my shoulders, eyes wide and hair wild. "Hide," he whispers, slinking to his bedroom door and clicking it closed.

I look around, panicked. Heavy footfalls are coming closer and closer to Steve's room.

Steve spins around, gives a strangled groan and grabs me again, pushing me down onto the unmade bed. Grabbing the comforter, he flops down on top of me and pulls the blanket over both of our heads—kneeing me in the stomach in the process. I try not to gasp for air—or knee him back in return.

"Shhh," he hisses above me under the cave of blankets. The footsteps stop right outside Steve's door. His chest is warm on mine, our breathing mingled. The memory of him looking at my lips just moments before comes back unbidden and I suppress a shiver. Not the creeped-out variety of shiver. The other kind.

The door creaks open, and the heavy feet take a few steps into the room. I smell musky cologne. Panic courses through me and the urge to scream bubbles in my throat. As if he can tell I'm about to freak out, Steve's arms tighten around me. He smells like cigarette smoke. The length of his body burns into mine in the summer heat. I have never been this close to a boy before. Let alone in bed. I wonder, wildly, what this would be like under other, less terrifying circumstances and my whole body floods with warmth. Then the chill eddies back as the feet start moving again. My mind begins an insistent mantra of *Fuck, Fuck, Fuck*, before I realize that they're heading away from the door, which clicks closed a few seconds later.

With a massive sigh, Steve collapses on top of me in relief, his whole body going limp. Then, he wraps his arms around me, letting out a kind of strangled sound as he squeezes. I catch my breath in surprise before returning his hug, tentatively, breathing in his earthy smell.

He's warm and his arms are solid. I wonder if he'll kiss me now. I blink hard, banishing the thought from my mind—just in time for a much more horrifying thought to creep in. Steve's dad had closed the door.

I sit up and fling the covers off of us both. Steve looks up at me, startled and, surprisingly, more than a little hurt. I shake my head to clear it and whisper, "The door. Your dad—he closed the door. What are we going to do?"

Steve's face falls and he sits up on his elbows, so that our chests almost touch. I flush and roll off of him to sit on the end of the bed. "Oh, God, I can't—I mean, your dad... Oh God." I drop my head to my hands.

I'm going to be stuck here until morning. Steve's dad will find me and call my parents. My parents—despite their overall malaise—will lock me in my room. I will never get to meet Haze. The thought of him banishes all memories of Steve's lips from my head. I have to meet him. I have to go to that show. Something dark and ancient deep down in my soul tells me so.

I look at Steve, who watches me with a weird, dreamy look on his face that doesn't look nearly panicked enough for the situation at hand.

"Well?" I say, raising my eyebrows.

"What we were just doing... That wasn't so bad. We could just keep doing that."

I choke a little. "*What*? What are you talking about? If your dad—and the show—*What*?"

"Do you have a boyfriend?" The words seem to burst from Steve's lips.

"I, uh..." I mutter, thrown off by the question—the weirdness of its context. "Yeah..."

It seems like a lie, even to me, but something about the declaration also seems right. There's ZZZ. Haze. Whoever. One message from him seems equivalent to a thousand warm touches from a boy like Steve. I am not available.

Steve sighs. A brief look of hurt flutters across his face before he regains his demeanor with a crooked smile. "Undiagnosed Tourette's. I told you. Ignore me."

Before I can say anything in return—specifically that he doesn't seem to know what Tourette's is—Steve kicks on his boots and dashes to the window.

"Is that your car out there?" Steve says, not looking at me. I can see his face reflected in the window, though. The grim line of his mouth and the dark bruise marring his face. On some people, scars and marks were ruinous, on Steve, the imperfections are oddly beautiful.

"Yeah," I say. "Sarah's out there waiting."

Steve turns around and raises an eyebrow. "Well, tell her to get in here, then—and fast."

I nod and tap out a series of rapid instructions in a text message. Calling Sarah would just lead to a lot of questions and protestations that I really don't need right now. I press "send" and sit back on Steve's bed with a sigh. He gets up as soon as I sit down and starts carefully depositing clothes into a duffel bag, avoiding my gaze all together. After a few minutes of overly meticulous packing, I realize that there will be no talking until Sarah gets here.

I study his hunched form, bending over the duffel bag, the sinews in his arms and his curling hair.

Then, the door creaks open. Steve and I both whirl around, and then sigh with relief. Sarah's slight frame stands in the doorway, her face cast in shadows.

"OK, kids, slumber party is over," she whispers. "Let's get the fuck out of here."

EIGHT

"All the little artifacts on your shelf mean something/ Mean something/ Mean something,"

—"Mummified," *Masking Tape* —Haze

I'm making out with a man without a face, his hands roving all over my body as it burns, burns, burns. I gasp, throw my head back. The man's mask-like face—like one of those creepy Amish dolls with the blank white features—turns toward me and his head cocks to the side before a loud beep emanates from the vicinity of his mouth. I jerk away, my head banging against a chilly pane of glass as my eyes pop open.

My entire body cramps and aches, as it had been curled up like a cat in the backseat of Sarah's brother's car. I blink rapidly and sit up, look around, trying to remember how I got here. The whole thing seems like an even more unlikely dream than the one I just woke out of. I can still feel the faceless man's non-lips on mine and I shiver a little.

Something skitters to the floor as I shift in the back of the car, which I just now notice isn't moving. My phone, the screen still glowing with evidence of a received message. That explained the beeping noise the faceless man made—real-life spillover into my dream world.

I reach for the phone, but someone taps on the window. I jump and my head hits the roof of the low-slung car. Rubbing my throbbing skull, I took toward the window, my heart pounding. Could it be the cops? My dad? A drifter? People were always talking about drifters stealing spleens and whatnot. Waking up packed in a bathtub full of ice, body parts missing like macabre puzzle pieces.

Steve waves at me with the tips of his fingers, crouching down to peer into the car. He unleashes an uneven smile and my heart lurches. This is definite progress from last night. After extricating ourselves from Steve's house—after Sarah arrived like a glorious, flaming deus ex machina—we had sat on opposite sides of the car, avoiding each other's eyes. Sarah, thankfully, had not pressed the matter—just drove for 40 minutes or so before announcing that she needed to crash "like, right now, unless you want me to literally crash." We had all decided to pull over into the parking lot of a highway-side diner and rest for the remainder of the night.

Steve bangs on the glass again and I roll my eyes and crank the window down. "What?" I ask. I can clearly see Steve's black eye in the morning light and my stomach does this horrible whirlpool thing. With his army jacket—donned in full heat, mind you—and wild hair, he looks like one of those aforementioned drifters. All he needs is a tattered sign warning passersby about the adverse effects of nuclear weapons. There used to be a man who stood downtown by the drawbridge with a sign like that. He disappeared a few years ago. I guess he either died or simply got tired of thinking about it all. I wonder if Steve is the kind to carry signs. I hope not. It all seems like a pantomime of principles to me, anyway. All artifice and no action. Steve seems more inclined to action than anything else.

Steve drapes an arm on the windowsill and leans in a little, jabbing a thumb back toward the diner. "Hungry?" he asks, his eyes meeting mine before sliding over my face to linger somewhere near my left ear. Not as much progress as I thought. I sigh and nod when my stomach grumbles, thinking of curling bacon and butter sliding seductively into the crevices of English muffins. I don't remember the last time I ate. There hadn't been time for food between jail and Dad's little speech about the hopelessness of love, that's for sure. Who has any kind of appetite after that? I miss Dad suddenly. Fiercely. But I kind of shake my head and shake it off and push it down. I'll think about all of that after. After what, I'm not sure.

I stretch and look for Sarah, who's slumped over the steering wheel in what looks like a spectacularly uncomfortable position. I jab my sleeping friend on the shoulder, wondering for a wild moment if she's dead. My eyes flicker down to her stomach, checking for an up and down kind of movement—or for the absence of kidneys.

"Sarah," I poke her in the back.

"Leemethefuckalone," Sarah groans and hugs the wheel tighter and I laugh with relief, patting her on the back. "OK," I say, as Sarah grumbles and shifts her weight. "Steve and I are getting food. I'll grab you a muffin."

"Fffffffffffuuu," Sarah hisses, and, apparently, falls asleep before she can finish cursing. Sarah can basically sleep anywhere. I've always admired that about her. Meanwhile, me—it's a wonder I had fallen asleep in the back of the car. I've always been a restless sleeper. Dad always said a shadow could wake me up.

Giving Sarah one last look, I open the car door and climb out to stand next to Steve. His hair has somehow gotten even wilder and his clothes are all rumpled.

He starts walking toward the diner without saying anything, his hands shoved deep into the pockets of his tight jeans. He doesn't even look back at me. "O...K," I mouth, rolling my eyes. This should be a pleasant dining experience. That rumination doubles its sarcasm factor when I fully take in the exterior of the diner—dirty siding and broken neon lights spelling out, "EAT HER."

Steve is already halfway across the parking lot, so I have to trot to catch up, reaching his side just as he pushes open the fingerprint-streaked door, still adorned with a dusty plastic Christmas wreath.

"Hey Lucy," Steve says, cracking a rare full smile—with teeth. The chip in his tooth is on full display and I wonder, with a little creeping, crawling feeling, how it happened.

For a moment, it seems like Steve is talking to himself, until a tiny woman appears from behind the podium at the front of the diner and clasps Steve's hand in her veined fingers, a red lipstick-grin splitting her face. I notice, with a little shudder that I immediately feel guilty about, that she's missing a few teeth.

"Oh, hello there, Hemingway!" Lucy exclaims, tucking his hand in the crook of her arm. "I certainly have missed you these past few weeks!" She looks at me then, a flash of confusion contorting her wrinkled features before a sly smile creeps across her face. "Well, there, this is new. She doesn't look like your usual date." She winks.

Before I can tell it to calm the fuck down, my heart drops kind of and I swallow hard. Steve has a girlfriend. The girl probably has a tattoo. And an eyebrow ring. And a penchant for throwing spectacularly dramatic scenes in public places that end with the two of them furiously making out on street corners in the rain. Her name is probably something like "Danah" (with an "h") and everyone calls her crazy–but she's not crazy. She's just passionate. And wild and free. And doesn't wear a bra. I hate those bitches. I hate "Danah."

Lucy laughs–a sound like a peal of church bells–pulling me out of my spiteful reverie. She elbows me lightly in the ribs and starts bustling toward an empty table. "Oh, your face!" she cries. "Oh, your face! I'm sorry, honey! It was a joke, because usually this boy's only company is his lappy computer thing."

Steve doesn't say anything, just follows closely at Lucy's heels. Still, it looks like the dick might be smiling. My face gets hot and I cough in a feeble attempt to cover my embarrassment.

"You come here at lot?" I ask, sitting down at the surprisingly clean red booth. Little pieces of foil glint in the vinyl like suffocated stars. Lucy runs a rag over Steve's side of the booth and he sits down, too, shrugging.

"Yeah, my brother and I used to before..." His voice trails off. "I mean I write here sometimes. Or I *did* before my dad took my car away." His voice is laced with bitterness and I flinch, my eyes flicking to the bruise.

"You don't need wheels to go places, kid," Lucy smiles and chucks Steve under the chin. She doesn't seem to notice the bruise–or maybe she knows better than to ask. Surprisingly, he looks up at her with affection instead of annoyance.

"Let's hope so," he says, a little wearily. "Can you get us two coffees and two number fives?"

I almost protest–I can order for myself–but no one's looking at me.

Lucy nods, then lets her veined hand drop to Steve's shoulder. "Your dad called here asking for you this morning..."

Steve stiffens, his eyes flicking toward the door–and escape.

"Don't worry." Lucy, giving his shoulder a pat, closes one eye. "I told him I didn't see you. And if he asks again, well, then, I'm legally blind outta one eye and I'm winking right now so I'll tell him the same."

Steve swallows hard and nods, but his back remains straight and rigid.

I open my mouth to ask him about it, about his dad, but he's pulling out his flip phone—the old-fashioned kind—and jabbing at the keypad with a really determined look on his face. Before he angles the device away from me I can see several missed calls from someone called "Devil Dad" filling the screen. My guts feel like worms. It feels like we should get out of here right now—before "Devil Dad" decides to take a roadtrip of his own.

Steve sticks his phone into the crook between his cheek and shoulder and starts drumming the table with his fingers—an impatient, staccato, punk rock beat. I close my eyes to calm myself and listen to the tapping with a sudden ache in my belly for my drumkit. I imagine an electric guitar coming in to race along with the beat, a rough voice taking the mic and layering words onto the whole mess—a cigarette-stained voice straining about lost love and over-extended youth. My dream filters back to me through the song I'm composing in my mind and I remember then the beep that woke me up. A message.

My heart bursts from my chest and flops on the table. Or at least it seems that way. Steve is still occupied with his phone, so I pull out mine. Two new messages. One text from Dad telling me that I'm grounded and to come home right now—he got my note about being at Sarah's, obviously. A knot of worry forms in my stomach. How soon until he goes over there himself to bring me home? I know he works today, so I have, like, 12 hours at least. And one new message. From ZZZ. Dad's text flies out of my mind. My pulse beats fast.

"Fucking, fuck, fuck, fuck," Steve exclaims and I look up from the unopened message reluctantly. He slams the "sleep" button on his phone and tosses it on the table, putting his head in his hands.

"What?" I ask, my attention back on Steve. He looks angry, not oh-my-God-my-dad-is-on-his-way-to-lock-me-in-the-attic-forever terrified, I note with relief.

"Alex. My fucking cousin. He's not picking up his phone. I'm—or I guess, *we're*—supposed to crash with him in the city. Haven't told him about you guys yet. But either way, he's not fucking answering," Steve says, his voice hard.

"Oh," I say, wrinkling my brow. "Is that all? I mean, just leave him a message. Or call him later or something."

"No, really?" Steve says, sarcasm leaking into his voice like poison. "Such technology exists? I had no fucking idea. Next you'll be telling me I can send electronic words to people through the air. I may be a little analog, but I'm not an idiot, Hallie."

"Jesus," I lean back in the booth. "Dude, I know... I'm just... What's the big deal? Why are you so upset?" I try not to feel hurt. Unsuccessfully.

Steve sighs. "Sorry. I'm pissed. I've left messages. Like ten messages. And nothing. No answer. Not since he disappeared during that party last night."

Worry coils in my stomach like a complicated knot. I am terrible at untying knots.

"What about your other cousin? Bethany?"

"She's not involved." Steve is kind of banging at the buttons of his phone now. I'm tempted to take it away so that he doesn't break it.

"What do you mean?"

He shrugs. "Alex said she's just not involved, OK? Like, she didn't want to be or whatever. He said to not even ask her about it because she'll get pissed or something. I guess they're fighting—brother/sister shit or whatever." He throws his phone across the table. "Fuck it! What are we going to do?"

"How about this," I say, trying for a calming voice and kind of failing. "We'll go to his place, ring the buzzer, and if he's not home we'll sit in a coffee shop or something until he is. He has to come home, right?"

"You don't understand," Steve says, putting his head in his hands. "Alex is a little... off..."

"Off how?" I say slowly. From what I recall, Alex seemed like a clean, put-together kind of guy. Maybe his eyes were a little far-away, but he definitely didn't seem deranged or anything. And he was cute. Crazy people can't be cute, right? "Off like, 'I'm a grown man who's really intensely into trains,' or, 'I like the taste of human flesh'?" I ask.

"Uh, somewhere in between," Steve says, wincing.

"Excuse me?"

"I mean, he's not dangerous or anything," Steve says quickly. "He's just weird."

"Define 'weird,' please." The whole idea of running away is starting to seem really stupid. Really, really stupid. Then I think of the unread message on my phone and swallow hard. I can pretend to like trains—I think I can, I think I can, I think I can.

"Like..." Steve starts drumming the table again. "Well, for example, he used to leave, like, these really weird messages on people's phones..."

"That doesn't sound too weird," I say, relief creeping tentatively into my brain. At least Alex wasn't an adult baby or something. I saw something about those dudes on TV once and it creeped me out for an entire week.

"Well, I'm not talking about, like, the normal kind of weird messages—like the kind that are a little too desperate or disjointed or rambling or whatever," Steve says, pouring salt on the table and pushing it into a line, like a mobster in a movie cutting cocaine.

"What kind of messages?" I ask. My skin is prickling a little and it's not because of the diner's crappy air conditioning.

"Like," Steve takes a deep breath and looks up at the ceiling. "Like... See Alex is like a computer genius. He was taking computers apart and putting them together when he was like six."

"Yeah, cool," I say, impatient. "Get to the weird shit, please."

Steve pours out another line of salt on the tabletop. "So he's good at computers, right? Which is why he was in the band in the first place. He's actually, like, pretty shit at the bass. He produced and mixed all the records and whatever. Which really saved the band a lot of cash, which is a pretty big boon in this fractured and dying musical economy."

I sigh, "The point is over there, please get to it."

Steve slams his hand lightly on the table, scattering the salt. I can't help thinking of bad luck. Sarah's weird predictions and superstitions creep into my mind even when she's not here now. "So he used to, like, fuck around—like record people talking and shit, make these weird-ass songs with their voices, then, like, call people and leave the songs on their machines."

I blink. That sounds weird, sure. But dude is a musician. I feel like all musicians are borderline psychotics. Actually, the whole thing seems like kind of an awesome art project—if your friends aren't totally lame, that is. Either way, it doesn't sound weird enough for Steve to look this worried. It isn't weird enough to stop me from going to see ZZZ—or Haze, rather. Whoever he is. Not a train or adult-sized diaper in sight.

Lucy swoops in and deposits two steaming cups of black coffee and two plates brimming with eggs and bacon in front of us and bustles away. The food smells amazing and my stomach whines for it, ignoring the whispering in my ventricles that says Steve is probably leaving something out. Something bad.

Steve takes a sip of coffee and shakes his head. "It really freaked people out. I never got one of the messages, but I heard about them and I guess they were pretty strange. I mean, Alex is a freak. But harmless. He's just always been really interested in other people, but kind of too shy to express that in a normal way. So he would do shit like that. And people just didn't get it, I think. B was always the social one, and he kind of just went along with her—made friends with her friends or whatever."

I take a deep breath to calm my nerves. I can understand that. I mean, I'm kind of the same, right? Fascinated with other people like the Anarchy Kids, but way too freaked out to actually speak to them. Until now, I guess. And aren't the songs I write kind of the same thing as Alex's weird art project shit? At least he's brave enough to share them. And fuck, did I understand being a tagalong in someone else's social sphere. Someone who I had left sleeping in a car in the parking lot, I remember with more than a little shame.

"So what's the problem then?" I ask. "You know he's weird. You're cool with it. Why are you so freaked? Do you think he'll bail on letting us stay with him?"

Steve sighs. "It's just that sometimes he gets really, really in his own head and kind of... disappears. Like, doesn't answer calls or emails or anything. He just ghosts on everyone. I guess he gets lost in projects and whatever. He does computer shit for work and you know how those guys are—like, they don't shower for days. Die playing online games and shit. Combine that with the sensibilities of a guy in a band and you have a lethal combo of obsession and ADD."

I nod slowly, looking down at my food. I'm not hungry now—at all. Sleeping in the car last night hadn't been bad, but I can't imagine doing that for the next three days. In the city, no less. Missing kidneys seemed like the least of our worries in that situation. I mean, we have two of those things, right?

Steve's hand falls on mine and suddenly his face is way close. His breath doesn't smell the best (mine probably doesn't either), but his hand is warm. It's kind of nice—and also wholly terrifying.

"Hey, Hallie. We'll figure it out, OK? I know other people and whatever. Fuck, I'll call Bethany. Alex can deal." His eyes meet mine and they're like a thousand summer leaves all latticed together—a thought I abolish from my mind all together because that is a ridiculous thing to think about a person. My voice kind of dries up then and I remember that I am a girl, sitting alone with a boy that I don't know that well. Something like stage fright kicks in and I stare at his hand to avoid looking at his face until he pulls it away, suddenly.

"I'm gonna go wash my hands," he says in a kind of strangled voice. "Be right back."

He's gone so quickly that I can see an afterimage of his form burned into my retinas. I melt back into the booth, my heart pounding, eyes slightly unfocused, and stare at the glinting foil stars embedded in the booth until I catch my breath. Apparently I could get arrested, run away from home, and break a guy out of his prison/house, but put me and the same dude alone for five seconds in a casual dining establishment and I become Lame Hallie all over again. *Haze, think of Haze,* my mind says firmly to my shaking body, and I push the last two minutes of awkwardness out of my cranium. He is all that matters here. Finding him. Meeting him. I don't know what will happen after. I don't even really know what I want from him. I just know I need it... whatever it is.

My hand shoots into my pocket again and I fumble to pull out my phone. There it is. The blue dot next to the unread message calms my racing mind immediately and I smile. He is here. He is listening. He doesn't know that I'm awkward sometimes. He doesn't know that I can be a shaking mess on stage. He wants to know me—the me somewhere inside that I know is the real one. I click on the message.

> I know I'm supposed to say something about me, but I'm not sure I'm ready to share something more right now. Maybe if you tell me something—if you tell me something you wouldn't tell anyone else—maybe then I could tell you something that I've never told anyone.

My mind whirls. What can I tell him? What can I say that no one else knows? What can I say that will be surprising and interesting and... enough? And what does he want to tell me? This is my chance. My chance to let him in. To let him know the me that I hide from everyone else. The one lurking in my atoms, waiting to come out. I take a deep breath, close my eyes, focus on the air going in and out. I let my mind wander through the ceiling of the decrepit diner and up toward the clouds and the sky. I try to let the words come to me, like ZZZ had said—like automatic writing. What do I have deep down inside?

I go back to read his message again, stalling, but before I can do so, a hand closes around the top of my arm. I look up with a start.

Steve's face looks a little wild. "Come on," he says, his voice ragged around the edges.

\\\\\\\\\\\

Shirts and jeans litter the asphalt, the empty fabric limbs askew as if they're attempting to escape. Blood smears Sarah's lip as she struggles against the chest of a dirty-looking man with a beard. Terror. Terror is the only word my mind can seize on and it forgets what it means. I forget how to think—to move. Luckily, Sarah seems to remember the basic rudiments.

"Fuck, no, asshole, you cannot take my..." Sarah's teeth sink into the man's hand and he pulls away with a yelp. "...car!" She spits in his face, blood spewing across his whiskered cheeks. I gasp, recoil. For the second time in two days I'm stunned by the violence my friend can muster. It terrifies me almost as much as the man squaring off against her—the man twice her size.

Sarah's fingers curl at her sides and the man growls low in his throat and reaches into his jeans pocket, flicking out a knife. Sunlight bursts from the blade and slivers of rainbow dance over Sarah's face. Terror clutches at me and I cry and stagger forward, only to find myself suspended mid-stride. Steve clings to the back of my T-shirt. I struggle against his grip.

"No," Steve hisses in my ear, his voice shot through with desperation. "*No*."

"Sarah," I choke. "We have to..."

Steve's arm wraps around my waist and he holds on. I'm surprised he's not shaking. My whole body seems like it's jerking out of control.

Sarah stands frozen, her chin jutting and all the cords standing out in her neck. Her face has gone pale in the summer sun and she's looking at the man with something like recognition in her eyes. Not like she knows him, really, but like she's familiar with the situation. I think of her father—whom I never met and had only ever heard whispers of—and erupt into even more shivers than before. Steve's arm tightens and he makes a strangled noise, then swallows it down and clears his throat.

"Sarah," he says loudly, slowly. "Leave it. Let him take it."

Sarah's eyes flick to Steve and she practically snarls through rigid lips. "It's my brother's. He'll kill me."

Steve juts his head toward the man with the knife, "So will that guy." I can feel his hand shaking against my back now.

The man's eyes are darting all over the place and his knife hand starts vibrating, sending the rainbows into crazy spirals across Sarah's face. He's not going to wait much longer. I recognize the look in his eye. It's in all of ours now, reflected back at us: fear.

His eyes flick over to Steve and me now, zero in on my phone, still clutched in my hand. "Give me that," he growls.

My eyes widen and my heart quickens even more. ZZZ's message still glows in my hand.

"No!" the word bursts from my lips and Sarah looks at me, aghast, the knife hovering right near her chest. "Hallie..." she whispers and my body floods with nausea.

"Give him your phone, Hallie," Steve barks.

I shake my head, dumbly, my skin buzzing and burning and

panic rising in my chest. My feet are locked in place, my spine rigid. I cannot give up my phone. I cannot give up ZZZ.

The man lurches toward Sarah and she shrieks and my eyes feel wild and wide and unseeing. A siren starts up in the distance and I wake up, kind of. My hand tightens on the phone and I squeeze. I have to do it. Of course I do. I'm a fucking idiot. I have to. What the fuck is wrong with me? I start to step forward, but Steve pushes in front of me.

He steps forward, slowly, his hand in the air. When he speaks, his voice is level and soothing.

"Sir."

The man looks around wildly as if the word is unfamiliar to him. As if he's looking for another person called "Sir."

"Sir," Steve says again, and the man turns to look at him. "Let's think rationally here. The diner called the cops. Even if you get in this car now, they'll find you—you don't have enough time to ditch the plates. Really, everything would be so much better for you if you put away the knife and walked away now—ran away, really. We won't turn you in. We never saw you. Just... put the knife away and spend the afternoon walking in this lovely sunshine." Steve's voice falls over us all like a warm blanket. It's like hot tea and lemonade all at once. A promise that everything will be OK.

The man with the knife looks torn for a second, but the sirens are coming closer. Apparently there's enough sanity left somewhere in there to realize the truth in Steve's words because he lopes off into the woods.

"How did you... how did you do that?" The words come out with a hysterical laugh and I press my phone to my chest to keep my heart inside, falling into a crouch on the pavement.

Steve doesn't look at me, just pulls open the car door and scowls. "You get used to calming people down when your dad's a violent asshole," he grunts. "Get in the car, Hallie."

Anger rolls off of him in waves and I shrink from it, pulling myself off the ground and climbing into the backseat. I watch through the window as Steve approaches Sarah, much more gently.

Sarah's eyes flick over to me briefly, and in that moment I see fear, sadness, and a sickening burst of anger reflected there. I start to open the door, to get out and hug her and say I'm sorry, but something in her face stops me. The sun glints off of grease spots on the asphalt, and for a moment the air is filled with the distant hum of cars and tentative birdsong. We look at each other. I can't read it—whatever it is there in her eyes.

"Hey, Sarah," I hear Steve say, muffled through the glass. "C'mon, let's go."

She shakes her head, looking down at her feet, breaking our eye contact. "I want to go home," she whispers, then shakes her head. "But not... home... Just somewhere else."

"I know," Steve says, placing a hand on her back. A little twinge of something like jealousy worms through my chest. "I know somewhere where we can go and calm down. Does that sound good to you?"

She nods slowly, looking at his hand. "Thanks..." she mutters. "I guess... you're not such a pants ferret after all." Steve kinds of awkwardly clasps one of her hands and laughs a little. Mutters something else. Sarah kind of smiles.

I smile slowly, my heart slowing down. Everything will be OK. We still have the car. Everyone is fine. Sarah even seems to be warming up to Steve. *Better hope she doesn't get too warm*, a nasty little voice says in my head. One that I tell to shut up. I look down at my phone, light up ZZZ's message anew. We're on our way to see him—or *maybe* him—and everything will be OK.

Steve slides into the driver's seat, without looking back at me, and Sarah gets in the backseat, also avoiding my gaze. I put my hand on her shoulder and try to pull her in for a hug, relieved that she's OK. Relieved that she's still here. But she shakes my hand away.

"Are you OK...?" I ask slowly, hurt.

"Yeah," she says. "I just... I just want to sit here by myself for a minute, OK?"

"Are you sure?"

"Yeah, Hallie, just give me some fucking room to breathe," she snaps, looking at the window.

I sit back, away from her, and stare out my own window, watching the diner pull away into the distance, the highway medians ticking by like islands in the sea. Give her some room to breathe? I'm not the one who's always there—always asking for help or complaining or crying about some guy. I'm not the one who needs to be fucking star of every show. I feel like I'm always letting her breathe. Always listening. Always standing in the background. The army with the pink flag starts retreating as the ZZZ army advances forward.

Angling myself away from Sarah, I take out my phone, read ZZZ's message again. Tell you something I've never told anyone before? Well, here goes.

Sometimes I feel like I let my best friend live my life for me. Like I reside in her shadow—like a stunted little tree. Sometimes I wish we had never met because sometimes I feel like she takes all

the nutrients up through her roots and grows tall and brave while
I cower and languish. Sometimes I wish I had my own band,
because without her there sucking up all the oxygen—all the
energy—I feel like I could really be alive.

**The words come back, shot through the airwaves like bullets,
almost immediately.**

I think you're right, Placid Girl. I think you need to break away
from all these people holding you back. You need to get out of
the forest. You need to cut back all the deadness in order to
grow. (I apologize for all the shitty tree metaphors—but I mean
it.) You don't need any of them, Placid Girl. You only need
yourself. And me.

**We're speeding through trailer parks and strip malls now. Steve's
fingers are tight on the wheel and Sarah is angled away from me, my
fingers tapping at the window. Then I notice she's clutching Steve's
sea glass in one hand, her thumb working away at the smooth surface like a nun with her rosary. Fire licks through my insides before
I can contain it.**

You're right, **I type back.** Now it's your turn to tell me something.

NINE

"Friendship is just a bracelet word,"

—"BF For Never," *Masking Tape* —Haze

My phone dies as I wait for ZZZ to respond, so I close my eyes and listen to the cars rushing by, rendered invisible by my eyelids. For a minute, I feel like I'm back in my room at home, listening to the motorcycles humming out on the highway, lying under laundry-fresh blankets. For a second I can imagine that this whole trip has just been a dream; then I open my eyes, watching the unfamiliar suburbs flying by.

Steve drums his fingers on the wheel and Sarah sits curled next to me, still rubbing the sea glass.

I reach into my bag and pull out my notebook, try to jot down some notes from the trip, try to turn some of this into a song, but all I can think of is my phone, dead in my bag, and what ZZZ might be revealing to me.

"Where are we going?" I call into the abyss of the car, my voice cracking a bit from disuse.

Silence fills the vehicle like a ton of feathers and I clear my throat to ask again, but Steve cuts me off. "It's a surprise."

To my immense relief, he sounds almost OK now—less gruff than he was with me before. Then, to Sarah, he says, softly, "You OK back there, Sarah?"

Sarah pulls herself up in her seat and tosses back her hair, as if she's just realized that it's time to go on stage and she's nowhere near ready. "Those are the only two letters I ever am—don't believe anyone who tells you differently," she crows, tossing the sea glass into Steve's lap. "Thanks for letting me play with your... thingie," she adds, lasciviously, smirking.

The car rolls onto a dirt road off the highway and stops in front of a low-slung house on the bank of a feeble river. The house is swimming-pool blue with a white trim that reminds me of an old lady's nightgown. Next to it—like a gaudier shirt on a clothesline snapping in the breeze—bobs something much more miraculous: a kind of carnival boat idling in the river, tacked together with brightly colored pieces of what look like scrap wood and metal. A robin's egg blue door here, a spray of yellow boards there, a green-painted smoke stack rising from the center, Christmas lights swaying in the summer breeze.

All of the boards gape at the seams and the whole thing looks like it's about to burst apart like a piñata and float away down the river. I can't tear my eyes away. It feels like the structure was tacked together with happiness. I only look back at the house when I hear a door slam somewhere inside—the sound echoing through the silent summer day.

I jump. There's a trio of white, white faces peering from the front window of the house, so devoid of color that they look like phantoms. They're standing so stoically still and I blink to clear my vision, realizing that the faces are some kind of statues or mannequins.

"Where are we?" Sarah says, asking the question that's currently reverberating through my mind.

Steve smiles his crooked smile again and waves an arm at the house. "This is B's place."

My mind blinks. Like, it literally feels like it opens and closes and clears itself. "Seriously?" I ask, my voice squeaking.

"And who the hell is B?" Sarah asks. Steve looks at me from the front seat then and a sly smile creeps across his face, like he and I share a secret. I struggle to keep my face from twitching.

"Who is this person?" Sarah presses. "What's with the creepy mannequins and boat and whatever?"

Steve crosses his arms and gazes at the house. I look, too, at the peeling paint and unsettling figures. "She's my cousin—Haze's drummer. Or she was."

A tangle of emotions wrestle in my chest like snakes and mongooses. Excitement that I'll get to meet Bethany—who is probably the best drummer that I have ever come across in my life. And, you know, terror that I'll get to meet Bethany—who is probably the best drummer that I have ever come across in my life.

"Oh, yeah, everyone's favorite completely unknown rock god and contradiction in terms," Sarah drawls. "And you're related?"

"Yeah, I haven't seen her in a while, though. Not since Dad took my car away. He doesn't really approve of her—not that he likes Alex, either. But Alex can drive, so he can sometimes bust me out," Steve says, kind of babbling. He seems excited to see Bethany, which makes sense since most of his immediate family seems kind of... unhinged.

"She can't drive?" Sarah sneers, apparently back to hating Steve.

He shrugs. "She prefers other modes of transportation."

"Q!" A woman with long, black hair steps onto the lawn, white skirt billowing around her bare ankles. Steve throws himself out of the car and starts running toward her. Bethany is beautiful—the kind of no makeup, messy-haired beautiful that very few women can pull off. Letting the screen door slam behind her, she runs lightly over the patchy lawn and flings her arms around Steve, then spins him around the grass by his hands. Sarah and I clamor out of the car a bit more slowly and hang back a bit.

"Where have you been? I missed you!" Bethany exclaims, elbowing Steve in the ribs and smirking—but there's something not-so-jovial about her words. He rubs the spot where her skinny limb made contact and barely suppresses a grin.

"I missed you, too," Steve says, his green eyes firmly fixed on her face. He squints. Frowns.

"Steve..." Bethany says, her voice growing solemn and granite gray.

Steve ignores her, turning to me then, all the sun dapples he had spilled her way before glowing full force on me. "Hallie! Bethany is kind of my favorite cousin. She's the one who gave me their album in the first place. After they broke up, unfortunately." He kind of play-pushes her.

"What? No way!" I wrinkle my brow, looking from Steve to Bethany. "But... why? I mean, why after?"

Steve shrugs. "Probably because I was, like, a little kid and they didn't think I was cool enough to hang with them or something. She gave me *Masking Tape* last year for my birthday."

"Yup, you're finally a man now, kid," Bethany says, her smile like hummingbirds and birdsong. Transitory. Her eyes are getting hard again and her mouth is opening. It seems something unpleasant is about to leap out.

I'm too flummoxed to wait and see what it is. "But... That's insane! You've only known about Haze for that long? What about the Internet?" I ask.

Steve pulls out a cigarette and Bethany gives a little motherly "cluck," but Steve lights it anyway, his face smoky for a second in the sunshine.

"My dad got rid of the Internet after Gabriel left. Didn't get that again until Alex showed me how to steal it. Then I blogged the shit out of that thing."

"Wow, you're..." I trail off, watching the smoke curl out of Steve's nose like sulfur, trying to imagine the dark world from which he had come like some kind of sightless underwater thing.

"Incredibly progressed for a boy whose father stifled his maturation at every turn? Why, yes, I know. Thank you." He looks at his feet.

Bethany gives a little cough and suddenly I remember the older woman standing next to us. The boat bobbing in the water. Sarah.

"He called here, Q," Bethany says finally, unpleasant thing extracted, trying to catch Steve's eye.

Steve nods mutely, dropping his cigarette on the ground and grinding it out. "I thought he would. You didn't..."

"Of course not," Bethany interjects. "But, Steve..."

"I'm eighteen in two weeks, Bethany," Steve says flatly.

"And I told you that you could stay with me. I've *been* saying you could stay with me." She looks at Sarah and me sideways—likely unsure of how much we know. I wonder if she knows where we're going. If Steve called and told her when he left me at the diner.

Steve drops the cigarette on the ground, extinguishes it with his sneaker. "And *I've* told you he'll call the cops. He's almost done it before. He's come close. And with all the illegal shit you have going on here..." he turns to me, kind of rolls his eyes. "She grows pot. Like a lot of it." Then back to her, "...I'm not putting you in the middle. I can figure it all out. I can do it myself."

Bethany doesn't say anything for a second—her lips get all thin and her eyes hard. Then she seems to notice Sarah and me standing next to Steve, looking supremely awkward, I'm sure.

"I'm Bethany, by the way," she says with a tight smile, clasping my sweaty hand in a cool grip. I can feel her delicate bones moving beneath the skin and hope she doesn't notice that my palm's egregiously damp. Her hand feels like a sparrow.

"Hallie," I say, my voice barely cresting a whisper. The whole thing about Steve's dad has left my head churning. Plus, she's *Haze's drummer*—that's a thought that hasn't been wholly tamped down by all the drama.

"Sarah," Sarah grunts, not uncrossing her arms.

"So nice to meet some of Steve's friends!" Bethany says, apparently choosing to ignore the wholly awkward nature of the exchange.

I force a smile and nod. Sarah does not.

"Well, come on, guys, let's get you all inside. I bet you could use something cold to drink," Bethany says, gesturing expansively at her slumping abode. "I'll make some juice."

Bethany cracks open the door, letting a warm wash of sunlight spill all over the floor. Books line every surface of the wall not covered with curling prints whose lacerated edges suggest that they had been plucked out of art tomes. A massive record player hulks in the corner next to an even more massive shelf crammed with vinyl, and a parade of dying plants take up residence in the windowsill, their fading, leafy limbs grasping at the weak sunlight coming through the dirty windows. The floor lets out muffled groans of protest under faded oriental rugs as we troop into the house. Steve flops down at a dusty antique table and Bethany seems to glide toward the kitchen. I stop just short of the table and stick my hands in my pockets awkwardly, taking in the motley—though pleasant—wreckage of the room around me.

Sarah's shoulders have relaxed a little as she looks around at the books and art and music, her fight-or-flight instincts calmed by familiar things.

A glint by the windows catches my eye and I swing around to inspect the only dust-free addition to the room: a black and gold drumset, all shining metal and glitter-flecked grandness. I don't notice that I've gasped until Bethany looks up from slicing carrots and ginger and smiles.

"Like it?" she says, hitching her hand to her bony hip.

I nod.

"I won it in a contest like a hundred years ago. A drum solo thing. It belonged to Marky Ramone."

"No way..." I breathe.

"Way." Bethany smiles. "I'm planning on selling it someday. Start my own drum school with the money. In the meantime, I just like to look at how shiny it is."

"You don't play it?" I ask, stunned. My fingers are dancing at my sides like spiders. "I would all the freaking time if that were mine."

"Not often. I usually play the old beat-up kit in my room," Bethany gestures toward the back of the house—it only really appears to have three or so rooms—with her knife before slicing into a hunk of ginger. "I've molded that one perfectly to suit my eccentricities. Also, it has some pretty rad stickers on it." She laughs.

I nod, my eyes roving over the kit. I want it. I want it more than I want most things of a carnal nature.

"You want to try it out?" Bethany asks, tossing carrots and ginger into her juicer with a small smile.

"Really?" I croak. I can feel my face going slack and hungry.

"Sure," Bethany says, pressing "blend." "Let's see what you got."

Trying not to run, I move across the room to take a seat behind the glittering kit, retrieving a pair of sticks from the dusty windowsill as I go. I sit down on the glitter-flecked vinyl drum stool and try to ignore Bethany's inquisitive look, and the twin gazes of Sarah and Steve, who are leaning forward in their kitchen chairs. As I position the sticks in my hands, the familiar feel of splintery, waxed-up wood sends a rush of contentment washing over me, and all thoughts of ZZZ and Sarah and my dad and my mom and the faraway city are wiped away from my mind like spilled milk. I close my eyes, idly swinging one stick around my fingers, and let my mind wander still more, let my body do what it wants to. Let my mind relax and find the beat that it wants to make manifest. It's always easier when you let your mind go. It's only when you start trying that things go to hell.

A simple, blazing fast beat bursts from my hands and feet as I dance behind the kit. T-Rex on the pedals, birds on the sticks. Then

143

a cacophonous fill. Followed by still another bullet-fast beat. My whitewashed mind tries not to interfere, not to ruin the steadiness and sureness of my hands by letting worries wander in—but one thought manages to sidle past. I'm playing one of Haze's songs—"BF For Never." But I'm doing the revamped version—from the new tape. The drumbeat threatens to canter off into the abyss, then pulls back, then explodes from my fingers—a push and pull and battle of beats. Haze's voice eddies into the white space of my mind like oil in water and its harsh lushness unfolds behind the drumbeat. The corners of my memory fill in the howling guitars and thrumming bassline and sense memory recalls the stage sweat and stale beer of a dark cramped venue.

My head falls back and I start getting looser with my hands as the beat comes more easily, letting them swoop and swirl in a way that drives drum teachers crazy but just looks undeniably better on stage. My head falls forward again, my hair tickling my fingers, and I clench my hands around the sticks until the splintered wood cuts into them, pounding out the final tattoo of the song before swinging back and crashing both sticks onto the cymbals.

Slowly, I open my eyes, sweat prickling through my hair. The room is silent and three pairs of eyes are fixed squarely on me. Bethany's are wide, a sad, perplexed smile on her face. Sarah's are narrowed, accompanied by a contented smirk. And Steve's face has contorted into a weird kind of rapturous awe. I look away quickly, embarrassed.

"It's funny," Bethany says, looking out the window past the line of white mannequins. I notice now they're made of papier-mâché—half-finished and unpainted. "That almost sounds like one of our songs."

"It is," I say, confused. "'BF For Never'?"

Bethany tilts her head. "I mean, I know that song—but what you played isn't it. It's similar, but... you know. I like it, anyway."

I look at Steve. He looks uncomfortable. "It's from the new tape, B," he says.

Bethany shrugs. "What new tape?"

"Yeah," Steve says slowly. "Alex told me not to mention it..."

Bethany's face seems to crack down the middle for a brief second before she turns back to the juicer, pouring the lurid orange drink into a quartet of glasses. "Not to mention what?" she asks.

She stands facing the juicer for a moment, leaning her hands against the counter. I can see her shoulders rising and falling a little faster, a tattooed flower bobbing up and down on her back.

When she turns around, Bethany seems to have pulled her lovely self together. I notice, though, that she now sports an orange stain on her dress from the juicing and the messiness only makes her more endearing.

"That's where we're going. The show—the Haze reunion thing. Alex said you didn't want to be involved. That we shouldn't mention it to you..." Steve trails off and when I look at Bethany I understand. She looks hurt. Confused. Something else.

"Alex told you *what*? That's not the plan." The sentence shoots out of her mouth before she can stop it and a stricken look passes over her face. Before anyone can ask what she means, however, Bethany fixes a smile on her face and cocks her head to the side with a shrug. "If there's a show this weekend, no one asked me to be in it." The words are tight. Her smile is, too.

"But Alex told me..." Steve starts.

Something slams closed behind Bethany's eyes. "Ah, Alex. Well,

I'm not talking to Alex right now." She comes around and sits at the table.

"What?" Steve asks, panic starting to creep into his voice. "Why not?"

"I don't want to talk about it right now. It's sibling shit. Don't worry about it." I don't know Bethany well, but there's something about her voice that seems to command, "Do not press me further."

Steve, however, ignores that command. "But what happened, Bethany? I haven't heard from Alex in a few days now and we're on our way down there."

"You're on your way to the city, by yourself? And Alex isn't even bothering to pick up the phone?" Bethany asks, and I remember that she's older than us—probably by about ten years. I push down the thought that Haze is also 10 years older than us. Than me.

"Yes," Steve says, attempting to sound confident and coming off as a bit petulant. "There's this magazine—they want me to write about the show. They want this story. They want to know who Haze is. And you and Alex won't tell me, so..."

"You know that's not my story to tell, Q," Bethany says, sounding hurt—and mad. "I've asked him. I've asked him so many times..."

"And you know what he does to me," Steve says quietly, icily. No one asks who "he" is.

Bethany takes a deep, harsh breath—like she's swallowing daggers. "I know, Q. Which is why if you won't just fucking leave—if you won't just come stay with me—I'm going with you."

"What do you mean?" Steve asks, his eyes still narrowed and fists still tightened at his sides.

"To the show. I'm coming with you to the show," Bethany says, although she looks like she's just offered to go dancing off a cliff.

"I'll come with you to the show and then you can talk to Haze. I will introduce you. I will get him to take the mask off if I have to pull it off myself. This has gone on far too long."

I can almost hear both of our hearts stop—Steve's and mine. We're going to see him. We're going to see his face. It feels like someone has just told me that God himself is going to come careening off the clouds to shake my hand.

"You will?" Steve asks.

"Yes." Bethany takes a sip of juice and looks at the table.

"Why now?" Steve asks. "I've asked so many times before."

Bethany shrugs and takes another sip. None of us have touched our drinks. I stare down at a chunk of carrot clinging to the rim of the glass and decide I'm going to keep it that way. Not that I don't appreciate the effort.

"Sorry to interrupt 'VH1 Behind The Music,' but can I use an outlet or something?" Sarah asks. "My phone's dead."

Even though Sarah actually does sound kind of sorry, annoyance canters in. Can't she recognize an emotionally fraught moment when she's sitting awkwardly in the middle of one?

"Sure, kid, there's one over there." Bethany smiles, pointing to the mannequins.

I think of the dead phone in my pocket—and ZZZ—and sheepishly get to my feet to charge mine, too, leaving Steve to stare at Bethany.

Sarah and I kneel down together, plugging in our phones side by side.

"Sorry I interrupted back there," Sarah says, her voice uncharacteristically soft. "I just want to check in with Tim real quick—make sure that everything is OK back at home. My phone died in the car."

I nod, kind of awkwardly. "Mine did, too." Sarah never really talks about what goes on at home—with her mom—but she hints at it. And I had heard a fair amount of yelling and crying when I was over for sleepovers in the past.

My phone glows to life first, and a barrage of messages appear on the screen—all from ZZZ—a longer missive broken up into separate dings. I grin. There's also a text from my dad—he's probably called Sarah's house by now. He's probably freaking out. My heart clenches a little, but the messages from ZZZ make it skip in my chest and I click through and read them hungrily.

I think you're right, Placid Girl.

You have come to realize in such a short span of time what has taken me years to learn.

Collaborators are not often our friends. They are people who drag our coattails until we're down there on the ground with them.

Oscar Wilde said we're all in the gutter, but some of us are looking at the stars—well, Oscar, some of us have had our faces ground too far into the gutter to look up.

And I don't want you to be one of us, Placid Girl. I want you to be the one that snags a grappling hook into the surface on the moon and hangs on. I think you can be that one, PG. I think you can.

You told me to tell you something and I really want to. I really do.
But first I want to show you something. I want you to know me.
And I want you to know yourself. Do you trust me?

Yes, I type back so fast my fingers shake. I trust you.

"Who sent you like a million messages?" Sarah asks, craning her head to see the screen. I press the phone against my chest and sit back on my heels. She looks hurt.

"Ah, lay off, Sarah," Steve says, coming up behind her with a glass of juice, an orange mustache and a wry smile. "She's probably texting her boyfriend. Or sexting or whatever."

Sarah's eyebrows practically touch her hairline. "*Boyfriend?* Hallie doesn't have a boyfriend."

Steve laughs. "Um, yeah she does. She told me back in my room. That's why we didn't..." He coughs, slinking back to his chair and taking a huge gulp of juice.

"Who is this boyfriend, Hallie?" Sarah asks, laughing in disbelief. "Why didn't you tell me you had a *boyfriend?*" She spits the word.

"I... I can't tell you," I sputter.

She glares at me. "You can't *tell* me? Are you serious?"

"I just..." I trail off. I know we're both thinking of Nick—what happened last time I told her about a guy that I liked.

"Sarah," Bethany says suddenly, but Sarah's eyes don't leave my face—they're burning into my cheekbones like frostbite. "Want to come out and take a look at Lazarus with me?" She gets to her feet and dusts her hands off on her dress.

Sarah blinks, looking at Bethany finally, then back at me, then back at Bethany. "What now?"

"The boat. Want to come take a closer look with me?" Bethany smiles and reaches for Sarah's hand. Sarah looks down at Bethany's palm as if it is a scorpion fixing to sting.

"Sure..." Sarah says, getting to her feet and walking toward the door, ignoring Bethany's outstretched hand. Bethany follows and the door clicks closed, leaving Steve and me in sunny silence, examining the grain of the table before us.

"Bethany is good at that," Steve says softly, after what seems like seventeen hours.

"What?" I look down into my juice and sigh.

"Deflecting. Avoiding fights. She's a pacifist like that. She can't stand to see anyone not getting along. It must be bad with Alex, then..." The last part he says to himself.

I nod and for lack of anything else to say, mutter, "I should thank her when she gets back."

For a few moments the room is all sunlight and dust motes dancing on the breeze. The art book pictures of jungle cats and fat angels lift away from the wall and flutter and I think of the photos in my room. Of Haze. I close my eyes and let the sun work its way through my eyelids, lighting the room up red.

"Why didn't you tell her?" Steve says, a little too loudly. Then, "Does that guy actually exist?"

I look at him. He's looking at the table.

"Yeah, he exists," I say, kicking at one of the rugs swaddling the floorboards. "And I don't know why I didn't tell her."

I do know why. Because I don't know what there is to tell. And because somehow, somewhere in the tiniest cavity of my heart, I know she would ruin it. She would drag down my happiness so I'd be down in the gutter, too.

"She's mad at you," Steve says simply.

"I noticed." I snort.

"I don't mean to be rude and point it out or anything, but it just makes me really anxious when people leave angry, you know?" Steve gets up and wanders in a little circle on the carpet. There's a tread worn there and I wonder if he's tracing it or if he's made it over the years.

"She'll get over it, I'm guessing," I say, watching his sneakers scuff the swirls of red and blue. "We've had fights before." Still, this feels different. The dissent that's growing between us seems more serious—more bordering on permanent. And I'm really not sure how I feel about it. ZZZ's words ring in my mind.

"I just..." Steve stops. "I know what it's like. To have the last words you say to someone suck. My brother—Gabriel—one time a few years after he left I just went off on him..."

"About what?" I shift in my chair to watch him, the sunlight streaming across his bruised face, catching in the little threads of gold in his hair—on his freckles.

"My dad. My dad went off on me so I went off on Gabe. The last word I said to him was 'cocksucker.' The last thing I called my brother was a really lame insult..."

"What happened?" I ask, watching Steve's eye flick all around the room, like he's looking for ghosts.

"What happened was..." Steve takes a deep breath and his eyes tick over to me for a second. "I was thirteen and I had this girlfriend. She was a little older. She wanted to see what sex was like..."

"At thirteen?" I ask, my mouth hanging open.

"Yeah, I dunno, she was precocious. Anyway, so we did it—on the floor at some lame kids concert—like a Christian rock band or something. It was gross. Her mouth tasted like Sour Patch Kids and I had popcorn stuck all down my back. We got caught."

"By the ushers or whatever?" I ask, still gaping.

"By her mom. She was in the back of the theater, chaperoning or whatever. We were idiots."

"Oh, fuck."

"Exactly," Steve says, sitting down in the chair next to me. "Anyway, she told my dad and it was obviously all my fault because I'm a boy, and he... well," he points to the bruise. "I had a few more of these in a few more places."

I realize that my hand is over my mouth and my eyes are practically spilling over and I try to compose my face. Steve's voice has been very matter-of-fact thus far. Very composed. I don't understand how he can keep it together.

"Anyway," he says, with a little gulp of air. "Anyway, I called my brother then. When Dad was asleep. And I told him that the way Dad is was all his fault. That he made him that way. That he had killed Mom and fucked up our lives. And I told him I wished he were dead instead of Mom. And I called him a cocksucker. And..." Steve closes his eyes and takes a deep breath. "That was the last time I talked to him."

The dust motes undulate in the obscenely happy sunbeams and I don't know what to say. My brain has died and my throat has dried up. So I just put my hand on Steve's shoulder and immediately feel inadequate.

He shakes himself a little and I let my hand fall away. "I don't know why I told you that story, really..." Steve says, blinking, like he's coming out of some opium-induced dream. "It was a little dramatic in this circumstance. It's just that... I don't like to see anyone leave angry. Anyone that really loves each other. Because what if... you know... That's the last time?"

He looks up at me, his green eyes all shiny and sad. "And, you know, Hallie, I don't want you to have to feel that way. I don't want you to feel like you fucked up a friendship and never got the chance to say you're sorry."

I open my mouth to say something—I'm not sure what—but the door swings open with a crash and sunlight streams across the room before my vocal chords can commence working. Sarah and Bethany tumble into the kitchen, bringing with them the scent of summer and cool water.

"Hallie!" Sarah yells brightly. She sounds almost like her old self—like she didn't just get robbed at knifepoint and suffer through all my idiocy. "You have to come see Lazarus! She's amazing—apparently it's a she, because boats are all bitches! And guess what?" Sarah dances to a stop in front of me, her cheeks bright and her pink hair all tumbled around her face.

"What?" I say softly, still trying to process Steve's story—this fragile, sad boy and his advice.

"Bethany is going to help us get to the city! Tomorrow!" Sarah cries.

I raise my eyebrows. Where did this sudden enthusiasm for our mission come from?

Bethany stands by the doorframe, her arms wrapped around her thin chest. She's smiling an expectant smile.

"And here's the best part," Sarah says with a grin, looking toward Bethany for confirmation. Bethany gives a silent nod of assent. "We're taking the boat, you guys! We're rolling up to the city in a fucking gypsy barge!"

\\\\\\\\

I've never been one to spend a ton of time staring into mirrors. I mean, I obviously care what I look like to some degree, but

I've never been into makeup or hairstyling or any of that mess. That all seems kind of pointless when you live in a town devoid of any romantic prospects. I always told myself that I would start caring when I got to college where, inevitably, there would be someone worth brushing one's hair for. Now, however, looking at my entirely un-sunkissed face in Bethany's fly-specked bathroom mirror I am underwhelmed to say the least. There are dark circles under my eyes—doubtless due to the immense lack of good sleep we've all been suffering the past few days—and my hair hangs dark around my face, all one length. My mom was always begging me to go the hairdresser with her and "get something done," but I never understood why we would waste money I could spend on new cymbals on having someone do what I could with a pair of kitchen scissors.

Now, I wish I had sprung for a trim at least. Especially when Bethany is floating around the living room in an ethereal white dress, all ringlets and bracelets, getting ready for the impromptu party she's apparently throwing tonight to celebrate our impending departure. Usually, Sarah would be buzzing around me, trying to get me to "*at least* take off the baggy denim vest," but after the initial excitement over the boat had worn off, she hasn't really spoken to me. She'd just retreated into Bethany's room with her phone.

I look down at myself and sigh. My customary black T-shirt and jeans are practical, sure, but I'm hardly floating like Bethany. With her in the room, I don't stand a chance. Not that I'm attempting to stand a chance doing anything tonight. It's just that I could—*will*—be meeting Haze in mere days, and now I'm pretty starkly aware how plain and utterly messy I look. And it's an awareness that's made even more acute by the message ZZZ sent me moments before: Send me another photo of you. And I'll send one back.

"Do you want to borrow something?" Bethany appears behind me with a clinking of bracelets and suddenly her hands are in my hair. I recoil slightly, not really that big on mass hair-braiding parties or things of the sort.

"Um," I say, feeling, instantly, like my tongue is too big for my mouth.

"I'll be right back," she says, not waiting for me to elaborate on my eloquent response. There's a rustling in the back of the house, presumably where Bethany's room is, and seconds later she's back with an armload of clothes. She smiles and holds up a short dark blue silk dress with a pattern of flying birds.

"This would be great with your skin tone—all porcelain like it is. It always makes me look kind of yellow." She smiles. I have a hard time believing that she looks anything less than gorgeous in everything—garbage bags and hair shirts included—but I appreciate her attempt at humility. I think about rejecting the offer and stepping out in my usual bleak uniform, but she looks so hopeful and happy that I take the dress from her with a weak smile. (Plus, what die-hard Haze fan would pass up the chance of sharing clothes with the drummer?)

Suddenly—as if taking the dress had acted as permission to make me over—Bethany's hands are in my hair again, twisting the mess into a high topknot.

"Oh, and you should wear your hair up more often like this. You have pretty much the best cheekbones I've ever seen—apart from Cleopatra," Bethany says. "I'm not down with a lot of makeup and stuff, but I'm pretty much convinced that with the right hair and dress, you can get any Antony you want."

I study myself in the mirror, shyly and–silently–agree with Bethany's fussing. Ponytails I've done, sure, but drastic topknots always seemed way too fussy to me–like I'm trying too hard. But this looked all right.

"What makes you think I want an Antony?" I say softly, holding the dress up in front of me and smiling. OK, fine, this blue is pretty.

Bethany laughs and shoves a pile of silver bangles into my hands. "I didn't say you did," she says slyly, slinking out of the bathroom. "But if you ever wanted one, Cleo, you'd have one in a regal snap–is all I'm saying."

I laugh, surrounded by Bethany's collection of pots and potions, everything smelling like wisteria and honeysuckle. "Sure," I mutter, stripping off my T-shirt and jeans and wriggling into the dress, which flutters around my thighs like night moths. "Sure."

But when I look at myself in the mirror I'm glowing and almost pretty, so I frame my face and torso with my camera and take a snap. A photo of me for what, ZZZ? What do you have to show me?

\\\\\\\\\\

The smell of wood smoke crackles through the cooling summer air and tickles my nose. As day turned into night, the heat definitely slowed down, but my skin still feels like the underside of a stamp. The blazing campfire Bethany and her friends built is a good 50 feet away, but I can feel the heat emanating off of the woodpile on my cheeks and forehead. All the figures up ahead are silhouettes–cut-paper people like shadow puppets moving in front of the fire. The only ones I can see clearly are Bethany and Steve, who are sitting close to the blaze, smoking cigarettes, and Sarah, who leans close to one of Bethany's more clean-cut friends. The rest are more on the ragged side—cut-off jeans and old T-shirts on the men, sun-washed dresses and bare feet for the women. Somehow Bethany managed to conjure up this array of friends at the last minute. I have no idea how. I don't even know if I know this many people.

The whole "christening" of the voyage thing—as Bethany dubbed it—has pretty much consisted of drinking PBRs and smoking weed. I roll a warm can of beer between my hands. It's unopened—I don't really like beer. Also, I'm kind of distracted, letting my eyes wander over to Steve and Bethany. Steve's leaning in close to hear what she's saying, the fire dancing over his bruised face. Bethany's reclining on a rock, her hair all around her face and her cheeks flushed from the heat. Steve looks happy—his smile is wide and real. I'm thinking, absently, that he looks nice that way when a ping erupts from my pocket.

A jolt dances through me.

You are lovely. So lovely. But that's not the kind of photo I meant...

I wrinkle my brow. What kind of photo did you mean?

A couple seconds later: You're sweet. Should I show you?

Please, I type.

"You texting your boyfriend?" The smell of smoke and booze settles down to my right and I quickly put my phone—facedown—on my lap. The guy next to me is wearing denim cut-offs, a beard crawling down to meet the chest hair peeking out of the neck of his white wifebeater. His eyes are bright and blue—although a bit unfocused—and his muscled, tan arms are thick with hair.

I shake my head before I realize that I should nod it.

"Ah, good. Everyone here is all coupled up, you know. Except Bethany, and she's basically an impenetrable fortress. Not that I haven't tried to penetrate her," the man says with a boozy laugh, his eyes roving over me freely. I suppress a shudder, then give a little shrug in response and fiddle with my phone.

"Hey," the man says, reaching out and putting a hand on my waist—I recoil a little—"I'm not trying to do anything here you know; I'm just trying to be friendly. I'm just being friendly, so there's really no need to be all standoffish. We're all friends here, lady."

"I don't think she wants to be your friend, dude," a voice comes from above me in the dark. Steve steps out of the shadows and glowers down at the bearded man.

The man snakes his arm even further around my waist. "Who the fuck asked you, kid?" The man's eyes flick over Steve's slight frame, his curled fists, and he laughs. "Jesus Christ, who invited all these fucking kids? It's like a fucking middle school dance up in here." The man's hand wanders up my ribcage and I flinch, a lick of hot rage searing through me—the kind of crazy adrenaline that courses through me when I'm drumming joining the fray. Suddenly, I'm dancing under the circle of his sweaty arm, spinning around, and slam-dancing my knee into his groin.

The man chokes out an expletive and crumples on the ground, but I don't stay to gloat over his fallen frame. My heart threatening to tear through my chest, I sprint toward Bethany's house and fling open the door, only letting out my pent-up breath when I flop, safely, on the couch. My phone, which I had been clutching in my hand, falls on the floor and I stare at it absently, my eyes blurry and my head pounding. I had never really felt threatened in that way by a man before. Sure, there's been the occasional catcall, but no one had ever tried to touch me like that. I know that on the scale of things, he hadn't done much, but it made me feel cold all the same. A sob threatens to shake its way out of my throat, so I take a deep, sucking breath to steady my nerves and put my head down on my knees.

"Hey," Steve says slowly, sitting down next to me on the couch. He tentatively puts his hand on my back. "I'm sorry about that... I shouldn't have left you alone out there in the dark. Although," he says and laughs slightly, "you certainly can take care of yourself. That dude's hand is gonna be pret-ty lonely for the next week or two."

I look up, my eyes narrowing. "It's not funny."

Steve sighs. "I know it's not. I'm guessing that was pretty scary. You look really pretty, by the way," he says suddenly. "I know it's probably not the best time to say that—after that guy sexually menaced you and all."

"Thanks," I mutter.

"Do you want some water?" Steve asks, his hand making slow circles on my back. "Or, like, a shot of whiskey or something?"

I laugh. "No, I'm fine. Thanks for standing up for me."

He smirks at me. "I think you handled it all pretty well yourself. All I did was make some vague comment about leaving you alone."

I shake my head, hug myself. "I'm not usually like that, you know. I'm kind of a wimp."

"I don't think you're a wimp." When I turn to Steve he's looking at me, levelly, his eyes serious. "I think you underestimate how much you're capable of, sure, and sometimes you probably let people talk for you, but I can see you're not a wimp. I mean, you broke me out of my house. You drum like a motherfucker. You just castrated that guy... But you don't need me to tell you who you are. You know it."

I let my eyes wander over Steve's face—to the bruise, his green eyes, the freckle at the corner of his mouth. Do I know it? Most of the time I feel like an asshole. I know hearing this boy say otherwise isn't going to really convince me, but it's nice to watch his lips form the words.

Although I don't see him moving, Steve is suddenly much closer to me, his arm along the back of the couch, his warmth tugging at mine.

"Also," he murmurs, his lips suddenly millimeters from mine. "Did I mention how pretty you look?"

"Yes," I whisper, leaning forward, some kind of weird electricity stirring up a heat lighting storm in my guts. "I think you said something..."

A flash of light and a loud chime erupt from the floor, sending us flying apart.

Steve laughs and scoops up my phone, then moves closer to me with a lazy smile.

"Shut up, i-thingy." He glances down at the screen.

"Don't pretend you don't know what an iPhone is," I say, laughing, but Steve isn't listening. He's looking down at the phone with an expression of horror etched on his face.

"Uhhhh.... What the fuck?" he croaks, holding up the phone.

I squint at the screen and then feel my face go slack. There's a picture. A man in a white mask in a red room. The muscles of his stomach taper down to his hips and beyond. He's only wearing a mask. Nothing else. It's shady. You can't see much. But he's definitely only wearing a mask.

I reach for the phone, but Steve snatches it back and looks down at the screen again. That burning feeling in my stomach is now replaced with a burning feeling of a wholly other nature. He has my phone. His brow furrows. "Is this... Is this who I think it is?" he says slowly, his eyes fixed on the photo. "The tattoo..." he mutters to himself. He swallows and looks up at me, confusion crinkling his brow.

"Where did you get this, Hallie? I've never seen this picture before. Where did you get this and who sent it you?" He looks so hopeful. "Sorry I freaked out before. I just saw all the skin and figured... Well..." He looks at my lips again, all anger apparently forgotten.

"That some guy had sent me a naked picture?" I ask, shame creeping through me.

A plethora of emotions war within my chest. On one hand, there's ZZZ... Intriguing, longing, lonely ZZZ. ZZZ who trusts me with secrets and feelings and seems to understand me. And, of course, there's his body... his naked body in a photo he had taken just for me. And then there's Steve. The bruise stands out even more than usual on his hopeful face, his lips—which had hovered so close to mine moments before—parted in expectation. He'll know soon enough. When Bethany introduces us to Haze. Provided ZZZ is Haze. Provided so many things.

I swallow hard. "You were right. Some guy did send me a picture—the guy in the photo did. The one I told you about before. And I think he's Haze."

Steve just blinks. I swallow, an effort like choking down sand, a barely audible clicking noise emanating from the back of my throat that somehow seems grossly amplified by the silence in the room.

Steve's eyes widen and then narrow abruptly and he clears his throat. "So you know him, then?" he says stiffly. "You know him and you didn't think to tell me that?" His voice is like crackling newsprint, but I can sense the hurt coursing underneath. I choke down my own disappointment. He's mad that I'm talking to Haze— or someone who *could* be Haze. Not that I'm talking to another guy. Obviously, that lip slip before was some kind of fluke.

"What the fuck, Hallie?" he says, his voice cracking. "What the fuck is going on? Is Haze your... *boyfriend*?"

I sigh. "I...I don't know... I just... We started talking, that's all. Before you and I really met. And then I wasn't sure. I mean, how can you really be sure, right? I thought I could go to the show and be sure... I don't even know if it's really him."

Steve picks up the phone and jabs at the center button with a force that makes me instinctively lean away from him. He stabs at the screen. "The tattoo, Hallie. He has the tattoo. And the mask. It's him." My heart soars inappropriately. If Steve thinks so, too...

Then I look at my lap, my insides churning. It feels like someone is ripping into my mind. ZZZ was my secret. What he said to me, what he sent to me, it was mine alone. And now Steve is taking that away. Making me feel guilty. For what? Talking to someone and not telling him about it? Fuck that.

"Give me back my phone," I say slowly, extending my hand.

Steve snorts, "No fucking way. I want to see what else Haze has to say. You owe me that."

I choke, "I don't owe you anything. Give me back my phone! Now!"

Steve stands, scrolling furiously through the messages as I lunge at him, but he's got a few inches on me and he's much faster. "What the... What the fuck? Are you, like, *in love* with him? What the hell is going on here? This is really twisted, man. You haven't even met?"

"No," I growl, finally snatching the phone from Steve, my nails grazing the back of his hand. He pulls it back sharply. "We haven't. And I don't know."

"You don't know what?" Steve snaps.

"I don't know if I'm in love with him. I like talking to him. And at least he can say what he's feeling without blaming it on some fake version of Tourette's! At least he's not a child!" I yell, glaring at Steve.

Steve's face gets hard. "No, he's not a child, Hallie. He's a man. Like an actual adult man. And I think it's seriously fucked up that you think this man has feelings for you. Just because you sent some guy a fan letter and he took pity on you, you think he's your boy–"

"He sent me a message!" I snarl. "He sought me out. Not you. Me!" I cry, my voice tinged with a kind of triumph that makes me hate myself.

Steve's eyes widen. "He just... wrote to you?"

"Yes."

"Out of nowhere?"

"Yes."

Steve furrows his brow. "But... why?"

"I don't... know," I say slowly, rage seeping out of me as I mull over the question. I still don't understand why he chose to talk to me–plucked me out of the Internet ether to murmur things into my ear. The room goes quiet–silence stretching on and on like some kind of unending highway. Then Steve takes a shuddering breath and his face gets hard.

"Well, we'll just use this then," he says, with a single nod.

"What?" What is he talking about? "What are you talking about?"

"He obviously likes you... or something—we can use this to get my interview." Steve isn't looking at me anymore. And he doesn't look happy at the prospect of the interview.

"But Bethany said..."

"I know, but this is more direct. You heard what she said. No one even told her about the show. Who's to say he'll even talk to her?" Steve's voice is colder than I've ever heard it and my summer-sticky skin is flushed with gooseflesh.

I nod. Despite his coldness, what he's saying makes sense. Haze might run from Bethany. We don't know what happened between them. We don't know why she wasn't invited to play with the rest. We don't know why Alex lied and said she was. Still, the fact that Steve seems more upset that I didn't tell him about Haze than the other man's possible affection makes my stomach sink. Despite my inner protestations that I don't care.

"Oh, and don't tell Sarah," Steve says, "She might tell Bethany. We should really start figuring out how we're going to do this..."

"Do what?" My head snaps up. Had I missed something?

"Approach Haze. Get my interview," Steve says evenly. "Maybe we could find out where his house is... Maybe we could use the photos?" Steve asks, looking at me like I'm an instruction manual.

I swallow hard. "Steve?" My voice cracks and I hate, hate, hate myself.

"Yeah?" he says, brusquely.

"Can we... I'm tired. Can we talk about this, like, tomorrow?" I say, looking down at the phone, trying to decide what I should say to Haze. If I should respond to Haze at all.

"Sure," Steve says, almost kindly, snapping out his weird trance for a moment. "We should all rest. This is gonna be fucking epic and we all need to be super sharp. Why don't you go sleep in Bethany's room? She said something about sleeping on the boat tonight—as part of the christening or something."

I nod slowly and get up, holding my phone limply at my side. I turn to go toward the little bedroom.

"Oh and Hallie?" Steve says.

"Yeah," I say, turning around slightly.

His face is smooth, impassive, but something cracks through for a second. Something like a wild animal moving in the dark trees. "Never mind. Goodnight."

TEN

"If I be the big spoon and you be the little spoon/ Will you take the fork in the road and run away with me?"

—"Morning After Breath," *Masking Tape* —Haze

Bethany's room smells like herbs—sage and rosemary and lavender, bunches of which hang from the beams of the ceiling like ingredients for a spell. My skin feels all cool and slick now—I had taken a shower after what happened with Steve, eager to wash off all the grime, both mental and physical, that had collected all over me. I had made liberal use of Bethany's lavender body wash and shampoo and now my hair is drying in loose waves on my shoulders. I don't think I'll wear it up like that again, no matter what anyone says about my cheekbones. I have a headache.

I flop on the bed and hug an embroidered pillow to my chest, looking around the dark room, the walls washed in opal moonlight and the herbs all swaying in the night breeze like lazy ghosts. It's always weird to sleep in someone else's bed. It makes me feel like

I'll wake up partly them—partly myself. It just feels a little sad, you know? It's silly, but it's true.

I watch the moon out the window and tick the days off in my head. Two nights since I had been home. (I worry briefly about Dad and then push it down. My mind can't handle that right now.) It seems like much longer ago that I had slipped into the night—broken my dull little life narrative in half. One time Sarah read my palm and declared that my life would be long—but mundane. I wonder if that's still true. If I can carve my own path, or if the grooves that I pressed into my palms as a baby sealed my fate. If that one little soulmate line that Sarah had told me about—there on the side of my hand by my pinkie—was accurate. Is there only one out there for me? Is it Haze? Or is that just insane?

I can't deny at this point that he's not the only one making it hard to sleep right now. The other reason is splayed out on the couch, snoring lightly, sleeping on his stomach like a little kid. With his quiet eyes and ropey arms and smoky breath and curling hair—locks that tumble over his forehead, barely concealing his bruise and scars. It's stupid to lie to yourself when there's no one eaves-dropping into your mind. To tell the inside of my brain that I didn't want something to happen. That it felt like he was ripping me down the middle when he promptly forgot about our almost-kiss when Haze came into the picture. In all the books and movies the guy is never selfish, you know? But I guess, in real life, people are. And everything doesn't always work out OK.

He probably wasn't feeling anything. He had probably seen an opportunity for physical contact—comfort—and instinctively wandered toward it. Sarah is always saying that no man in his right mind will ever turn down sex—no matter how homely the girl.

I pull a pillow over my face in an attempt to shut out the

moonlight, but a soft "ping!" from the bedside table makes me fling off the cushion before I can get comfortable. I pop from bed and scoop up my phone, anger and urgency and coldness surging through me as I look at the screen. Was that too much? I didn't mean to freak you out…

The corners of my mouth pull up in an in-spite-of-myself smile before I remember what Steve had said. Asking why Haze—or ZZZ, or whoever—is talking to me. It doesn't make any sense. It all seems so random—that this grown man could just happen to be interested in me. I look down at the message seared across my screen. If he's just bored, if he's only lonely, why would he apologize? Why ask about my comfort? If he really didn't care, he would just dash, magpie-like, after his next distraction.

I look down at the message again, scrolling back to the picture. His arms are long and lean, but the muscles in his biceps are rounded and firm-looking. He doesn't have bodybuilder six-pack abs—a look that has never appealed to me—but he does have that V-shaped cut common to lifeguards that Sarah swoons over at the beach when the days are long and hot. The V leading down into the danger zone that I am wholly unfamiliar with. My cheeks are getting hot and I turn my phone over on the bed, imagining that somehow, some way, someone will come up to me and chide me for looking. For thinking the things that I had just been thinking. Steve would say ZZZ is too old for me.

But when I look at the image, imagine the possibilities of dark lips and dark hands and things I don't know anything about, something inside of me surges. Fear, sure, but something else.

You didn't freak me out, I type back, only semi-lying. What did you want in return?

I want to see you.

The words reflect blue on the walls and ceiling and swaying herbs.

I look down at my loose T-shirt and pajama pants and fears coils around my belly again like a cat looking to settle down and sleep and stay. But something deeper, something darker, bares its claws and lashes out. Wanting blood.

I feel frozen. Locked in place. Like if I don't move time won't go forward. I won't have to make a decision. And this feels like a big one. One that will make me into a different version of myself—and I'll never get the old version back. But that old version... that's the one I've been trying to escape. The one that's scared. The one that can extricate itself from situations like with that creepy dude, but freaks out in the meantime. Feels guilty for freaking out. The one that's angry because a boy didn't kiss her. The one that's always angry and wanting more. It's comfortable to be that girl—like it's comfortable to stay in your pajamas all day. But I don't want to be her anymore. Finally, finally, I move, look down at myself—and at those clawed things eyeing each other across the chasm of my mind.

Quickly, so that I don't back out, I whip off my shirt and stand in my bra in the moonlight, staring at the whiteness of my body in the full-length mirror on the wall. The room is dark, dark, dark, so all I can see is my flesh, blooming bright like a nighttime flower. Or a darting fish beneath the surface of the water. I try to pose for a second or two—parodies of stances I've seen in fashion magazines, but finally I just shift my hips to the side and snap a photo, sending it into the night without looking at the screen. Pixels and pings that once were a girl flying through the night to reform somewhere, out there, on another screen. Terror. Oh, God, terror.

Moments pass and in them I curl on the edge of the bed, feeling warm and scared and weird and awkward and different, river-scented air wandering in from outside to curl around my skin. Then.

Lovely. You are so lovely. If you would do just one more thing for me—with me—I'll tell you my secret. Do you think you can do that?

I swallow—relieved. Scared even deeper. What is it?

I want you to lie back on your bed as you are now. Without your clothes. With all of your true and lovely beauty shining through. I want you to think about me. I want you think about my chest against your chest. I want you to wander until you see the stars that no one has let you see before. And while you do this, I want you to think of me, thinking of you, doing the same thing and moaning your name...

The words hit me in the chest and stomach and other places and I sit back in bed, pulling the covers around me and blinking at the ceiling. I want him. I think I want him. My body certainly feels like it does. But I can't. My arms and legs are cement and glue and other things that do not budge. I can't jump into the roaring abyss, not untethered here, alone in the night. Perhaps if he were here with me... Perhaps then... The old version of me crawls back into my skin and clings to it.

For several moments I blink into the darkness. Thinking. Willing my body to move. For my body to follow ZZZ's instructions. But I can't. All my mind and body can manage to say is, "I can't."

The edge of my bed lights up. I washed away to the stars and back thinking of you. You can know my secret now, you know, if you feel the same...

My fingers kind of numb I type back. I do.

The phone chimes again.

Good girl.

Then I can tell you, Placid Girl, I can tell you finally... I am who you think I am. I am Haze. And I am yours. All yours.

ELEVEN

"So when I die put a bell on me/ Put a bell on me/ So when this cat comes back you'll know/ You'll know,"

—"Dead Ringer," *Masking Tape* —Haze

The city seems much closer—there across the sunlit water—than it did when there was only concrete rolling out in front of us. I lean against the bright blue wood of the railing on deck and trace the outline of the skyscrapers with my eyes—a few towers piercing the sky like angels' needles, the other buildings hunching in the shadows and concentrating on throwing their shadows on the sidewalks below. By the water, all is red rust and smoke, the smell of plastic and chemicals and paint clinging to the sea salt and worming its way into my nostrils. It's not an unpleasant smell—just unnatural.

Somewhere in the middle of all that stone and smoke and shadow is Haze. And he wants me. And I want him, too. Or at least some part of my mind screams that it's so. Another looks askance at that portion and almost-whispers "hush." Scared. That's the word my mind clings to somehow—despite the elation. *Scared.*

Steve appears at my elbow on the deck. Bethany is somewhere in the guts of the ship, doing whatever it takes to get it to run. Sarah is, presumably, helping. I try not to feel jealous that my best friend seems to like Bethany better than me. I still haven't spoken with her—not since yesterday—and Steve's words are ringing in my ears again. I should really try to get a moment alone to apologize—although the voice from before is sneering at me and asking, *For what? How many times has she done something shitty and failed to say she was sorry to you?*

"What do you think we should do—when we get there?" Steve asks. I look over at him, the wind making his hair wild and his cheeks red. He looks like he should be standing on some Irish cliff in a cable-knit sweater. Instead, he's squinting at me, wearing a Bad Brains T-shirt, his nose peeling slightly in the sun. My plan of slipping backstage at the show tomorrow—of locking eyes with a man whose face I don't even know—basically ends at the "locking eyes" part. That's curtain down. The end of the film. I don't know what comes after that.

I shrug.

Steve squints at the rapidly approaching skyline. "Maybe we can use the photos to find out where he is. That way, we have a better chance of catching him. We could try, like, scoping out his place and then, after the show, if we can't grab him, we can always camp out outside his apartment or whatever and see if he'll talk to us then," he says, his voice lighter than I've ever heard it. It bothers me—the lightness. How he thinks Haze will solve all of his problems. How he feels like the man somehow owes him something. I want to tell him to fuck off. To go home. I want to jump over the side of the boat and paddle toward shore. But instead I just set my mouth into a grim line and try not to growl. It's also a good idea. Using the photos. I wish I had thought of it.

"Are there any identifying details or whatever?" Steve asks, gesturing toward my pocket where my phone is. I don't want to take it out in front of him. Share Haze any more than I have to. But I'm curious, too. I pull out the phone, scroll through the shots. The same red background in every photo. I don't know what we expecting. A street sign of some sort?

"Damn," Steve mutters. "I guess that's a wash." He looks hard at my phone. Like he thinks by doing so it will offer up its secrets. It starts ringing, as if in answer, and I jump. "Oh, you're blowing up!" Steve says.

My stomach surges with anticipation before I remember that Haze doesn't have my number. It's my dad. Guilt gets at my gut—hard. I should really let Dad know I'm alive at least. He must be freaking out by now. He might have even called the police. I snatch back the phone, press "ignore" then fire off a quick text. Can't talk now, Dad. Call u later. I'm safe. I promise. I block his number before he can call again—fully aware that this will send him into an even more intense panic. But I can't do this. Not right now. I think back to the greenhouse—sitting on the floor, watching him make things grow back when he noticed me sitting there, both of us singing along to the radio. I miss him. My gut clenches with guilt. He trusts me. Always has. Never put one of those tracking thingies on my phone like a lot of parents did... which gives me an idea interesting enough to make the guilt recede into the background like a fading headache.

"There's data in photos," I say, slowly.

"Huh? I actually have no idea how to use one of those things. I still have a flip phone," Steve says, although I was mostly talking to myself.

"Photos—taken on iPhones and whatever—they have data in them. If you use the right tools or whatever, you can find out where and when they were taken and everything. Super creepy, I know," I say, while typing "find photo location data" into Google. Within seconds, a litany of different sites come up.

"How did you know that?" Steve asks, I don't look at him, but it sounds kind of like he's smiling—laughing at me, maybe. I bristle.

I shrug. "I'm smart? I dunno." I do know. I watch a ton of crime shows and shit on Saturday nights when Sarah has dates and my parents sit in their separate rooms waiting for their relationship to finally expire. That's all that's on super late at night—and my mind usually keeps me up *super* late. I'm lame. I watch TV like a geriatric insomniac. Guess it finally paid off.

I click on one of the first links, upload one of Haze's photos—one he sent directly to me, because social networks strip all that data when you upload a snap—and within seconds the tool spits out a list of info including the make and model of the musician's phone, what time and day the photo was taken, the fact that he had not used flash and, there at the end, coordinates and a link to Google maps containing the location of Haze's home.

"Whoa," I breathe.

"What is it?" Steve strains to look over her shoulder.

"Nothing. That was just surprisingly easy..." I say slowly, clicking on the maps link. "Remind me never to do anything that would draw the attention of a stalker." The page loads slowly on the tiny screen, little by little revealing a map of the city with a red icon denoting Haze's home. Steve holds his breath, leaning over the phone, his hands unthinkingly clenched on my shoulders. I grit my teeth, trying not to think about his hands or his earthy smell—or anything about him. As the image of the map finally comes into focus, that endeavor becomes rather easy.

"Looks like he lives pretty close to the water... Right here it says 593 Shore Street." Steve says gleefully, pointing at the map and then at the approaching land. I take in the row of desolate-looking warehouses gazing sadly into the water and frown.

"He lives in a warehouse?" That sounds pretty sketchy to me. And possibly incorrect. Maybe the tool didn't work after all.

"Sure," Steve laughs, as if I'm some kind of idiot. "This is the city and he's a musician. All of those guys live in, like, lofts and abandoned storefronts and storage spaces and whatever. Spaces like that are cheap and no one bothers you if you play your music too loud."

"Is that legal?" I ask, my eyes still fixed on the horizon ahead. For a moment, the image in my head of Haze flips from brooding, romantic singer to deranged vagrant warming his hands by an oil drum fire. The things he said to me last night twist like tapeworms in my stomach.

Steve laughs. "No. I'm guessing it's really, really not legal. I went to a party with Alex once and it was in one of those buildings. The place those dudes were living in didn't even have any windows. And I think they got robbed a few times."

All ideas of ditching Steve to go find Haze immediately flee from my head. Fine, he and I will stake out the situation first and make sure Haze is not some coked-out horrorshow— even though I know he's not—and then I'll find him after the show. He'll see me and he'll know it's me and then... Whatever will happen will happen. Maybe Steve can even get his story. I look at him, squinting across the water and smiling. Irritation bubbles anew.

"Why do you need this story so badly?" I ask, my eyes fixed on his profile. The words feel like rusted metal or something, but for the moment I don't care. I want to know. His face falls then, his lips thinning until they almost disappear.

"I told you, I need to get out of my house," he says slowly, not looking at me.

"I know that," I say, ignoring the little sock in my guts when I think of the bruise. "But why do you need the story to do that? Why do you need Haze? Couldn't you just go stay with Bethany or Alex? Couldn't you have run away a while ago?"

Steve still doesn't look at me for a few long seconds and I think he's ignoring me. Then he starts speaking, his voice low and steely, his eyes fixed on the city ahead. "I told you before, if you run away right the first time, you only have to run away once. I don't want to mess up my chance. I want to do it right. I want to be someone. I want to make something. I want to start off out there on my own already ahead." The words are coming fast now, like robots clinking down an assembly line. "I don't want to be a fuck-up. I don't want to be a loser. I don't want to be like my brother. He ran away, and look what happened to him. He's dead."

Steve isn't talking to me. I know that. He's talking to someone inside himself. Someone half-alive, half-dead. Half-him, half-Gabriel. I search my mind for something to say back but my brain seems empty.

The cracked blue door to the wheelhouse flies open, and Bethany barrels through, her hair wild around her face and her cheeks wet with tears.

"Q!" she yells, looking around the deck frantically until Steve rushes forward and puts his hands on her shoulders.

"Q," Bethany moans, burying her face into Steve's neck, her shoulders heaving up and down, her throat erupting with ugly sobs.

I look on aghast, Steve meeting my eyes above Bethany's head, his face shocked and concerned and a little embarrassed.

The door creaks open again behind them and I watch speechless as Sarah comes through, her face somber and scared. The dark roots show through her pink hair, and there are circles under her eyes. Her face is pale. She looks young. Young and tired, like a sick child. I want to wrap my arms around her and tell her it's all going to be OK—that we're going home now. We're too young to look this sad. We should try to do all this living five years from now when we're ready.

"What's going on?" Steve says at last, his voice cracking. "What happened?"

Bethany keeps sobbing, so all eyes swivel to Sarah, searching for some kind of answer.

She clears her throat and looks back at Bethany, who seems unable to speak. "She got a call," she says, her eyes roving over everyone, but not meeting anyone's gaze.

"From the police."

"And?" Steve asks, more than a touch of anger and impatience creeping into his voice.

Sarah just looks at him sadly and my stomach lurches and drops. Sarah isn't getting angry. For once, she isn't snapping back with her usual rage. The kind that she channels when she's on stage, wailing the songs that she writes—the ones about lost love. If anything, she just looks sorry. Very, very sorry.

"They found Alex," she says slowly.

"And? What the fuck is going on?" Steve practically yells. Bethany is silent now, her fingers digging deep into Steve's back.

"Their parents didn't pick up. So they called her," Sarah says, looking down at the deck.

"Sarah, just please tell me what the *hell* happened?" Steve's voice takes on a pleading tone.

"It burned down," Sarah says in a dead voice. "Your cousin's apartment building burned down. All of it. He was inside. Or they think he was. They need his medical records. They called her..."

Steve just stares at her, his mouth open, his arms limp around Bethany. He looks shocked by the bluntness of Sarah's tone, but I know that she's not trying to be cruel. When things were bad, when situations were so utterly sad, Sarah could only really function if she shut down. If she robotted out. I know Sarah feels very, very bad for Steve. And it scares me. I remember Alex then, his faraway eyes and dreamy smile. It's hard to picture him no longer...being.

Slowly, I walk over to Sarah and put my arms around her steely frame. She stands rigid for a moment or two, like a cold corpse, and then gradually relaxes into me, putting an arm around my waist and resting her head on my shoulder.

"Oh, Hallie," she whispers. "What are we going to do?"

I open my mouth to say something—I have no idea what—but this flat voice, a voice that sounds like it's coming out of someone possessed, starts murmuring "I knew it was coming. I knew it was coming and it's my fault," Bethany drones.

Steve looks at me, then down at Bethany. "What are you talking about, B?"

"He was talking... That's why I stopped... I couldn't do it any-more. I couldn't. He was getting worse... We just couldn't... We... And he was talking," she says in a fast, cold monotone. The hair stands up on my arms.

"I think you better go lie down," Steve says. He looks so calm. He looks so collected. I realize then he's a lot like Sarah. He knows when he needs to shut down. So that he doesn't break apart.

"No," Bethany tears herself from Steve's arms, but that creepy monotone persists. "He was talking about things. About death and things and becoming what he was meant to be. About how we... I was stopping him," she pauses, looking down at her hands, biting her trembling lip.

"How could you stop him from doing anything, Bethany?" Steve says, reaching for her again. "You didn't do anything. I know you didn't."

Bethany shakes her head. "I did. He was always talking about how he was meant to be something more than he was. How he needed to be something or he would just fall apart. But I didn't listen. I told him he was scaring me and to stop. To take a trip, see a therapist, just... stop. And then he did stop. Talking to me. And I didn't try. I didn't try to... We told..." her voice breaks and the tears keep rolling down her cheeks.

"This isn't your fault," Sarah says, moving out of my arms and putting her hand on Bethany's shoulder. "Why would you think this is your fault?"

Bethany chokes down a giant sob and sinks to the deck, her flowy dress pooling around her like a blue shadow. "Because Alex killed himself, obviously. He killed himself and I did nothing to stop it. Everything is fucked. And Steve," she whirls toward him. "The cops asked about you. They said they'd talked to your dad. He's looking for you, Steve, and I can't stop him either."

\\\\\\\\\

Heat licks the side of my face, but I don't move away from the boat's engine—something about the stinging warmth is comforting. It proves, somehow, that we're still in the real world, where fire can burn and skin can hurt and moving away from danger will have a positive effect. As I stare into the glowing fire that is—somehow—powering the boat, I realize I never messaged Haze back last night. I wonder if he's waiting plaintively by the phone, jolting at every ping and ring. Or if he has forgotten about me. If he has 20 girls with whom he does...what he did last night. That might not matter now, though—Haze might not. How can this trip have any meaning anymore when death is here? Its dark shadow has fallen over the boat, sucking Steve and Bethany into its vortex and leaving me and Sarah—those who didn't know Alex—alone.

"I can't believe she has to go down there," Sarah says quietly.

"Where?" I start, kind of dazed, finally turning my burning cheek away from the fire. Cool air rushes up and brushes its fingers against my skin.

"To the police station. They asked Bethany to come. I feel so fucking bad for her."

I think then of my own family, back home, unraveling. How they must feel right now. I wonder if they even miss me. What would it be like for them—if I were really gone? If they had to come to some faraway police station and sign papers or whatever? I shake my head. That's too much to think about right now. Besides, they've been shutting me out for months. It's time they understand what that feels like. To worry. To be alone.

"No other family?" I ask, snapping back to the present. "Didn't he... Alex, have parents and whatever?"

Sarah shakes her head. "I guess not. I guess they don't talk or something. I guess he's estranged from pretty much everyone."

"So where does that leave us?" I ask. "Should we..." My stomach falls as I force out the words. "Should we just go home? Let them figure this out?"

"No," Sarah says. I sit back on my heels. Did I hear her right? Does Sarah really want to stick around? This whole thing is getting to be too much—even for me.

"To hear that someone you love died. To have to... It would be hard. It would be really fucking hard. We can't leave them now. Anyway..." she takes a deep, shuddering breath. "I just *really* don't want to go home right now."

I nod. "Yeah, me neither. I get it."

"Do you really?" Sarah snaps, looking at me with slitted eyes. "You haven't asked me once what's up at home. You've been too busy texting some boyfriend I've never heard of. What is that, Hallie? What the hell is going on?"

I swallow. "It's complicated..."

"No, it isn't," Sarah says, exasperated. "I don't know what's wrong with you, but suddenly you're just... shutting me out. I thought we were over the whole Nick thing. I thought we had moved past that. My life is fucking hard enough without having to feel bad for one stupid mistake."

Something inside me breaks. "Everything always has to be about you, doesn't it?" I snarl. "I'm sick of it. The band, guys, everything—you have to have it all! You couldn't even see anything in the review past the shit about you. Like, you don't fucking care about me at all—my needs! The Nick thing is just one of the classic hits in the string of shitty things you've done to me."

Sarah's eyes are hard, hard, hard and her face is red—from the furnace or anger, I don't know. "I was fucking protecting you," she says, her voice strained.

"What?"

"I was fucking protecting you from that *asshole*, Nick. He was hooking up with underage girls left and right like a total fucking loser and I didn't want you to be next. I didn't want you to lose it to some grimy jobless dickhead who didn't give a fuck about you."

"What are you talking about?" I snap, my brain whirling. "Protect me? What does that even mean?"

"None of those bitches were gonna step forward and get him fired because they were too scared, too worried about looking uncool or whatever in front of all those punk idiots. So I fucking set him up. Sure, it wasn't the most elegant of plans—I was drunk and sad and mad about my mom that night—but it did the trick. He never got his fucking hands on you." Sarah crosses her arms and stares into the licking fires of the furnace.

I blink. "But you were jealous... you couldn't stand that someone was interested in me and not you." I hate my voice right now but I keep talking. "You just couldn't stand it."

"Hallie, that you would think that... Jesus fucking Christ. I just explained it to you. I literally just told you why I did it. I support the fuck out of you. Who the fuck is the one who is always trying to make you sing your songs? Talk to dudes? Take off the fucking baggy clothing and be brave? How could you even... Je-sus."

I look down at my toes. I want to scream and cry that she's wrong. That she *was* trying to hurt me. That she *was* jealous. But I can't. I can't because I know that she's right. And it makes me mad. Mad because if I can't blame her anymore, who can I blame?

I shake my head, "I don't believe you." The words fly out of my mouth and strike Sarah in the chest.

The fire crackles and the water laps and the Christmas lights strung up for illumination sway and sway.

"Fuck you," Sarah whispers, then turns away from me and walks—straight spine—up the steps to the deck.

I sit and stare into the fire for what feels like forever. I click on my phone to write something to Haze—to get some kind of reassurance that I'm not a horrible person. That I'm right. But there's no signal out on the water anymore, so I just stare at nothing until the vessel bumps against the shore and everything shudders to a stop.

When I come out on deck the sky hangs low above us, gray like unwashed, sagging linen, and Bethany is on shore, tying up the boat to a dock. There are no other boats bobbing around us—just tangles of barbed wire fence on shore and a bunch of broken stone angels reaching empty wrists to the heavens. The building next to the water has a faded sign half spelling out something about memorials. It appears to be some kind of abandoned tombstone factory. I shiver in the warm, humid air, thinking about death and where we're headed. Trying not to think of Sarah. How final that "fuck you" had sounded.

Steve stands on the cracked sidewalk, staring at the concrete.

He barely looks up when I get off the boat. I don't even think he's seen me until his hand shoots out, encircling my wrist.

"Can we go after?" he asks, staring down into my face with a pleading look. His eyes are dry.

I squint at him. "Where?"

"To find him? Bethany wants to go to their old practice space to sit for a while. I'm guessing Sarah will want to go with her or something. We can split up and go find him."

I try not to feel the surge of relief that courses through me when I think of getting away from Sarah, the way she looked at me like I had hurt her so fucking much; instead, I focus on Haze. I will see Haze. Haze understands me. Even if I wasn't ready last night for... whatever... there's still that. I will see him. And I will have to bring Steve with me.

I swallow hard and nod. His face almost relaxes into a smile and at that moment he looks so tired and sad and relieved that I feel like reaching out and touching his cheek, but he turns away then and starts walking with Bethany down the sidewalk, toward what looks like the subway. That seems apt. Neither of them seems like the type to waste money on cabs. It's fine with me, too—I think I only have about 50 in my wallet from when my mom last pressed some cash into my hand to go buy new clothes. As if new clothes could be purchased for $50. I hadn't spent it, though. I figured I would just buy some records when the new shipment came in at Picture Disc.

I reach into my pocket, pulling out my phone. There's a new message from Haze: How are you today, Placid Girl? I imagined your skin on my skin all night...

A shudder runs through me all bone-deep and my finger hovers over the message, but Sarah and Bethany and Steve are descending into the bowels of the subway now and I run to catch up.

He wants me to know him, he said. But I already do. More than he knows. I know his words and his voice and some aspects of his heart. I know his address. And I'm planning on tipping the scales to woefully uneven proportions by camping outside his home and waiting to catch him unawares. And what's more—I'm planning on doing so with Steve. With someone who wants to reveal all his secrets. And he trusts me. I swallow hard and throw myself into the shadows of the subway. I'll have to find some way to make it up to him.

The subway ride defies logic somehow, racing forward and slowing down to a crawl all at the same time—Bethany and Steve aren't talking, and Sarah is pretending that I don't exist. The police station is only a few stops away, Bethany says, and in the meantime, I try not to make eye contact with any of the other occupants of my train—a couple holding each other, their hands thrust deep into each other's back pockets, a homeless man sleeping across a row of seats, a businessman in a wrinkled, cheap suit reading a paper. I sit carefully on the edge of my seat—even though I'm probably dirty enough after being on the boat all day—trying not to lean back into the hard plastic. I think of the message of my phone. What my next moves will be. How I will avoid disappointing that sad, dark man. And that word again, *scared*, as I think of his skin... him thinking of his skin on my skin.

When the doors open, I almost miss our stop—I'm so lost in thought. Steve grabs my arm and I shoot up, angling myself through the closing doors and earning some exasperated glares from the other denizens of the train. I shrug and quirk my face into a mask of apology, but the couple has already gone back to grabbing ass, the businessman has resumed reading, and the homeless man's slumber was never interrupted in the first place.

Minutes later—it seems—we're standing near a set of heavy double doors, breathing in that sickening antiseptic smell common to schools and other government buildings, and Bethany is gone—back behind some gated doors leading somewhere cold and terrifying. Bethany had tried to convince Steve to stay outside in case the police recognized him, but he wanted to come in, insisting that he wouldn't leave her alone. So now he's slumped against the wall by the exit wearing sunglasses, a hat pulled low over his eyes.

Sarah sprawls in a chair, avoiding me, so I walk back and forth across the waiting room floor and examine the posters on the wall. There's a brightly colored painting hanging above the receptionist's desk of a Parisian apartment bursting with gilt furniture and plants, the Eiffel tower glinting outside the balcony windows. It's a weird picture to have next to all the anti-drug posters; I wonder how many people stare at it every day while they're waiting to get booked or whatever, wishing they were standing on that balcony. Or wishing they could jump off it. The hairs stand up on my arms. This is the second time in the last few days I've been in a police station, and I decide (pretty obviously) that I'm not down with these joints. My head starts to go all starry like the sky in the painting, so I turn to go sit down with Sarah—then freeze when Bethany comes slouching through the door, crying.

Steve rushes forward and grabs Bethany's arm, forgetting that he said he would not draw any attention to himself. I wish I could reach out and grab his arm, too, or put mine around him. But I hang back, awkward, feeling like an intruder.

"It happened a day or two ago..." Bethany says quietly, without anyone asking. "I guess he had moved without telling anyone, so it took a while to figure out it was him. The lease was in his name, though."

"So... it's really him?" Steve asks.

Bethany shakes her head slowly, "I mean, they can't be sure... They didn't find much... a tooth and some... They asked me about his dental records, but I didn't know... They're looking into it," her voice catches. "But it looks that way. He signed a lease. He lived in that apartment." Bethany stops and closes her eyes, her breath ragged. "There is something else, though, Steve..."

"What?" he asks.

"The way it looked... in the apartment... there was kerosene..." Bethany says, forcing out the words.

"So you were right..." Steve says, his voice barely cresting a whisper.

"There were traces of kerosene all over the floor... They don't think it was an accident. They're investigating, but I know... I'm pretty sure... he killed himself," Bethany says, and leans heavily against the receptionist's desk, staring at the painting behind it. I wish I could rip it off the wall. It seems like a mockery in a place where basically all anyone gets is bad news.

Bethany's face falls, her lip quivering as tears pour down her face. She takes a deep anguished breath and whispers, "It's all my fault..."

"No," Steve says, "No." But before he can say anything else the doors in back open with a smattering of radio static and heavy boots. A pair of policemen stand by the door, scanning the room.

Steve's eyes widen and he starts backing toward the exit sideways like a crab. I grab his arm. "What are you doing?"

He doesn't answer, just narrows his eyes and jerks his head

toward the doors. The cops aren't paying much attention to us—at least at first—but they glance over now, probably because Steve looks like he's about to have a seizure. A curious look passes over the shorter one's face and he lags behind a little bit as the taller one strides to the desk. I remember then that Steve's dad had called the police, and suddenly it seems like a supremely stupid idea that we had all decided to go with Bethany to the station—even if she did need the moral support. Do they know what Steve looks like? Do they know what I look like? Did my dad call the police, too? Just how fucked, exactly, are we?

Steve's hand tightens on my arm, pressing painfully into my skin, and I fight the urge to yelp. "Come on, Hallie, we need to get out of here now," he whispers, and pulls me toward the door, leaving Bethany and Sarah to scuttle behind us.

We tear through the parking lot, no looking back, and pretty soon my side is on fire. I've never been able to successfully run the mile in gym class. "The only time I'll run is when I'm trying to get something I want," I always joked with Sarah as we plodded around the track, watching the athletic kids strive toward six-minute miles and high school glory. Are they chasing us? Is anyone? I don't want to turn around.

"Hallie, come ON!" Steve yells, grabbing my arm and hauling me across the blacktop. I fling myself past the burning legs and cramps and catch up with the rest, who gracefully lope ahead like African beasts. There's a steep hill ahead and down below I can hear cars rushing by—a highway. My heart careens into my ribs as I realize we're heading right toward it. Steve is still running, though, so I throw myself down the embankment, my legs pumping faster and faster without my accord, sending me flying down the steep, rocky hill. It feels like one of those dreams where you're running but your feet aren't touching the ground—just skimming the surface like a water bug on a pond.

I trip and fall and my jeans rip at the knee. Steve's hand shoots out and steadies me and he looks at me with concern. My heart thuds—not out of fatigue—but he looks away quickly, setting his sights on the highway in front of us.

In seconds, the grass and stone turn once more to solid road and I'm dashing across the highway, gripping onto Steve's arm as the cars rush by, honking and swerving. My ears pound and I taste blood. My legs jolt with every step and electricity in my veins propels me faster, away from the giant hurtling hunks of metal bearing down on me as they rush toward wherever they have to go. I tumble onto the grass on the other side of the highway, my sides heaving and veins pumping away like geysers. I glance across the road as the blood throbs in my forehead, but before I can get a good look at the other side, Steve grabs my arm and pulls me down the embankment further so that we're all hidden by trees.

Laughing, Steve flings himself down behind a rock and clutches his sides, breathing heavily. "Ah, fuck! Ah, fuuuuuuck." He starts laughing harder then.

"Fuck!" he yells, his voice careening all over the place. Sarah and Bethany look on, their faces red and horrified, but I take a deep breath and sit down next to Steve against the rock. Slowly, as if I'm reaching out to a feral dog, I put my arm around Steve and force a smile. His shoulders are shaking now and all the laughter melts away, leaving only tears and convulsions.

"Yeah," I say in a quiet voice that I didn't know I had inside myself. "I know." But I don't, really. I don't. And that's a fucking understatement.

Steve stops laughing after a few minutes, but his face is still wet and his shoulders shake at intervals. I realize that I'm rubbing his shoulder and snatch my hand away. He looks at me with a flash of shock in his eyes, then glances up toward the embankment. No one. Bethany and Sarah had excused themselves a few minutes into Steve's manic fit with mumbled mutterings about needing to pee.

Steve rubs his wet face with his hand, leaving a streak of dirt across his forehead—right near the bruises—and before I can stop myself, I reach up and wipe the grime away. His eyes are filled with tears.

"Hallie," he whispers.

"Yeah," I croak, pulling my hand away from his forehead.

"I want to—I mean, I need to –" His eyes widen and flicker down to my lips. My heart bangs against my ribs and my stomach threatens to tear itself through my throat.

"I need to find him," Steve says, his eyes flicking back up to mine. I am not even wholly sure where my mind was going back there, but it was nowhere rational.

"Oh," I whisper.

"I need to find him now. You saw those cops up there."

"Do you think they were after us?" I ask, finally.

"I don't know. I didn't want to stay and find out. But sooner or later, they will be, won't they?" he says, his eyes darting all around.

"Probably."

"But we need to ditch them—now," Steve says, jutting his chin toward where Bethany and Sarah had disappeared through the trees. "I don't want to leave Bethany. I really don't. But I just... I just feel like he would, I dunno, spook easy or something if we all showed up. I think..."

"What?" I ask.

"Haze. I think we should go down there and then you should go and knock on his door. Talk to him alone. He trusts you," Steve says, then adds gruffly, "I guess..."

I feel my phone in my pocket now, all heavy and slick. There's still that unanswered message. There's still that fear and promise and everything else.

"Will you do it?" Steve asks, leaning close to me. I can smell his earthy smell—intensified by the run but somehow not unpleasant. I can see the fine down on his temples, where his hair hangs damp from sweat. The muscles in his arms stand out from anticipation. And, fuck it, I want to kiss him. It's a stupid thought in a stupid time. A thought that makes no sense. But a thought all the same. Yes, there's Haze and, yes, Steve seems mostly interested in finding the musician—and only sometimes interested in me—but my whole body (the part that doesn't like listening to my brain) just wants to fling my arms around his neck and find out what his lips taste like. To feel his whole thin body pressed against mine. I shudder in the afternoon heat and swallow hard.

"Yeah, I'll do it," I say, pushing any tremors from my voice. "But how do we distract Bethany and Sarah? How do we split away? The cops may be after us. They must be freaked."

Steve's face falls. "Yeah, that's the problem... Bethany will still want to go to the practice space now... To look around, maybe see if there's anything there that could explain why he... A note or some-thing." Steve looks down at the ground and scuffs a rock with his toe, digs the sea glass out of his pocket and squeezes.

"But we can't go there," I say, shaking my head. "The cops—don't you think that's where they would look—if they're looking? You know, somewhere that Alex used to go? They would find you in a second."

"I got it," Steve says, looking up with almost a smile.

"What?"

"That's how we can split up without pissing anyone off or anything," Steve says. "I'll say that I need to go back to the boat—to hide out, you know, until the show. If there's still a show... After..." Steve shakes his head a little. Swallows.

It hadn't occurred me before that Haze might cancel the show now that Alex is (the word fails to complete itself in my mind) but now that it does I understand Steve's urgency. And my own anxiety about not getting to meet Haze begins to mount, in what I realize is a horrible way. It's just a show. Alex is dead. There, my mind managed to finish the phrase. And I realize Steve is still talking.

"...I mean, if we explain the whole thing about the cops that you just said they wouldn't be all that weirded out if I took off for a while."

"But what about me?" I ask, doubt wriggling through my brain. "What's my excuse?"

Steve shrugs slightly, busting out his crooked smile, "Moral support? I mean, I'm a fucking mess, I shouldn't be alone. Who knows what I'll do?" His voice cracks and I don't smile back.

All this shit—his dad, Alex, the cops—I don't know if I could handle it. I don't really understand how Steve is still standing. Probably because he has to. Probably because when things get so bad that you feel like lying down and sleeping forever, that's when your heart kicks in, sends some kind of electric shock shooting through your veins to keep you going. Some people have that. Others, like

Alex, apparently, don't. They just lie down on a funeral pyre of their own making and let the flames burn everything away. I shudder, thinking of what it must be like to feel your skin dusting away, heat gnawing on your bones and your blood turning to smoke. I think about him asking me to smoke weed with him on the roof. His white hands. Gone now.

"I'm going to go find them," Steve says somewhere near my head. I nod. He moves silently away through the trees and I dig around in my pocket for my phone.

When the screen flickers to life, I raise my eyebrows. Another message from Haze: Placid Girl. Please don't ignore me.

The words send a jolt through my veins. There's something off about them. Like one of those visual games where you're supposed to find the discrepancies between two pictures. It hasn't been that long since he sent the message. Why does he sound—the idea makes my eyes prick—upset? I made him upset. Maybe I should just send him a response so that he knows I care. That way, when I show up at his doorstep, there'll be no weirdness—aside from the whole showing-up-at-the-doorstep-of-a-stranger thing. I flick back to the last message and take a deep breath, trying to think of something of worth to say. What will happen after what happened last night? What will happen when I show up at his door and he sees me—the real me—in front of him? Will he be disappointed? Is he expecting someone older? Someone who knows how to do... things? Someone who can actually say the words instead of just "things"? These thoughts have me paralyzed.

"Did you get another message?" Steve says, dropping down next to me on the rock. Bethany and Sarah are heading off through the trees behind him, presumably on their way back to civilization. I notice with a little jolt that Sarah doesn't even look back at me.

I shove the phone back into my bag as Steve cranes his neck toward me and he looks a little hurt.

"You scared me," I mutter, by way of explanation, then draw my shoulders square, "No, just my dad. Freaking out."

Steve nods and gets to his feet, dusting off the seat of his jeans. "Ready to go? I told Bethany and Sarah we'd call them later."

"Do you think the cops will find the show—look for us there? I mean, if there's still a show..." I ask, hauling myself off the ground. My leg is asleep and a veil of fatigue is beginning to weave itself around my face. It's hard to remember life before these last couple of days. It's like we've always been chasing Haze.

"I dunno," Steve says. "All I know is that I have to find him—no matter what it takes. I'll figure out the rest later."

I nod and scan the road in front of us, my hand over my eyes. My phone buzzes in my pocket. I check it when Steve's back is turned. Placid Girl, please...

My stomach sinks. He's getting upset. He's getting upset because of me. I tell myself I'll make it up to him when I see him, but my mind whirs with worry all the same.

"Are you coming?" Steve calls. He's standing in a patch of sunlight breaking through the trees. His curls look all tinged with fire, his eyes dark in shadow—like a painting of an angel that has been desecrated. I trot to catch up with him. Just as I'm pulling up alongside him, breathing more heavily than I should be after a short jog, my pocket buzzes again. You're making my heart hurt, Placid Girl...

Before the words can really sink in, however, Steve is pulling me across the road.

The smell of Mexican corn and hot sauce tickles my nose as Steve and I turn away from the taco truck and take a seat on the curb. Until right now, really, I hadn't had any urge to consume anything, but as I look down at the warm tortilla curling over the paper container my mouth starts watering. Sure, we all had had some of Bethany's homemade granola this morning, but night is bleeding into day now and I realize we haven't eaten for hours. Absently, I watch a terrier begging for scraps from its tan owner. I wonder what her evening entails. Certainly not a stakeout.

Steve allows us barely enough time to finish our tacos before grabbing my phone and attempting to enter Haze's address into the Maps app—until he gets frustrated and presses it back into my greasy hands. How a modern-day teenager still insists on carrying around a flip phone like a grandma is beyond me. I hate that I kind of find it cute. I tap in the coordinates and squint at the screen as the phone's little brain chugs away. The warehouse is not too far from the boat, really—but far enough that you'd probably have to go out of your way to actually see it. I look off in the distance toward the row of buildings, and before I can pocket my phone all the way, Steve is off and walking fast.

We haven't said anything in a while now. Maybe because we're both holding our breath. Maybe it's because we don't know what waits for us out there among the warehouses and broken angels. As we wander by the water I let my eyes run over the stone walls, most plastered with graffiti—a mermaid under which is scrawled "my friend got arrested for this," a tag reading "vapidface loves you," an endless parade of "fuck yous."

Soon, too soon—we're standing across the street from Haze's—well, "home" isn't the right word. In fact, it doesn't look like anyone lives here. Unless you count rats. There's a big garage door—like the kind where trucks unload things—and a bunch of broken, blacked-out windows at the front. A coldness commences wandering up my spine. The place just feels... empty.

"I don't know about this," I say, pressing myself against the adjacent wall. "Maybe we got the coordinates wrong... You know how GPS is... always fucking up." At least that's what I'm hoping.

I look at Steve, but he's just shaking his head, staring at the building. "This is it. I know it is." He seems so sure, I almost believe him. I mean, he could be right. If you were trying to hide from the world, where would you go? Probably somewhere no one went to look for the living. The thought sends another unbidden shiver through me. Steve starts to move toward the building, but I grab his sleeve.

"What are you going to do?" I ask.

"What do you mean?" He stops and retreats back into the shadows with me.

"When you get the story. What are you going to do? I mean, you're seventeen, right? Won't your dad just keep looking for you?" I'm stalling, sure, but I'm curious.

Steve shakes his head and cops a wry smile. "My birthday is in a few weeks. All I have to do is hide out until then. I think I can manage. I just want to do it right, like I said."

"So we're both Leos, then," I say without thinking. Sarah and all her astrology shit. Gets stuck in my brain.

"What?"

My face flushes. "I just had my birthday, which makes us both Leos, which, according to Sarah, makes us super romantic or something." The words trip off my tongue as if I'm the ventriloquist's dummy and, well, something else is the master. "Anyway," I say quickly grabbing Steve's arm. "Shouldn't I knock or something?" Then I look at the door to the warehouse and feel chilled all over. "How do I even knock?"

We both turn and consider the garage door. It's not like there's a doorbell. It's not like there's a peephole. Steve gives me a little push forward and retreats into the shadows.

"Just go knock on the big door. Remember, you have to go by yourself. He knows you."

I detect a slight tinge of jealousy in his voice. Ignoring the feeling of ridiculousness rising in my stomach that's telling me this is all a waste of time—that Haze isn't in there—I advance toward the building. My phone has been quiet for the last hour or so and I wonder if he's given up on me—if he's decided that I don't care. I should have answered. I should have let him know I heard him. That thought propels me toward the building, pushing me through the feeling in my brain and gut and toes that's telling me this is insane. That's telling me that showing up—unannounced—at someone's door (however unconventional) is the stuff of stupid romantic comedies that, if attempted in real life, would result in restraining orders. I try to push all of that out of my head now as I stand in front of the garage door, hold my fist in the air for one indecisive second, and then pound on the reverberating metal once...twice... three times.

The seconds tick by. No one comes. I count to 120 and still nothing. Without looking back at Steve I move slowly away from the door. Maybe the knocking doesn't register. Maybe neighborhood kids walk by and pound on the door all the time with rocks and sticks. Feeling like some kind of Peeping Tom I creep over to the blacked-out windows and try to peer through. Nothing. I give one of them a tentative pull, surprised to find the frame lifting away like the top of a box. Haze—or someone—has left the windows unlocked, trusting, no doubt, in the black paint to keep the prying eyes away.

I peer into the room, but all I can see is blackness—no lights on anywhere—which makes me bold. Pulling the window up all the way, I climb onto the sill, leaning forward into the room to gaze into the pitch black before a face materializes from the shadows. Muffling a scream, I fall onto the concrete floor. My head pounds. I'm inside Haze's house—and someone else is here.

My eyes adjust quickly, catlike, and as they do I see more and more faces loom out of the shadows—white and blank and unflinching. A scream is rising in my throat that I know I won't be able to control if it makes it past a certain point so I clap my hands over my mouth. The faces don't seem to see me, though. Or if they do, they're not doing anything about it. A flash of the mannequins in Bethany's house careens through my head then and it occurs to me—these faces can't see me because they're not real. They're masks.

I sit in the dust for ten more seconds—slowly counting them off in my head—listening in the blackness for any sign of life. My eyes have fully adjusted now and I see the jumble of stuff spilling across the warehouse floor—books and clothes and furniture scattered across the concrete, like someone has been digging through it all looking for something. There's an oil drum in the middle of the floor, an acrid smell rising from inside. Still, it doesn't look like whoever lives here actually lives in disarray. It's more as if a neatly arranged room had been ransacked. There's a bed in the back of the warehouse—my skin tingles when I think what he did there last night—and a table with chairs pulled in around it. And above it all, a row of white masks stares and stares on a red, red wall.

"Hallie."

I scuttle across the floor toward the pile of clothes and papers, scraping the palms of my hands and cursing before I realize that the voice came from behind me—that it's reedy and gentle. Steve. He falls to the floor behind me, landing neatly on both feet like a cat, and looks around the room.

"So this is it..." He looks around slowly, as if memorizing it all for his story, drinking in every crumpled piece of paper and discarded sock. His fingers twitching, he moves toward the giant pile of stuff like a goat looking for lunch. Kneeling down among the debris, he starts sifting through, examining pieces of paper and tossing them aside.

"Should you be doing that?" I ask, moving to stand next to him, looking all around the room. What if he comes back and finds us here? Finds us squatting in a pile of his stuff and... is that underwear? I flush.

"Of course. The most interesting stuff about people is in their trash. Sure, that's kind of a tabloid journalist mentality, but, still." He picks up a stack of newspapers, shining the weak glow from his phone across the pages, and sighs. "Anyway, most of this is junk. Just old papers and magazines and shit. Nothing addressed to anyone. Obviously purchased at a newsstand."

Steve stands up and dusts off his jeans, noticing the oil drum in the middle of the room. "This looks more interesting." We peer into it, taking in the charred pile of papers and things inside. Steve frowns and reaches into the depths of the container, shoving his hands into the grime and dust and burned debris, and pulls out a handful of crumbling ash. He watches the black flakes dust between his fingers for a second, disappointed, then plunges his hand in again and roots around. I watch for a few seconds, fascinated. His face lights up and he pulls out his hand with a grin.

"Missed something," he says, fishing out a dark lump. He spits on the surface and jerks up his T-shirt, rubbing at the black. I try not to notice the soft blond hair on his stomach and wholly fail.

After a few seconds of concentrated rubbing, Steve stops, his hand going rigid. I can almost hear his heart pounding from a few feet away.

"What is it?"

Instead of answering me, Steve digs in his pocket and pulls out the sea glass, then holds up the object—another piece of blue glass. Slowly, he pushes them together like puzzle pieces, then sinks to the ground.

"My brother," he says, so quiet I can barely hear him.

"Gabriel?" I ask, a thought just rippling in the corner of my mind.

Steve nods. "My mom gave me and my brother two pieces of sea glass—two pieces broken from one bigger whole. She said we could always find her in the glass—and each other, because here were these two pieces of glass tossed by the sea that still managed to fit together. 'Miraculous,' she said." He turns to me then, as if just noticing me. "Why would Haze have this, Hallie?"

"And why would he be trying to get rid of it?" I say quietly.

"Something is seriously fucked here," Steve says, clutching the twin pieces of glass in his hands.

"Do you think Haze knew Gabriel?" I ask. "I mean, if Alex knew him that would make sense..." I hate mentioning his cousin, but it seems like an important point somehow.

Steve shakes his head. "I need to think about this. I just need...

like ten seconds to think about this. None of this makes sense."

I reach out to touch his shoulder, but there's a massive shuddering then, like a robot having a full body fit, right there in front of the garage door. A car door slams and there are footsteps, heavy footsteps approaching the warehouse—then a key and chain rattling. I look at Steve, still white and confused, and grab him. "Steve, there's someone here. We have to hide."

The room is open though. There are no corners—no closets that I can see. There's only the bed—which appears to be a mattress on the ground—and the pile of shit we're sitting on. Wondering if we can possibly pull this off, I grab Steve and burrow up under all the clothes and things, pulling sweatshirts and jeans and papers and books over us and hold my breath. "Stay still," I hiss in Steve's ear, but it doesn't really seem necessary. He's not moving. I wonder wildly if he's even breathing and press my ear to his lips, feeling his soft, warm breath. I give a little shudder, and then force myself to lie still. The thought that this isn't the first time Steve and I have been pressed together in close quarters when faced with possible danger dances through my head and I wonder, for the 500th time, how I arrived here.

There's a final jingling—and muffled cursing—outside the door and then the sheet of metal rattles like a giant peal of thunder. I can feel Haze standing there, surveying the room, and fear grips my throat. What if he notices something amiss? What if he's some photographic memory freak who remembers just where he tossed that one sock? I hold my breath, waiting for the "What the hell?" exclamation, but none comes. The garage door shudders closed again, and the footsteps—boots, by the sound of them—advance into the room. There's an acrid smell like birthdays, and I realize he's lit a match. An irrational fear that he's going to drop the flame on the pile of stuff we're huddled in surges through me before I smell the skunky scent of pot undulating through the air. There's a clunk, like he's put down a load of stuff, and then a softer thud as Haze, presumably, sits on the floor.

He's mere feet away now. I can almost feel him through the air. Soon. I will see him soon. Then the sea glass flits back into my head. It doesn't make any sense. The only person who would have that glass is dead. It's a stark thought—and I move my arm slowly, slowly to press against Steve's. He returns the pressure and I wonder if he knows what I'm thinking. If he gets that I understand. Not that I do, wholly.

There's a scraping—and then footsteps scuffling toward the pile of stuff. I clamp my mouth closed and grind my teeth. The footsteps keep coming, and then there's a rustling, like papers being picked up and sorted through. I hear—and smell—another match being lit and then there's a crackling, a bigger fire. Haze is dropping more things into the oil drum. He's burning more stuff. The footsteps keep up without pause—wandering to the pile and then back to the drum, more papers rustling and clothes whispering off of the heap.

Oh, fuck. He'll find us. If he keeps sorting and burning he'll find us. My whole body erupts in goosebumps. I can't let him see me like this—pressed under a pile of shit like a crazed fan, my knee bleeding and my hands all scraped up. All feelings—if he has any for me— would abruptly evaporate. I know it. They would burn away like the socks and jeans and papers that are curling as smoke toward the ceiling. Something in the back of my mind is concerned with why Haze appears to be burning all of his worldly possessions in an oil drum in a warehouse, but I push it down. It's probably some kind of release ceremony or something. Sarah was always doing those when some dude ditched her—she'd burn all of his notes and clothes she wore on dates and cry and scream and then walk around her room, waving a burning stick of sage that she said was supposed to "purify" the place. I don't know about purifying, but it did make her room smell pleasant and foresty for weeks afterward.

Steve stiffens next to me. Haze has made quite a dent in the pile already. It won't be long before he reaches us. My mind grasps for things to say but nothing occurs to me. What do you say in a situation like this? How would I explain the wannabe journalist currently pressed against me under all of Haze's—Jesus, he has a lot of underwear. Just then the footsteps stop—halfway back to the pile. The boots shuffle and scrape and there's a loud "Fuck" from above us. The curse seems extra obscene in the silence and crackling and I suppress the urge to let out a "Shhh." Haze has no need to shhh—he's not the one hiding.

"I fucking forgot... the tape," the voice continues, in that half-formed way you say things when there's no one there to hear you. "How could I... Fuck!" The voice is soft—gentle, almost. I try to hear his songs in there, but it's hard. But, then, a singing voice doesn't sound like a speaking voice. It's like a secret voice hidden inside you, you know. Like the voice of something deep and ancient burbling inside.

Haze's feet stomp toward the garage door now, curses erupting like popping flames under his breath, and I hear the metal rattling down again, leaving us in darkness. Steve bursts from the pile, dashing toward the window and pressing his face to a chink in the black paint.

"Come on," he hisses. "He's almost around the corner now. We need to move."

I pull myself from the pile of clothing, brushing a sock from my shoulder, and run to his side. "What does he look like?" I ask, before I can think or worry about Haze seeing us. I need to know.

"I dunno," Steve says, "He's wearing a hoodie. Come on, he's out of range now, let's go."

"Wait," I pick up Gabriel's sea glass from the pile where we were just nestled and hold it out to him.

Steve looks down at it for a second, a spasm of pain crossing his face, hesitating. Then he snatches it and shoves it into his pocket, his eyes trained on where Haze disappeared.

"Do you want to talk about it?" I ask, immediately feeling lame. "I mean, do you want to... I dunno..." What, Hallie? I mentally smack myself in the head. Discuss why our favorite musician was discarding something that belonged to his dead brother? What exactly do I have to contribute to that conversation that's productive? Nothing, that's what. Idiot.

Steve shakes his head. "Let's just go. Now."

"Where?" I ask, clamoring after Steve out the window and dropping to the ground.

"We're going to follow him," Steve says over his shoulder, rushing toward the corner that Haze has presumably just rounded. There's a van parked outside the building and I wonder why Haze didn't take it, dimly noting that there's no license plate. That doesn't seem legal. But I don't have too much time to think about vehicular laws—Steve is already out of sight. I run to catch up, my scraped-up knee aching, and pull up next to him. He's just standing there, staring at the sea of warehouses.

"Where did he go?" I ask.

Night had fallen big time while we were crouching under Haze's stuff and there are barely any streetlights studding the asphalt. Everything is black—except for a door a little further down the way that keeps opening and closing, bursts of music and laughing and feedback belching into the night.

Steve shakes his head.

"Maybe he went in there?" I point at the door. There's a little group of men in tight black jeans and hoodies standing outside, puffs of cigarette smoke blooming into the night.

Steve just shrugs.

"We'll find him," I say. "We know he's here now. We can wait outside the building all night if you want, and when he comes home..."

"I need a drink," Steve says abruptly and starts stalking toward the door and the smokers and the noise. I hang back, stunned. Doesn't he want to wait for Haze? Isn't this why we came all this way?

"You coming?" Steve says, without turning around, and I trot after him, weaving around the smokers. Steve pulls up short in front of me and I crane around him to see what he's looking at. There's a big man all in black sitting on a comically small stool by the door—a bouncer, probably. The kind that checks IDs. Game over, I guess. I turn to say as much to Steve, but he's stalking around the corner again, lighting up a cigarette and heading for a mesh trashcan overflowing on the street corner. As I pull up beside him, he starts rooting through it.

"Dude, I think we've gone through enough trash for one night," I say, watching as Steve tosses soda bottles and papers onto the street. Luckily, we're out of sight of the smokers now and they can't see Steve getting down and personal with the debris.

"Shut up for a second, Hallie," Steve says, fishing around in the trash. Finally, he pulls a hand out, holding aloft two green rings of paper. "Fuck yeah."

"What's that?"

"Old trick. At all-ages parties, you get a wristband if you're old enough to drink. You get stamped if you're a baby. Now we have wristbands, and are therefore not babies—meaning we can get as wasted as we want," Steve says, a kind of mirthless smile splitting his face. I can see his chipped tooth—it looks a little sinister in the half-light.

"How did you know they'd be in the trash?"

He shrugs. "No one wants to wear a paper wristband if they don't have to. Most people trash them as soon as they're out the door. Just a little party trick Ale—." He stops, looking down at the papers in his hands.

"Steve." I move toward him, but he just shoves one of the wristbands at me and starts moving back toward the door. "Come on," he says.

I wriggle the wristband over my fist and trot after him. At the door, the bouncer gives us a wary look as we show him our wrinkled paper bracelets, then rolls his eyes and waves us in. Something tells me he's used to shit like this. How many kids in there are currently sporting knockoff proof of maturity? Steve grabs my hand as we sidle into the room, pressing ourselves between the bodies toward the makeshift bar in the back. I glance at the stage, where a group of four guys in leather are leaping around, writhing through a Beastie Boys cover. Sweaty, red-faced dudes keep climbing onto the stage and leaping off into the front row, which, more often than not, lets the crowdsurfers fall to the floor, only to leap up moments later and try it all again. The scene isn't that much different from shows at

Picture Disc—or that warehouse party Steve invited me to. The kids just appear to be a little older. The Christmas lights swaying from the ceiling seem wistful somehow—like something left over from another time. I watch them silently, a smile creeping across my face.

Steve taps my shoulder and hands me a giant cup of something amber and fizzy. "What's this?" I ask, taking a sip and pulling a face. About 3/4 whiskey, apparently.

"Just some ginger ale," Steve says, with his sideways smile. "To settle your stomach." He waggles his eyebrows and takes a big sip from his own cup, which appears to contain 4/4 whiskey. "Come on," Steve says and grabs my hand, pulling me through the sea of shaggy-haired dudes and girls with bangs to where all the guys are throwing themselves around and laughing in the pit. I pull back a little, watching a 200-pound guy with a giant mustache throw himself bodily into another 200-pound man with a knit cap, but Steve wraps his arm around my waist and pulls me to the front of the stage. He laughs, smiling down at me kind of wildly, and we start throwing ourselves around, too, in our own separate mosh pit. The guys on stage are done with their cover now and they're playing something that seems original—something fast and fraught and sneering that gets stuck in my head immediately even though I can't make out the words, and I take a giant sip of my whiskey ginger ale and close my eyes, the room spinning around me in a nice, warm way. Hands push me from behind and I spin around and push back and Steve and I get lost in the warm crowd of surging bodies, pinballing off of laughing faces and arms and torsos. It makes me feel like I'm back home at the beach, way out in the ocean waiting for a wave to come. You stand there in the surf, watching behind you for the white, cresting water, and when it hits you let yourself go, soaring through the sea until you crash on the shore like a shipwreck.

My hair sticks to my face and sweat runs into my eyes, but I'm laughing. I feel lost but no longer alone and sad, the bass thudding in my chest like another heartbeat and the whiskey disappearing from my cup as Steve fills it again and again. The band tears into song after song and my throat hurts from singing along to the words I can make out. Suddenly, an arm snakes around me and I tense for a second before I realize it's Steve's. He presses another drink into my hand and I take a huge gulp, thirsty from all the dancing. It doesn't taste so strong anymore—just sweet and cold on my lips. Steve's arm is still around me and I feel it all hot through my damp T-shirt. A mosher pushes against my back and I'm pressed nearer to Steve and he pulls me even closer against his chest. I burn there, too, and I look up at his face, shining from sweat, his eyes hazy and green and soft. I feel a tingling in my scalp, as I look up and up and up into his eyes, his face so close to mine. So close I can smell cigarettes and whiskey and the foresty smell of his skin. He gives me a look all packed with questions and something about my eyes must have answered them all because he leans close and presses his lips to mine. I feel my arms snake around Steve's waist. His lips part slightly and then he presses me closer, biting my lip and pulling me into his chest, my back pressing against the edge of the stage and my knees feeling all rubbery and not-mine. He tastes like whiskey and something dark and fierce and like something I don't ever want to stop tasting. I want, I want, I want and then everything is swirling and lips and sweat and the room careens off into the corner of my mind into blackness.

TWELVE

"And all the rest is silence/ I didn't write that/ I think,"
—"Shakes Beer," *Masking Tape* —Haze

I'm thirsty. So thirsty. But opening my eyes seems like a massive effort and procuring water even more so. My body rocks gently and I'm the most comfortable I think I've ever been, my limbs all splayed on some soft surface and the gently snoring warmth of someone behind me. Someone? I sit up with a start and put my hand to my head. Apparently, the majority of that rocking had not, in fact, been outside my body—although the room around us is, indeed, swaying back and forth. Us. I look back at Steve, his hand curled under his cheek and his hair in his eyes. His mouth is slightly open and every time he breathes out, his hair wisps away from his face. He shifts a little and the blanket pulls, revealing his bare chest. It's smooth and kind of sunburned and very, very bare. Panicked, I look down at myself, but I appear to be wearing all of my clothes—even my sneakers. I kick them off now and flop back on the mattress, sud-denly unable to keep upright without swaying.

Given the rocking of the room and the engine cold over to the right, I have ascertained that we're in the hold of Lazarus, but have no recollection of how we got here. The last thing I remember is laughing in the front row of the show and then... Oh God, we kissed. Steve and I kissed. I sneak a sidelong glance at his sleeping form, his chest rising and falling, his hand resting there. What had happened after we kissed? Did I pass out? Did he carry me here? Did anything else happen? Sure, I'm fully dressed, but... Slowly, I turn over on the mattress and lift the blanket carefully away from our bodies. It's too dark, though for me to see much, so, holding my breath, I inch under the blanket more, peering, peering into the blackness.

"Oh, hey there," Steve's sleepy voice comes from above me and I shoot out of the covers. "Don't let me stop you," Steve says, cross-ing his hands behind his head.

Face flaming I sit all the way up, flinging the covers off as I go. Relieved, I see that Steve's legs are still clad in his skintight jeans—and I've seen how hard those are to get on and off.

"Shut up," I mutter, swinging my legs off the side of the bed and trying to twist my hair into a ponytail sans hair tie.

There's a rustling behind me as Steve pulls on his T-shirt and then he puts his hand of my shoulder. "Hey, sorry, Hallie. I was just kidding," he says. I can feel his breath stirring my hair and I try not to shiver again—to remember his lips on mine and our bodies pressed close together. It all seems so absurd now—everything had happened in a kind of haze. I think then of the messages on my phone and tense up. I still haven't answered him.

Steve must take my sudden stiff-backed routine as a reaction to his touch, because he takes his hand off my shoulder quickly and moves to sit next to me. "Hey, nothing happened OK? We were dancing and we were... Then you started stumbling and whatever and I kind of carried you back here. We've just been sleeping, OK?"

I shake my head, turning to look at him. "No, I was just thinking... Haze." I stop at the expression that crosses his face—his eyes kind of narrow and he frowns. I wonder if I've messed up. Maybe he wanted to talk about it more—the kiss. I just assumed he'd want to forget it. Forget any distraction that gets in the way of his story. That's how he'd handled anything coming close to last night over the past few days—by just pretending it didn't happen. I didn't want to pretend it didn't happen. That had been my first kiss—and no matter how whiskey-soused and moshy it had still been... well, my skin tingles and everything goes warm now that I think of it. But I don't know what to say. It's not like we're back home. It's not like I can just go back to my house and wait for him to call me and invite me to a movie or something. We're so far away from normalcy and, to be honest, making out is not normal for me in the first place.

Neither of us had said anything in what feels like hours so I open my mouth again and sputter. "Our phones."

Steve stands up from the mattress abruptly and turns away from me. "What about them?"

"Has yours rung? I mean, have you got any messages or anything? Have Bethany or Sarah tried to..." I go kind of cold as I say it, as it just occurs to me. We forgot about Bethany and Sarah.

Steve turns around, a little worry line carved between his eyebrows, and digs in his pocket. I start rooting around in my bag for my phone. I jab at the top button when I find it, but it fails to illuminate.

"Dead," Steve says, and the word makes me shiver for some reason.

"Yeah, mine, too," I say, holding up my phone for Steve to see. "I don't suppose there's any outlets on this thing." I look around Lazarus and the room starts spinning for a second. So this is what being hungover feels like. Sure, I've drunk before, but never enough to feel this horrible. Everything I've ever worried about swims around in my head, fighting for a chance to voice its concerns and, simultaneously, I feel, quite genuinely, like I'm going to die.

I fall back on the pillows again—I can't help it—and half-moan. "What time is it anyway?"

Steve bends his wrist to look at his cheapo plastic watch—who wears a watch?—the word "Fuck!" bursting from his mouth like soda from an overly shook can.

"What?" I sit up, my head protesting the whole thing.

"It's 3 o'fucking clock in the afternoon!"

"You're kidding me," I gasp. "Is that thing right—I mean, do you even know if that thing works?"

Steve starts rooting around on the floor for his shoes, hopping on one foot as he pulls on his socks and sneakers. "Yeah, Hallie, it works. My brother gave it to me. Fuck!"

I stand up, thinking again of the sea glass and wonder if Steve is still thinking about it. He has to be. Then I think of Sarah and how pissed she must be right now. I will never hear the end of this when I see her again. Then it occurs to me.

"They never came back to the boat, did they?" I ask.

Steve kind of shrugs, pulling his shoelace into a sloppy knot, then climbs the ladder and pokes his head topside. He stands for a second, looking, then comes below deck. "No, I guess they didn't. I don't see them up there. But Bethany knows a lot of people in the city. They probably crashed somewhere. They probably left a message or something."

It sounds like a reasonable explanation, but something seems wrong. Wouldn't they come back to the boat if they hadn't heard from us?

"Let's go," Steve says, turning toward the ladder.

"Where?" I ask, putting my shoes on and tying them with an immense effort. I don't think I've had this hard a time tying my shoes since I first learned how.

"To a bodega," Steve says. "We can charge our phones there and call them—and also get an egg and cheese or something. Judging by how many knots you've just put in those laces, you need some serious sobering up." He sounds less brusque now—almost gentle—and I'm relieved that we're apparently moving past last night. Something down in the deep dark parts of me is disappointed, though, right to the bone, and I wonder if I'll ever stop feeling this way— never one way or another. My toes only dabbling in happy, but always halfway to sad.

When we come up on deck the sun burns my eyes like acid and I sway against the mast of the boat. The world smells like salt and splintered wood and oceans and oceans of garbage. I almost gag.

"Wow, you have never really been this hungover before, have you?" Steve says, grabbing my arm to steady me.

I squint at him. "Like you're the expert."

He frowns. "Sadly, yeah, kind of." He pulls at my elbow and I stagger after him onto shore. "I've eased up, though," he says, talking to the puffy sheep-like clouds on the horizon instead of me.

I sneak a glance at Steve's profile, his hair in his face again and his eyes tired. A kind of blooming, aching sadness erupts in my chest—a sadness that feels almost exactly like being happy—and I wonder what will happen with us after we find Haze. After the show is over and I head back home and he heads... wherever it is he's going. It doesn't seem like a safe thing to think about right now.

We stumble down the street in silence for a bit until Steve jingles into a corner store, holding the door for me. Old men line the windows—rat-faced in gold chains and stained white T-shirts, tucking into bagel and egg sandwiches dripping ketchup. It shouldn't look appealing, but I want one. I want one right now. An egg sandwich, I mean—not an old man. Steve orders two—his with extra bacon—and nods me over to the counter, where there's a plug close to the dusty floor.

"Lemme check mine first," Steve says. "It'll take less time than that mini-computer thing you have there."

"I've never seen a kid with one of those before," I say, pointing at Steve's cracked gray device. "What's the deal with that?"

Steve shrugs. "There's too much out in the world to look at without staring at a screen." It sounds like something he's said before—to many people—a kind of rehearsed speech.

I raise my eyebrows at him.

He sighs. "Fine. My dad won't let me have a fancy phone. He thinks I'll look at porn on it."

I laugh, suddenly, surprising myself. It doesn't seem right to laugh at something Steve's dad said, but I can't help it. "Well, would you?"

"What do you think?" We both laugh and the guy at the counter calls our number. As Steve goes to retrieve the sandwiches, I look down at his phone, which has come back to life. Five missed calls from Devil Dad. No other messages. I shiver. Someone must have tried to get ahold of us. Even if they decided to stay in the city. Something's wrong.

I stare at my screen, willing it to come to life, as Steve comes back and sits next to me, tossing a sandwich in front of me and unwrapping his own. He takes a big bite and picks up his phone. "Fuck," he mutters, scrolling through the missed calls, his face drawn and angry and worried. "You got anything? Where are they?"

I jerk my head at the black screen. Steve swallows his bite then puts the sandwich down. We're both staring at the screen, but out of the corner of my eye I can see Steve clutching something. The sea glass. The thought crosses my mind again: Why did Haze have it? What possible reason could he have? I know Steve must be thinking about it, too—even behind all this bravado.

I swallow, deciding to bring it up—even if he tells me to drop it. Even if he tells me he can't think about it right now. I know he must be. I know all these thoughts must be swirling around in his head—Alex, Haze, Gabriel. It must be so much to contain all on your own. It seems like way too many things to hold in one heart.

"Steve, I really think we should talk about..."

My phone lights up and rings then, a too-loud blare cutting through the static-y music piped into the bodega. "Dad" flashes on the screen, popping up after a parade of 10 missed calls from the same. I start to press ignore, but then think of all the missed calls on Steve's phone. How both of our dads are trying to get ahold of us—for different reasons.

"Hello," I put the phone to my ear. "Dad?"

"Hallie." His voice is harsh and ragged and surprises me. I hadn't heard him speak above a whisper in months. "About damn time you answered the phone. Where are you? I called Sarah's mom but the phone was dead. I went over there and you were both gone. You're grounded, Hallie. You shouldn't be anywhere but here. Where the *fuck* are you?"

I look around the bodega, at the old men slowly chewing, at Steve blinking at me, his bruised face, his hand clutching that sea glass like some kind of religious talisman—at the industrial wasteland of a city afternoon-snoozing outside. Good question.

"We went to the mall..." I say slowly, hoping he doesn't hear the old men speaking Polish in the background or the latest top 40 monstrosity crackling through the stereo.

"You shouldn't be anywhere but *here*!" he shouts, his voice cracking, and I look at the phone in shock. He never yells. I have fucked up. I have officially fucked up. I open my mouth to say something, anything, but Dad cuts me off. "Can you..." His voice cracks, then gets hard again. "I need you home. Now. There's something we need to discuss."

Something yanks at my heart and my throat and my skull. "Why?" I whisper.

"Just... Hallie ..." His voice sounds dead and flat. It's scarier than the tears all those nights ago. Scarier than the yelling.

"What's going on?" A parade of images march through my head: Dad helping me dig in the garden for ladybugs, the hot sun on the herb garden making the day smell like mint. Dad taking me to my first show—some old rock band he liked—hoisting me on his shoulders so that I could see all the people bobbing below, singing. Looking down and seeing his face all open and happy and enraptured and sad somehow because he probably wished that he was up there, too. I miss the smiling and joy and I don't like this deadness.

Dad coughs a little, trying to pull himself together. "Your mom left," he says quietly, simply.

My stomach drops into the subterranean depths of the earth and I can't swallow all of a sudden. "What do you mean?"

Silence pours from the phoneline and I can hear Little Edie meowing, plaintively, from somewhere in the echoing house.

"I want you to come home, Hallie." Dad tries for a firm voice again but he just sounds small in all those empty rooms.

I look up. Steve is looking at me, his brows knit. My breakfast doesn't smell appealing anymore, not at all. And it's not just the hangover. I want to go home but I don't want to go home and I want to stay here but I don't want to stay here.

"I..." I choke. "I can't right now, Dad... Um... Sarah needs me. But I'll be back tomorrow. I promise." The words catch in my throat like nettles.

More silence. More meowing. More echoes. Then the deluge. "No. This is not a discussion, Hallie. This is not a negotiation. This is not you telling me how things are. I am the parent here. You are the kid. I will come over there and drag you home if I need to, but I—"

The dial tone rings in my ear. I hung up. I hung up on my dad. I didn't want to hang up. Not really. It was refreshing, almost, to hear him yelling. To hear him having it out. But I can't right now. And he can't. He can't drag me home because I'm not there to drag. I'm far away. So far away from everything.

I put my head down on the counter. My eyes burn and my throat is a thousand grains of desert sand. Then my phone chimes again—and again and again and again and again. I snatch it up, relieved that something, at least, wasn't completely falling apart. Once we found them, once we got Steve's story, we could all go home. Figure out all the places we're bleeding and try to stitch them up.

I tap at the notifications page and relief sticks in my throat. No texts. No missed phonecalls. Just 15 new messages on my photo app, all reading, Please Placid Girl, please...

THIRTEEN

"Love will be your gravedigger/ Love won't save your soul/ Love will take its shovel/ And toss you in a hole,"

—"Embalm Me," *Masking Tape* —Haze

The practice space is totally empty. A trash can lies on its side in the corner, but there's nothing else inside. Even the carpet is immaculate, which is really weird considering people in bands hypothetically practice here.

"Where are they?" Steve asks no one, standing in the middle of the room, rotating slowly as if looking for clues. He hadn't said much after seeing the sea of messages from Haze pop up on my phone. I hadn't answered them. Everything is too fucked up. Everything is too confusing. The part of my mind that wants to figure out how I feel about, well, *anything* has shut down. It's like a hard drum pattern you tuck away in your brain and try to ignore until you have the mental energy to devote to it. But much, much more complicated. And much less fun.

We had walked by Haze's place on the way over here, but his van was gone. Neither one of us has mentioned our dads, but the ache in my chest has not abated. I tap the text screen on my phone again, but there's nothing new. I contemplate calling Sarah, but the previous 20 phonecalls and texts are still unanswered. She'd call back if she saw them, right? I guess we just have to wait. Bethany isn't picking up her phone, either.

"Where are they?" Steve repeats, his voice getting hard and strained.

"Do you know any of Bethany's friends here? Someone she might have crashed with?" I ask.

Steve shakes his head, still looking all around the room. "No. I mean, she's mentioned people, but I don't know their numbers or any—What the fuck is that?" He crouches at the baseboard of the wall, squinting at the white surface. I follow, more slowly, and kneel down beside him. There's a splatter of something red—something red and half-dried. Steve jabs at it with his finger and holds it up to his nose.

"Pennies," he says. "It smells like pennies..."

"You mean," I start to say, an idea forming in my head that seems way too horrifying to be real. I broke a drumstick once and sliced my hand and there was blood everywhere and it smelled just like copper.

"It's blood," Steve says, collapsing onto the carpet. "Jesus fucking Christ, what is going *on* here?"

I sink down next to him and stare at the splatter—it's so small and insignificant-looking, but there's a coldness spreading through my limbs that could render this entire room a meat locker. Sarah. Her face flashes in my mind and then every day we've ever spent together. Sun-splattered mundane days and the smell of water fresh from the sprinkler. Singing along drunkenly to '90s music in my room until my parents told us to shut it. Where the hell is she? Is she OK? What are we going to do? A parade of questions treks through my mind and it's full of scary clowns. I look over at Steve and see that he seems to be lost in the same dark bozo show. Then I think of what Steve said to me back at Bethany's—about not staying angry with people you love. How that's exactly what I did with Sarah.

"Steve," I say. "I think we need to call the police."

He starts shaking his head slowly, then so fast I think he's going to get whiplash. "No, no, no, my dad..." His whole body breaks out into shivers. "I can't let him find me."

"I know. I know, but what else are we going to do, Steve? Where are they? There's blood and they're gone and they're not answering their phones. What else can we do? We need to call the police."

Steve looks up at the clock on the wall—one of the only things left in the room—and turns to me, eyes practically spinning in their sockets. "It's seven now, Hallie. It's almost time for the show. Let's just go there. Let's go there and see if they're there and we can figure it out then."

"But they're not answering their phones," I cry, shoving my cell in his face. "They're obviously in some kind of trouble!"

Steve shakes his head again. "How do we know that? How? Our phones were dead until a few hours ago. How do we know they didn't just, like, get drunk like us and make out with someone like an idiot and wake up with no battery power? They could be fine. That blood could be from some drunk dude in a band who stumbled in here and hit his head. We don't know!"

I stare at him, all of his words slowly sinking in. "What did you just say?"

Steve cocks his head to the side. "Drunk dude in a band. Fell down. What?"

"No," I say, rocking forward on my heels. "About making out. Being an idiot. What are you talking about?"

Steve laughs, pressing his hand to his head. "I can't believe we're talking about this now..." He looks at his feet then kind of gives a strangled growl. "Goddamn. I'm obviously the idiot. For kissing you. Although you're kind of the idiot, too. You're a fucking idiot."

"What? Why?"

Steve smirks at me, an unkind smirk. "Because you have a 'boyfriend,' remember? Because you're in love with Haze. Because I can't fucking compete with him. And I'm stupid for thinking I could. And you're fucking stupid for letting me think that I could. But I've let you make me believe it because I love you—but now everything is fucked up. Everything is such a royal fucking mess and we're standing in the middle of it yelling like idiots." He's breathing hard now, staring into my eyes.

I'm frozen. Seriously, ice sculptured-out. It's just too much. Everything is too much. So instead of thinking or saying or shouting I move toward Steve and kiss him—hard. I kiss him in a way that is not nice. That is not gentle. I kiss him because everything hurts and I am selfish and I am not nice and there's a lot inside me that I hate. I kiss him because I kind of love him or something, too—even though I don't know what that means, but what it seems to mean is that I don't want bad things to happen to him. That I don't want to lose him. That I can see all the things fading from my life and going all wonky and I don't want him to be one of them.

His arms go around me and he's crushing me to his chest. He's crushing me and kissing me and I notice that even without all the whiskey and music and pulsing bodies I still feel weak and spinny and like I'm going to explode and melt and fall apart all at the same time. I grab his shirt and pull him closer and closer until I'm pressed against the wall with him against me and I don't remember anything. Then there's a ping in my pocket and we fly away from each other.

My hands shaking, I dig for my phone, relief already flooding through my limbs and making my heart pound and my head swim and everything seem sharper and more alive and singing. I pull it out, expecting a message from Sarah—something chastising and angry and all-together beautiful—and my heart almost bursts from my T-shirt when I see her name on the screen.

"It's OK," I say, shaking and laughing, looping my arm around Steve's neck. "It's Sarah." I look up into his face and he's smiling now, too. Everything will be fine. We'll meet up with Sarah and Bethany. We'll find Haze. And then we'll figure everything out later. I tap the screen, my face hurting from smiling and kissing—the release of worries melting away. There's a picture.

I click on the message and wait for it to load, squinting at the screen. Then I almost drop the phone—the image doesn't make sense. It can't be real. It has to be some kind of stupid, terrible joke. Steve comes around when he sees my face and looks over my shoulder, his body going still as he takes in what's on the screen. It's Bethany, lying on the practice room floor, beautiful eyes closed, a trickle of blood marring her cheek. Then a bubble of words immediately after:

I said please, Placid Girl. You heard me say please. Come to the show tonight or your friends will end up like Alex. I won't ask nicely again. And if I see any cops, Placid Girl, show's off. I disappear. And they do, too.

FOURTEEN

"I don't know who I am/ I don't know /I don't know who I am/ Who are you?"

—"Call Me Sometime," *Masking Tape* —Haze

All the faces lined up outside where the show is slated to go down swim in the shadows, featureless, mouths moving without words like monsters hiding in the corner of a kid's room. Night throbs all around us, all the noises in the world melting together and pulsating in my ears like I'm underwater. The faceless beasts sigh and screech and check their phones, lighting up cigarettes and joints and taking surreptitious sips from flasks.

It all seems so obscene, somehow. All the excitement pulsing in the air outside the makeshift venue—what appears to be an abandoned Chinese restaurant. Not that any of them know. Not that they saw Bethany broken like a doll. Not that they suspect anything dark looming behind Haze's mask.

He didn't answer when I called Sarah's phone. After he sent the picture. Hasn't said anything else. The string of "please, please, please" messages has ended—and their silence, their absence, seems to be full of screams. How could I have thought... How could I have imagined... How could I *believed* this man knew me? We all made the same mistake, though—me, Steve, and Bethany. I shiver—a full-body shiver—but Steve doesn't move to comfort me. He just stands next to me, watching the line outside of the show buzz like a bug zapper with excitement.

"You should go to the police," I say, voice flat, eyes fixed on the crowd. "Give them a different name. Anything. He's only expecting me."

Steve shakes his head. "Fuck if I'm making you go alone... Fuck that. Also... Jesus. I can't believe this..."

"What does it solve if we both..." I say, my voice trailing off. I don't know what's going to happen and I won't even pretend to. I just know we have to get to Sarah and Bethany before anything else dark slithers onto my phone. Someone has to get to them, and that someone should probably be the police, with guns.

"I think... I don't know, but I think..." Steve says, eyes locked on the venue.

"What?" I press, my voice getting high and shrill. My heart is beating too fast. My hands are shaking.

Steve looks at his boots. "The sea glass, Hallie..." I tense. He hasn't mentioned the glass since we found it. Why now? "What if... I mean, where would he have gotten it if he wasn't...?"

"Wasn't what?" I ask, then an idea blooms in my mind like an impossible kind of flower. "Gabriel? Do you think Haze is Gabriel?"

Steve shakes his head and shrugs. "I don't know. I mean... I don't—it doesn't make any sense, but..."

"But he's dead," I sputter, probably not gently enough.

Steve is just staring at the venue, his hands shoved deep in his pockets. I tentatively put my arm around him and he leans into me after a moment or two. "It can't be him, Steve. It can't be," I say. "Why would he do this to Bethany? To Alex?"

He nods. "Yeah. Maybe. We're going on my dad's word here, though—that he died. And my dad's word is very unholy for a holy man."

I squeeze him tighter. "I know, though, Steve. I know it's not him. Somewhere deep down in my bones." And I do. Somehow. I know that Steve's brother could never do something like that. My mind skitters away from what "that" is.

Steve nods again and gives a humorless kind of laugh. "The funny thing is—my mind is all torn up with hoping it is him—and hoping it's not. But if it is him—and it really, really could be—I don't think he would do this. I don't think he would hurt anyone. If we can just see him, if we can just talk to him, maybe everything will be OK."

I don't know what to say. I know what he means, but I don't know what I want to be true. So I just squint toward the club. "How much longer?"

"Ten minutes or so..." Steve says softly. "Doors open at eight." He tugs on my hand and I fall into step next to him on the sidewalk, pulling up at the tail end of the line just a few feet away from the last few people. There's a girl with her arm around her boyfriend's waist, her hand thrust deep in the back of his jeans pocket. He's wearing a red mask pushed up on his head and he's laughing. He swoops down, his tongue leading the way, and I look away quickly as they start making out. It feels like they're having sex on a grave or something.

"How are we going to make it through the show?" I ask. "When do you think he'll... He'll find me?"

Steve shakes his head. "I'm hoping we can find *him* first—pull him away from everyone else when he's not expecting it."

The conversation is so close to the one we originally had back on the boat that I almost laugh. How could Haze—how could this man that we both admired and that I had... (my mind shuts down)—be a monster? Maybe it's all a mistake. Maybe there's some kind of explanation. Maybe Bethany is OK. Or maybe we're just fucking idiots. I don't know.

The door cracks open with a jingling of bells, a paper dragon swinging from the doorway with a lecherous grin, and the crowd surges forward, pushing against us, forcing us toward the door. It feels like I'm lost in a sea of lemmings, all pushing and rushing to jump off the cliff. I can't see a doorman up ahead, just a stream of bodies wrapped in leather and denim disappearing into the restaurant.

Too soon we're at the door, where the doorman finally emerges from the shadows, draped on a stool in a leather jacket. He's wearing a white mask—like the ones Haze had hanging on his wall—and when I crane forward to look further into the room my heart sinks. Everyone is wearing a mask. The same mask. There's a pile of them sitting by the door and everyone pauses to pull one over their faces as they enter. I look back at Steve, panic surging in my chest, then there's a hand in front of my face—the doorman. He holds out his palm to me and Steve and my panic triples. IDs. We don't have any bracelets this time. The doorman snaps his fingers, not saying anything, and Steve and I reluctantly reach into our pockets. If he doesn't let us in we'll find a way. We'll have to.

Keeping my face as neutral as possible, I extend my school ID to the bouncer, Steve his license, and he takes them, holding the cards up to his eyeholes. Behind the mask his eyes are shadowed. I see the whites ticking in the eyeholes like a cat clock. He cocks his head to the side and I'm sure we're done for, but he just wordlessly hands them back and jerks his head toward the door. I look at Steve and he shrugs, pulling me into the restaurant. The bouncer grabs my elbow before I can get all the way in, though, and I start, sure that we're going to be thrown out, but he just jabs a finger at the table laden with masks and then points at Steve and me. Steve gives him a look and then picks up a mask, trying to smile as he fixes the strap around my head before putting on his own.

For a moment we just look at each other: two faceless people wiped clean of identity. Two people who could easily be lost in the crowd. As if sensing my unease, Steve takes my hand—gentler this time—and leads me into the room.

Inside, red light pours down from the ceiling, blood-colored lights swinging from the rafters, which are laden with paper lanterns and dancing golden dragons with the same leering faces as the one at the door. A crowd putters around the bar—which is set up where the buffet usually is, whiskey and beer replacing hot dishes of sweet and sour pork and rice. They all look ominous in their white masks, rendered somehow silent by the costumes. It's a much more solemn scene than the one outside. Even the drinking has settled down, as people are having a difficult time figuring out how to imbibe through their masks.

As I scan the room, looking for Haze's tall, wiry frame, I realize that it's going to be much harder to find him among the masses than I had previously thought. Before, he was the only one wearing a mask. Now, we all are. Maybe we'll have to wait until after the show after all. Steve interrupts my thoughts then, pulling me toward the outskirts of the room.

"We should check all the doors," he says. "He's probably waiting out there until it's time to go onstage." I nod, then look to the makeshift stage at the front of the room, set up under some kind of red and gold lacquered altar. It's all a mass of wires and boxes and keypads—no guitars or drums. I shiver again, more violently this time. Bethany was wrong. He hadn't kicked her out of the band. He'd gotten rid of the band entirely. I think of Alex, burning in his apartment, and worry for her, fiercely.

Steve isn't even attempting to be casual, pulling me around the room, jiggling door handles to no avail. Finally, one swings open—the bathroom—but a shaggy-haired dude with his mask pushed back on his head, nose dusty, just gives a giant sniff and pushes it closed, almost crushing Steve's fingers.

"He's thought of everything," Steve says bitterly, leaning against the wall and drawing me close to him. "He's jiggered it all so it's on his terms." He looks so worn out. Close to broken.

Anger surges in me. At Haze. At the man I thought I knew—who knew me. For doing this to us. For doing this to Steve. I loop my arm around Steve's waist and squeeze. "I don't know who he is, Steve, and I hate that you think he's someone that you love—I hate that he's added that to all the fucked-up shit he's already heaped on us both. But I know he's not Gabriel. I know it. And we're going to beat him. We're going to take him down."

Steve laughs, the sound muffled behind his mask. "Take him down?"

I shrug. I know I sound ridiculous. But I feel like we need ridiculous now. So we don't go insane.

"Yeah, take him down. Just what I said." I rest my head on his shoulder for a second, then start dragging him toward the stage. "Come on," I say firmly. "We should get up in the front row."

"Why?" Steve says, a kind of humorless humor in his voice. "Because we're his number-one fans?"

"No," I say. "Because it'll be easier to kick his ass from there."

Steve laughs—or at least I think he does—and we make our way up to the stage, pushing past the faceless masses, who seem to have finally nailed the whole inebriation thing after discovering the wonders of the straw. After fewer "Watch its" and "Fuck yous" than I would have imagined, Steve and find ourselves at the front of the stage, staring into the sea of wires and cords.

"What do you think this is all about?" I ask, turning my masked face toward Steve and gesturing at the setup. I'm starting to sweat under the plastic, perspiration like tears running down my cheeks.

"No idea," Steve says. "Although that new tape... It *was* all just chopped and screwed."

I realize then that we're both still excited to see Haze play and shame floods my entire body. Even after everything, I still want to hear what he has to say. It feels sick and twisted and perverted to want to listen—like I'm one of those people who seek out snuff films and beheadings on the Internet because they're "curious." I vow not to enjoy the show—no matter how good it is. Evil doesn't make beautiful things, even though deep down inside I know that that's not true. Isn't that what Adam and Eve learned in the shady garden, listening to the sweet-talking snake? Also, Jim Morrison seemed like kind of an asshole.

The lights start to dim and the crowd melts into murmurs, all laughter and chatter hushing until we're all just a sea of white faces, staring at the empty stage—a grotesque, rapt audience. The lights pulse, but no one comes out and we all stare and stare and stare, waiting for Haze to appear. Silence stretches out ahead of us, and then there's a soft clatter near the door. All the faces swing toward the doorman, who has stood up from his stool. He takes off his jacket slowly and there's a sharp intake of breath all around us. There on his arm is tattooed a blackbird. Haze. Slowly, he reaches under the stool and takes out a slat of wood, sliding it through the door handle and clicking all the locks closed. The last metallic click makes my spine go porcupine-like with phantom needles. The crowd laughs nervously, like this is some kind of theatrical joke. Steve and I don't laugh.

Tucking his jacket under his arm, Haze walks toward the stage, unhurried, like he's alone here in the room. I watch the thin bones and muscles moving under his tight black T-shirt and wonder how I didn't know—how I didn't guess when he examined my ID. He let me in because he knew me. He let me in because he meant for me to be here. He let me in so he could... I don't know what. I think of the messages he sent me in the dark of night—about what he did while he thought of me—and my skin goes cold. I feel sick.

The audience begins to whisper, all the white faces turned toward each other like Kabuki actors, swirling in the darkness, and Haze pauses, standing completely still, watching us through the dark chasms of his eyeholes. We all feel his eyes on us and everyone stops buzzing. Only then does Haze complete his trek to the stage, his body sliding through the sea of boxes and cords. His fingers dance over the knobs and keys and he bows his head, his brown curls spilling over the top of the white mask. There's no microphone, I notice suddenly. Just the jumble of electronics. His fingers tense over the controls for a moment, then he sweeps in and starts twisting and pushing, feedback erupting from the speakers with a metallic whine. Everyone puts their hands over their ears and shrieks. Haze looks up, leveling where his eyes must be at us all and everything stills.

A dark, droning tone starts to emanate from the speakers as Haze focuses on the knobs and buttons again. I don't recognize the song at first and then it hits me like seasickness and a punch in the gut, "Placid Girl," but twisted somehow—even more so than on the new tape. Notes wash over each other like stormy waves and then a voice emanates from the speakers—obviously unconnected to Haze, as he doesn't appear to be wearing a mic or singing behind his mask. It's a crackly voice, a ghost of his normal groan, a dirge:

You'll be sorry when you're gone
You'll be sorry when the road
Rises up and swallows you.
Because the night ahead is long
And all the things that you once fled
Never stopped following you.

The room holds its breath and I feel Steve's fingers digging into my waist. Sure, Haze's songs are usually dark, but this version is jagged and cold—a warning. I press myself into Steve's side and stare up at the stage, transfixed. Haze looks up from the knobs and dials and I can feel his eyes on me, crawling all over my skin like spiders.

And the wind, yeah it blows cold
At your back as the skies roll and break and split, babe.

233

You think you know, you think you know
Where the lighthouse lies, but you're lost now, babe.

No one seems to be breathing—they're all lost in the fog of the song and the buzzing, too lost and hushed to notice Steve and I clutching each other like we're standing in some kind of invisible gale force wind.

Placid girl, placid girl
I'll tell you what
You can have me
Fill me up and make me whole
Wear my mask, hold me close
and we'll both be happy.

I squeeze Steve's waist hard, hard, hard and he looks at me. I don't know if he managed to read all the missives from Haze, if he's seen what he calls me, but I need him to understand. This song is a message. A message for me. Steve seems to understand something, at least, and puts his other arm around me so that we're full-on embracing in the stock-still pit, watching Haze poke at knobs and buttons like some kind of mad scientist as the machinery groans.

With chilling purpose, Haze turns one last knob, then looks down at me, the swinging lanterns overhead picking out the black sheen of his pupils behind the mask. Slowly, he kneels down at the edge of the stage and reaches out a hand to me, locking his eyes—bright green, I can see now—on mine. Steve holds on tighter, but I pull away—gently. I have to go with him. I have to go with him or something will happen to Sarah. Something bad.

The song drones on, overlapping vocals and sounds tornado-ing into a kind of dance beat, and all around the audience starts to move—as if awakening from a dream. Hips sway, hands float above heads, and all the masks turn toward the ceiling as if in supplication. Haze kneels still at the edge of the stage though, black eyes on me, hand outreached. "Placid Girl," he says quietly, his soft words cutting through all the noise and feedback somehow. "Please."

I reach for his hand, then feel Steve's tight around mine. I turn slowly, lifting my mask as I do. "Follow me," I mouth at Steve, turning toward Haze and his outreached hand and the unseen face behind the mask. I reach toward him and let his fingers wrap around mine. They're cold. "OK," I say nodding. "OK."

The crowd follows me on stage, jumping off the lip of it into the sea of twisting bodies, yelping behind their masks, reaching their hands out to Haze as he pulls me through a door at the back of the stage and slams it shut. The venue erupts with shouts and curses like explosions before we burst out into the night. The building shakes like boxed thunder.

FIFTEEN

"Tip-toe through the tombstones with me,"
      —"Everybody Do The Death Rattle," *Masking Tape* —Haze

The streets teem with shadows that never resolve into people, just lampposts, and I wonder if Steve is somewhere back in the gloom, following. I hope he is. I listen and feel for his breath or his skin in the night air, which reeks of seawater and sewage, and I think I can feel him back there, trailing us in the night. Haze glides ahead of me, the white of his mask glowing. I think of all he said to me and all I said to him and my heart and fists clench. All those feelings curl into something dark and ugly now, like paper turning to ash in a fire.

It would be so easy to run. He doesn't appear to have any weapons. My legs ache to run, but Sarah whispers into my head and I keep walking, my muscles protesting with every step. Haze says nothing and neither do I—I just follow behind with the mask still snug on my face. I don't want him to see me. I don't want him to see the tears swimming down my cheeks with my sweat.

I look up from the pavement unrolling in front of us like a moving walkway to see that Haze has stopped. We're standing in front of Lazarus. I examine the curve of his shoulders as he looks out at the water, his shoulder blades sharp under his gleaming leather jacket, like a statue of an angel whose wings have been snapped off—like the stone angels now lost in the blackness by the water. His waist tapers down to praying mantis legs, which end in heavy black motorcycle boots. Nothing about him seems attractive anymore, cut as a stark silhouette against the light-polluted dark blue of the city sky.

I shrink away from him almost unconsciously, then he turns around, pointing toward the gangplank to the boat. I look up at the swaying mass of scrap wood and metal and shake my head. He levels the eyeholes of his mask at me and points again, this time more insistently, and I pull my spine as tall as I can and start walking up the slant of wood, expecting every second that he's going to come up behind me and push me into the sea. He's doesn't, though. He just watches me from the shore, and when I swing myself onto the deck, he follows.

I look around the boat, searching for some sign of Sarah and Bethany, but there's nothing. Everything is just as we left it. As I gaze out at the glittering city, though, willing it to wake up and save me, I hear a soft whimpering down in the hold. Without waiting for orders from Haze, I stumble down the steps.

Sarah and Bethany lie splayed on the floor, their hands tied around a pole in the center of the boat, near the engine. Joy surges in my chest—she's alive, they're alive—before an acrid smell assaults my nose, making me cough and sputter. I compose myself as best I can and start to rush to Sarah's side—her nose is bleeding all down the front of her tank top and the gag in her mouth, and her eye looks bruised. Bethany is barely conscious. I doubt she even knows I'm here. I just stare at them as Sarah sniffles and glares at me, her eyes wide and shining. I realize that I'm still wearing the mask and pull it off.

Sarah struggles against the ropes, trying to call my name, trying to reach out to me. I reach out to touch her cheek. Her eyes get even wider and a hand clamps down on my shoulder. I swing around, staring up at the white, human-like face looking down at me. Behind the mask, Haze's eyes are all scrunched up, like he's smiling. He gives my shoulder a little squeeze and glides fluidly to the corner of the boat, pulling out a little stool and placing it near the engine. He gestures at it like some kind of gentleman, and I sit down.

"Placid Girl," he says slowly, the words rolling over his tongue like liquor he's savoring. "You're here."

I jut out my chin, searching my mind for something to say. Something to make everything OK. Something I can say to save Sarah. Instead, the word "Yes" croaks out of my throat like in that fairytale where the girl spits out frogs.

"I've been waiting for you. For a long time," Haze says, almost shyly, looking down at his boots. "I've waiting for someone to come along who... understands me like you do."

I swallow. A day ago that sentence would have filled me with joy. Now my insides feel knotted. What does he mean, "understands" him? I look at Bethany and Sarah and my legs turn into bone jelly under me.

"What do you..." I swallow again. "What do you want?"

There's a muffled laugh behind the mask and it's almost a pleasant sound. Like a fucking babbling brook, or something. "I want you to know me."

I just stare at him, not understanding. Is that some kind of innuendo? My skin crawls all over and I resist the urge to run topside and jump into the waves.

"Don't you want to know me?" He asks. "I know that you do. I knew after that night. That night when we left each other panting even from miles and miles away. I know that we are for each other. We're the same."

My insides are crawling now, twitchy like those of a zombified corpse.

"Now I want to show you something," Haze says, moving toward me, placing a hand on my shoulder, letting his fingers slide up and down my arm. I hear Sarah behind me, wrestling with her restraints, muffled curses erupting from behind her gag. I swear I can make out the words "pants ferret."

Haze pauses, glancing toward Sarah. His eyes grow narrow behind his mask. "She already knows. Which is too bad. She wasn't supposed to know. She doesn't understand me—not like you. You know that. You told me."

Sarah spits and struggles against her ropes, straining toward me, but Haze has stopped paying attention to her now, advancing toward me. Gracefully, everything he does is graceful—like he's made of porcelain and he might break—he kneels down in front of me, placing a hand on my knee, a hand that wanders up the inside of my thigh. I clench my jaw and try not to react.

Haze's eyes search my face for a moment, and it seems like he's smiling again behind his mask, and then he reaches behind his head, loosening the elastic tangled in his hair and pulling the plastic from his face.

I don't know what I was expecting– I never let myself expect too much—but I certainly wasn't expecting this. His nose is straight and fine. His eyes green and doe-like. His cheekbones sunken and chiseled and perfect. He looks like some old statue that somehow lasted it out through the centuries. He looks like someone I know. He smiles, wide, and there's a gaping hole in his smile. There was a tooth. A tooth in the smoldering apartment.

"Now," Alex whispers with full lips that curve at the corners—just slightly. "Now, you know me..." His face wanders closer to mine and I feel his breath warm on my neck, his lips parted like he's tasting the way I smell.

"What the fuck?" The voice breaks the palatably creepy spell and Alex whips around, his hand clenching my thigh. Relief floods over me like a hot shower after being out in the sub-zero and the snow.

"Steve!" The name erupts from my mouth and I struggle to stand up, but Alex's vise-like grip locks me to my seat.

"Steve..." Alex says quietly, brow furrowed. "Hey."

"What the fuck is the deal, Alex? Just—what the fucking *fuck*? I thought you were dead!" Steve yells.

I look down at Alex's slim white hand on my thigh. The hand that had held my drumsticks what seemed like years ago. I'm shaking. All-over shaking.

Steve walks further into the hold to stand next me, putting his hand on my shoulder and squeezing. "What's going on, Alex? Is this all some kind of joke? Some kind of stunt? Where's Beth—" he stops, seeing Sarah and Bethany tied to the pole. Bethany is slumped against the hold, blinking, trying to wake herself up.

Blood stains her dress. Sarah shakes her head slowly, opening her eyes wide.

"Oh, Alex..." he says, sadness tingeing his voice. "Oh... Alex. What did you do?"

"I'm sorry," Alex says, his voice genuine. "I'm sorry, but I had to do it. They were going to kick me out."

"Who was?" Steve says, pulling his eyes away from Bethany and Sarah.

"Gabe and her. They were going to come back and kick me out," Alex says, imploringly. "Like they didn't need me. Like I didn't matter. Like I hadn't been waiting. My own fucking sister and cousin."

"What?" Steve asks, his voice chilly and broken.

"They were going to take it all away," Alex says, almost wailing. "I wanted my turn for once. I wanted it."

"No," Steve says. "You said Gabe. Gabriel is dead, Alex. Gabriel died a long time ago, Alex. What are you talking about?"

Alex gives a little laugh. The kind of laugh that is not funny and is frightening as shit. "Well, he's dead *now*. But he wasn't—not before. He was just hiding. Hiding from your dad. And you."

"Before what?" Steve presses, "What the fuck are you talking about, Alex? What happened to you?"

"Gabriel wasn't dead," Alex says matter-of-factly, almost exasperated. "He ran away and we formed the band and then five years later he broke up the band. Threw it all away because he was *sad*. Then he wanted it back and he wanted me out. So I killed him, doused everything in kerosene and watched it burn. Because he was going to take it all away." He sounds like he's reading off a laundry list.

A stricken look passes over Steve's face and his mouth drops open.

"And you…" Alex says, leveling his dreamy gaze at me. "I was looking for someone like you ever since…"

"What do you mean?" Steve cries. "What are you talking about, Alex? Why are you dragging her into this?"

"She's my number-one fan. My 'HazeGirl.' My Placid Girl," Alex squeezes my thigh. "I deserve someone like her," he purrs, eyes flicking back up at Steve. "Gabe didn't. He never deserved anything he got. He was a lazy motherfucker, Steve. Gabe was a lazy mother-fucker and he didn't deserve anything he had. Which is why it's my turn. I get to be Haze now."

"And you do? You deserve it?" I say, not recognizing my own voice.

Alex looks down at me, a smile splitting his perfect face, the gap in his teeth horrible. "You see, Placid Girl? You understand me. And now you know me. Know it's me and what I can do. Know my mind and my body. Which is why you're coming with me."

I shiver and Alex takes off his jacket and drapes it over my shoulders. It smells acrid, like chemicals and hellfire. I shrink away, shrugging it onto the floor. I notice now, up close, that his blackbird tattoo is fresh and peeling.

"She's not going anywhere," Steve says, snarling.

"Oh, I think she's coming with me," Alex says, as if Steve has made some kind of idiotic joke. "She understands me. She loves me. I'll be famous and she'll be there to support me. You saw them out there—the crowd. They loved me. I have that love—now all I need is someone to understand me."

"I'm not letting you take her, Alex," Steve says, stepping between me and his cousin. "Sorry, dude, not gonna happen."

Alex laughs again—a musical, wholly not nice sound—and

reaches into his pocket, pulling out a lighter. "Do you smell that?" he asks, looking around the room calmly, his eyes hooded and dark.

Steve shrugs. "It smells like a boat. Stop it, Alex. Let her go."

"No," Alex says, patiently. "It smells like kerosene. I've soaked this entire boat. I saw it bobbing here and knew it was hers," he jerks his head at Bethany, who's still struggling to wake up. "Piece of junk. Knew that either way I wanted it to burn. She betrayed me. My own fucking sister."

Steve's eyes get wide and I can hear Sarah struggling behind me, the curses erupting anew. "Why would you do that?"

"Because I want what I want. I want what I want and I have spent *years* wanting it. And if I don't get what I want I will take everyone *the fuck down with me.* Don't think for a second I won't do it." His face cracks like a marble sculpture crumbling into dust and Steve stares at him, aghast, disbelieving.

I clear my throat. "What do you want, Alex?" I say as smoothly as I can, forcing as much tenderness as I can into my voice. Steve looks at me like I've just grown horns. I ignore him.

Alex looks at me, a slow, warm smile breaking over his face. "I want to be famous, Placid Girl. I want to leave these people behind," he casts a disgusted glance over Sarah and Steve, "and finally bask in it all. I want to be remembered. Known. I want to get out of the fucking gutter and look at the stars. And I want you to come with me. Because you and me, we're the same."

I force myself to look deep into his green eyes, seeing myself reflected there in the glassy darkness. A few days ago this had been my dream. I would have traded a thousand lifetimes for this. Now I have to force myself not to spit in his face. I tell the muscles in my face to smile. "OK."

"No, Hallie!" Steve cries, and from behind me I can hear Sarah choking something similar.

I ignore them. "Untie them. Let them go. And I'll come with you. They won't tell anyone about Gabe or any of this. You can be Haze. I'll go with you."

"You will?" Alex breathes, his eyes roving over me in a way that almost makes me gag.

"Yes," I say, through a manufactured smile. "Only if you untie Sarah and Bethany and let everyone go."

Alex stands still for a moment, his eyes crawling over Steve and Sarah and Bethany, then he looks at me and smiles. It's such a sweet smile. A smile that doesn't look like it's ever seen anything bad. My eyes track down to his discarded jacket and I see what looks like a knife glinting halfway out of the pocket.

"OK," he says, his eyes wandering over my lips. "I'll let them go." His eyes snap to Steve then and he laughs a little. I don't trust him. I don't trust him as far as I can throw his crazy ass. "But remember, I have the lighter—and if you try anything..." he says, scooping up his jacket and sidling into it, stowing his hand in his pocket.

Steve is staring at me, his eyes red-ringed and anguished. I stare right back, willing him to trust me. To trust the half-formed idea brewing in my mind.

Alex walks stiffly over to Sarah, holding the lighter aloft in his hand as he unties the knots around her wrists. Sarah immediately pulls the gag from her mouth, "*Hallie*," she spits, but Steve gives her a look and she stops cold.

"I'm sorry, Sarah," I say, softly. "I am so, so sorry. You've always been there—always been around to protect me. I know that. And now I have to protect you. I have to do it because I love you. You're my family and my friend and I love you."

Tears swim down Sarah's face and I realize that I've hardly ever seen her cry—at least not sober. And the urge to see her again, to see her smiling and not hurt and happy courses through me. I have to do this. I have to make it right. Because even if I thought it before, even if he thought it, too—I am not like Alex. I am not the same. I can love and care even if I make mistakes and I'm shitty sometimes. It's not too late for me.

Alex sidles up to me, extending the crook of his arm like an old-fashioned man in an old movie. Trying not to cringe, I place my hand on his arm.

"After them," I say in what I hope is a smooth, formal voice, gesturing for the others to go ahead of us on deck. Steve unties Sarah and Bethany and they drape the woman between them. I try to give Steve a meaningful look. Hoping he understands what I'm about to do. Hoping he forgives me.

Alex and I follow close behind Steve and Sarah and Bethany, his arm starting to curl around me as we hit the stairs, his head burrowing into my shoulder like I'm the older one—like I'm not the one scared and young here. I wonder, with a shudder, how I could have found kinship with this man—how I could have confused his rambling persona with, what it turns out, was Steve's older brother. The real Haze. The Haze he killed.

Up ahead, I see the others rushing onto the deck, heading toward the gangplank. Steve hesitates at the top of the plank and I lock eyes with him, willing him to understand. Willing him to get to safety. His eyes burn into mine for a second and I remember his lips on my lips—his body pressed against mine. I want to go on a date and be walked home and feel his lips on mine gentle and slow and soft. I try to convey all of this to him as he stands shrouded by darkness. I want him to know me. But I don't wait for him to give me a sign. I can't. Instead I turn to Alex, his perfect face white in the darkness.

"Oh, Placid Girl," he moans, his arms snaking around my waist. "Oh, Placid Girl, I've been *waiting*." His voice throbs and aches and he leans toward me, his eyes lingering on my lips. Close up I see Steve and Gabriel and Alex all merging into one and the world folds and melts into itself. It's easier this way.

I press myself into the curve of his body, against the broad chest and bony hips and mantis legs. He moans and I wind my arms around, around, around him, his lips wandering toward mine. "Haze," I whisper and he shivers, delighted, as I thought, that I've used the name he wanted so much. "Haze... I wanted to tell you..."

He swoops down, his lips just brushing against mine and I press myself closer, my hands wandering, lingering, plunging into his pocket. He gasps and pulls me closer as my fingers wrap around the lighter, and then I rip myself away, sparking it to life.

"I wanted to tell you," I shout. "I'm not your fucking 'Placid Girl.'" I push the lighter into his chest and he roars, fire spreading faster than I would have thought across his shirt, singeing my fingers as I propel myself into the water, horrified. Falling backward, I watch him scream, fire licking his body as he bashes himself with his palms and screams and screams and screams. He tears the knife out of his pocket, but it's too late—I'm tumbling over the side of the boat. Water swallows me whole and sucks at my lungs and for a moment, a dark kind of moment, I relax and float down into the cold.

Arms close around me and for a second I struggle, thinking he's followed me. Then, as the arms tighten, I feel the familiarity of Steve's form and stop fighting, kicking up toward the surface beside him, black water rushing over my face and into my nose and mouth.

We break the surface, and I cough, Steve holding me above the water. My limbs are weak and my body convulses with shivers, heat pulsating on my cheeks and forehead. I cough again, extracting the last bit of seawater from my lungs, and start treading water, taking some of my weight off of Steve.

"Is he...?" I choke, as Steve starts towing us toward shore. The boat is wreathed with flames now, the fire spreading rapidly across the deck. I guess he wasn't kidding about the kerosene.

"I don't know," Steve says, his voice wracked with shivers, pulling us onto an outcropping of rocks about 100 feet from the burning boat. We crawl onto the dry stones, still warm from a day spent in the summer sun, and lie on our backs, panting. I reach out and close my fingers over Steve's. His hand lies limp for a minute and then he squeezes—hard.

Feet flap the pavement above us and I stiffen against Steve.

"Hallie!" Sarah yells. "Hallie! Fuck it, Hallie, where are you?"

I let go of Steve's hand and crawl toward Sarah, tripping as I go, my knees banging against the ground. But I don't care. I fling myself at Sarah, knocking her off balance and clinging to her, her familiar perfume filling my nose. "Fuck it, Sarah," I mutter into her snarled pink hair. "Just fuck it. You're OK."

She shoves me away then, her face twisted, tears running down her cheeks. "And you're fucking lucky, bitch. You're fucking *lucky* you're OK!"

I pull her toward me again. "I know. I'm sorry... I'm sorry for everything."

I feel her nod against my shoulder and hug her tighter. I know my apology is hardly enough, but now I have time to make it enough. I have more time than I could ever want. But I want it all. A siren wails in the distance, screaming louder and louder as it approaches. The police. The fire department. The real world is coming. And it's coming fast. I look around for Bethany, relieved to see her sitting on a rock, her head in her hands and looking rough, but alive. I try not to imagine what she's thinking right now.

"Hallie," Steve says, his voice insistent and sad.

I extricate myself from Sarah's embrace, but give her hand a squeeze as I turn to Steve.

"You have to go, don't you?"

He looks off into the distance, where the sirens are wailing and crying. He doesn't have much time before they pull up and start asking questions. He nods. "I have to. They'll send me back..."

I nod, looking at the glints of gold in his green eyes. There's so much to talk about. So much to say. But nothing comes to mind. Everything has fled from my brain.

"I'll see you again?"

He nods. "Yeah. You will."

I look back at Sarah, my friend and bandmate. I think of my dad, dark eyes in a dark car cutting through a dark night. My mom, a wilting paper flower in her Greta Garbo stupor. I think of my life, which always seemed on the verge of starting, now more than begun. Then I move toward Steve and press my lips to his. Awkward. But real.

The sirens are wailing closer now, red lights flashing above the warehouses and painting the night a garish kind of red. Steve gives me a crushing hug, and turns around, running into the night.

The night is full of noise and sound now, Lazarus burning and sinking into the river. I wonder if Alex made it out alive and shiver. I don't know if I hope he did or not. The glassy surface of the water winks and undulates with flames and my eyes hurt from staring. But I don't look away. I just put my arm around Sarah's shoulder, pulling her down next to Bethany, and cling to them both down among the rocks, watching as the vessel floats out to sea, an exploding star drifting out into the universe.

SIXTEEN

"You kept me in the holding cell in your heart, babe/ And I used my skeleton as a key,"

—"Lock Up And Go Down," *Masking Tape*, Haze

A lot of things happened after we watched the remains of Lazarus sinking into the river that I could tell you about—mostly the fact that after you throw a lighter at a self-proclaimed murderer, there's a lot of paperwork. And questions. There were definitely a lot of those.

My ass is asleep but my brain is not after hours of slumping in one of the police station's hard, plastic chairs, my eyes unfocused from staring at the same anti-drug posters until the words are just nonsense shapes. Sarah's brother just picked her up and Bethany has long since been carted away to the hospital; we watched as they loaded her into a red-light-washed ambulance, watched one white hand waving away into blackness. All of those images are repeating in my head like flicking ceiling fan blades.

"Hallie." My dad's voice and the squeaking of his sneakers on linoleum and his face under his knit cap all lined and tired swim into view. He pulls me up from my chair and wraps me against his sweater, wool scratching at my face and warm tears falling on my cheeks. His body vibrates like a small dog's and I realize mine is shaking, too. Shaking and relaxing even though I hadn't realized how rigid it had been. Corpse limbs, baby.

"Are you OK?" He asks my hair, his arms crushing my ribs.

I nod against his shoulder, blink, then blink again as another hand falls on my back. Mom stands beside him, all white and tumbled hair. Her eyes are red but alive and flashing and my dad opens his arms to let her in. And we all stand, arms and hair and tears all tangled and shaking. And I feel really young. And safe. And kind of OK with feeling young.

"Where is he?" The voice cracks open our knot of limbs and it seems as if all the ambient sounds of the police station—typing and phones and heavy footfalls—pause. The voice echoes and booms, rich and aggressive like yawning ceilings and deep, old wine.

I rub the tears from my eyes and shiver, the voice caught in my ears and brain and chest.

"Where is he? Where is Steven Quilty?" The voice comes from a slim man, thinning hair and green eyes and sharp features. I had expected him to be huge. Huge and sinister like that preacher in the movie with "love" and "hate" tattooed on his knuckles. He looks like Steve from the future, though. Steve beaten down and haunted and old.

The police officers who had handed us all blankets and hot drinks down by the water start to jangle out of their offices, but Steve's dad sees me before them and his eyes narrow—his eyes so much like Steve's but watery and cold—and pin me to the wall.

"You..." The word flies from his mouth wreathed in spittle and I shrink back into my dad as he advances toward me, suddenly taller and suddenly bigger and his fists clenching and unclenching at his sides. I check them for tattoos.

"Where is my son? What did you do to my son?" he says, rendering me a pinned specimen with his eyes—eyes that also don't seem to see me at all, only red. "Say something you little bitch..." My dad's fingers tighten on my shoulders until it hurts and he moves in front of me.

"You will get the *fuck* away from my daughter right now," he says in a voice that's cold and level—one I've never heard before.

The police swarm forward like beetles then and usher the preacher into a little room all buzzing with fluorescent lights, but he twists against them and stares at me and all of the anger and pain caught in his corneas buffet against me like getting too close to a campfire. Then he's gone. Hidden behind a metal door. Contained. And I wonder if I put my hand against the metal, if it would burn. And I wonder where Steve is now. And hope he's far away.

Later, after the papers and questions and scalding cups of tea proffered by hangdog-faced cops, my dad puts his arm around me as we head out into the morning-tinged night.

SEVENTEEN

"You can fall in love in the dark/ I know you can/ But you can also just fall asleep,"

—"Smaller Town," *Untitled*, My Friend's Band

"You can't," Sarah says sternly, fixing me with eyes ringed with blue liner, her freshly dyed hair falling all green around her face. "You can't puss out tonight."

I give her arm a squeeze and nod. "I won't. I promise."

I tip my head back and the stuffed marlin on the wall gazes blankly down at me as if to say, "I heard you. Now you have to keep your promise." I narrow my eyes at the fish and shrug further into my jean jacket. I can make a promise and still be nervous. It's not like you can control the freaked-out shakes with sheer force of mind. Still, I had been working on the song for months, tweaking and fixing and tinkering with the bare bones of what it had been before. Now it feels like all the notes are encoded into my DNA. It feels more like breathing now than it does gasping for air.

"And if you do puss out, it's not my fault," Sarah says with a fake sneer, punching me in the arm, but still kind of meaning it.

"No, I know," I laugh. "My failures are my fault from now on. Entirely my fault."

"Damn fucking right they are," Sarah half-roars, falling onto the ratty couch and readjusting her heels. She looks up at me with a shy kind of smile then and shrugs. "But, you know, if someone likes your crappy song better than mine, well, then, I'll say something nice about it, I promise. I won't be an asshole."

I raise an eyebrow.

Sarah sighs. "And it's not crappy. It's really good. It's, like, actually really good."

I smile, flopping back on the couch next to her, resting my head against the back, breathing in years of dust and spilled beer and other smells I'd rather not think too hard about.

Things aren't back to normal between me and Sarah. But that isn't necessarily a bad thing. We are more careful now. More careful with each other's feelings. Sure, it doesn't make for the most free-flowing of conversations, but it's like we're training ourselves to have a different kind of friendship—to be the kind of friends who don't just take what they need from each other. The kind that offer it up before it's asked of us.

"Bethany's coming, right?" I ask, looking up at the cracked ceiling, at the stars painted there and the tagged names and dates.

"Yeah, she'll be here. She says she has a surprise, too," Sarah says, pulling out her phone and checking her messages. "She'll be here soon."

Sarah has been spending a lot of time with Bethany lately and I try to be OK with it. She needs it. She needs to be around a woman like Bethany—a quiet woman who listens and cares. Someone less chaotic than her mother. And I think Bethany likes to feel needed—after everything that happened with Alex. After Steve went away. Bethany invites me over, too, but I've been spending a lot of time with my dad. When he showed up that night at the police station, tears streaming down his face, and wrapped his arms around me, it was like he had finally thawed—like one of those prehistoric men trapped in a glacier. He had grounded me, sure—for months—but all that time at home hadn't been so bad. We listened to music and went for drives and sat together quietly and watched his plants grow. I saw Mom a few times a week at her new apartment with the white walls and white carpeting and white furniture. They didn't get back together. Not everything works out. Not everything should.

I know Dad misses her, but it's also like the house has been exorcised. Like they are no longer possessing each other with their sadness. We are far from ghost-free, but at least we aren't as haunted.

"Should we go through the set list again?" I ask, looking around the room, nervousness starting to dance around in my stomach. I arrived extra early to set up our gear, so there isn't much to mess with.

"I can think of a more fun option," Sarah says with a smile, nudging me in the ribs.

"What?"

She juts her thumb toward the door. Steve stands there, an unlit cigarette hanging from the corner of his mouth, his hair falling all down his face, red plaid shirt drooping from his shoulders. He shifts from foot to foot and kind of lifts a hand awkwardly. Looks at me. Looks away.

I jump up. Take a few steps toward him. I haven't heard from him in months. No one has. There had just been one message right after he left: I will see you again. I promise. Then nothing. I tried to call him a few times, but his phone had been disconnected.

He stands in the doorframe now, kicking at the floor. The venue is empty save for us three—not even the bartender is here yet. Anger and nerves and other deep-down feelings war in my stomach, trying to clamber their way up to my throat, and both of us stare at the ground. Seconds smother each other.

Sarah rolls her eyes. "As fun as this standing awkwardly is, I'm going to go stand awkwardly on the balcony by *myself* for a bit." She stops right before she pulls open the door. "And no snarky reviews this time, OK pants ferret?"

Steve looks up and gives a wry smile. A small nod.

After she shimmies outside I turn to Steve, shove my hands in my pockets. "Do you want to... sit down?"

Steve nods, looking at his feet, then slowly shuffles over and sits next to me on the couch. He smells like cloves and cigarettes and fresh laundry.

I can't imagine where he's been, what he's been doing for the last few months. The cops hadn't found Alex. They'd dragged the river for weeks. They asked if Steve had been with us and we lied, saying he'd left before we got to the boat. It was a big story. A national story. The crazy musician who killed his bandmate and disappeared. Burned down a homemade barge in the river. There were tasteless jokes about hipsters on snarky blogs. But I had never seen a story by Steve Quilty—even though I checked that magazine he'd mentioned every month.

"So..." I say slowly, immediately feeling like an idiot who doesn't know how to use words. "Did you write that story?"

Steve shakes his head. "I'm sorry..."

"Don't be. I was more worried about you than anything else. Since we didn't hear anything..."

He looks at me, green eyes dark, "I should have called or something, but everything..."

I shake my head, tightening my grip. "Everything" indeed. Everything that had happened... I couldn't be mad about a few months of silence. I could only hope he'd been OK. And I had. I had spent a lot of nights looking out my window at his room, dark in the night, thinking of him existing somewhere out there, feeling my atoms connected to his and the tug that his absence left behind.

"So what happened?" I ask; the words feel like insufficient change. "What's... going on?"

"I talked to my dad," he says, looking at me finally.

"You did?" The image of the thin, sad preacher had whirred in my dreams for weeks afterwards.

He nods. "I called him the day I turned eighteen. I told him that I don't want to see him anymore. That I don't want him in my life. That he's poison." He takes a shaky breath. "But that I won't be hiding from him. I'll be living my life the way I want to be living it and he's to stay out of it."

"What did he say?"

Steve gives a weak little laugh. "Nothing nice. But he hasn't called me since."

I sigh, relieved. I hadn't seen much of the preacher since Steve left. Church went on as usual, as far as I could tell, but the lights were often out at the Quilty house, all of the lights—they went out as night fell while all the other houses winked in the darkness.

"I'm sorry I didn't call you after... I've been trying to sort everything else out," Steve says, picking at a hole in his jeans. He looks up with an echo of a smile. "I got a job at that magazine."

"That's great!" I fight the urge to hug him. He still hasn't touched me.

"As an intern," Steve says with a little nod, looking back at his jeans. "I'll be doing service industry shit to pay the bills. And, in the meantime, I'm writing a book. About Haze. I'm getting to know my brother," Steve looks at me then, his eyes heavy and sad and kind of hopeful.

My heart thuds. I still haven't quite been able to separate Haze the band from Alex. From the darkness there. I haven't listened to *Masking Tape* since the night on the boat and I don't know if I'll be able to again. Not in the same way at least. I know it's not fair to conflate Alex with Haze, but something deep in my stomach still does.

"What happened?" I ask, the question that I had been running over in my head for months burning up my lips. "With Gabriel? With... everything?"

"I talked to Bethany pretty soon after," Steve says, his voice heavy. "She told me that after that fight Gabriel and I had he broke up the band—Gabe told my father that he was right. That he should stay away from me. That he had ruined everything. I didn't even know about Haze then, and I wasn't supposed to. Until Bethany gave me that first tape. Let me know my brother. Or at least a part of him. But by then it was too late; Gabriel had already let me think he was dead."

"But he was coming back, right? That's what Alex said," I say, wincing as Steve's face gets darker and sadder at the mention of his cousin.

He nods. "Yeah. Bethany showed Gabriel my blog a few months ago. She showed him how much he meant to me—at least abstractly. Told him that I missed him. She convinced him that even if he didn't know it, he had made me stronger. Made me braver in the face of my dad and all his bullshit. So he wanted to come back, for me..."

"And Alex...?" I press tentatively.

Steve shakes his head. "He was wrong. They weren't kicking him out, really. They wanted him to produce—focus on what he was best at instead of just kind of sucking at bass. I guess that wasn't enough for him."

A tear rolls slowly down his cheek and I reach out to brush it away. He catches my hand and holds it in his lap, his body finally softening, relaxing. He rubs his thumb against the back of my hand and a soft sigh escapes his lips.

"Anyway, now I need to do this for Gabe. I need to tell his story."

I nod. "I'm sure he would have liked that."

I stare at Steve's profile for a few moments—his long nose, his freckles, his face, now unblemished by bruises. There's so much I want to say, but instead I put my arms around him and let him melt into me. I realize, my arms wrapped around this flesh and blood boy, that Haze was never a deity—or the monster that Alex made him. He wasn't some kind of all-seeing being who knew my heart. He was another flesh and blood boy. A sad boy with secrets and worries and scars—with a heart that beat like mine and Steve's. A boy who felt alone like everyone else. A boy who didn't need to feel so alone, at all, in the end.

Steve stirs in my arms and turns to face me, his lips parting slightly to reveal the chipped tooth, a tentative smile. "I missed you," he says, and kisses me quickly, tentatively. I kiss him back. I don't know what will happen with us. Where we'll end up, but we're both fumbling through and, at least for now, we can be bright spots for each other in the dark.

We sit, tangled together, talking on the couch, until the doorman arrives and the bartender and the soundman—and until Sarah bashes through the sliding doors and pulls us apart, muttering about sound check. I give Steve an apologetic smile and join Sarah on stage, this time stalking the lip of it instead of retreating back behind my drumkit.

The room seems to fill in fast-forward time, bursting at the seams with kids in leather and jean jackets and sweaters to fight off the fall chill. I can see Bethany in the back of the room, joining Steve on the couch. I wave and she flutters her fingers at me, her face melting into a smile. All of her bruises and scars have faded and her face is lovely and unlined, although her eyes are still sad.

Soon the lights dim and the room is full of the dull roar and din of 50 people all talking at once and laughing and coughing and sighing and shouting. Sarah taps the microphone once and then shouts into the chasm of bodies and blackness, "Hi, we're My Friend's Band and we've got some new songs for you!"

I can see Steve and Bethany whooping in the back, smiling.

"Our drummer here, Hallie, is gonna start off the night with an original song. What's it called, Hallie?"

My heart hammers my chest, but I step up to the microphone, anyway. I cough. "It's called 'Smaller Town,'" I mutter, my lips bumping into the mic, hair falling all around my face.

Sarah gives me a little push and I laugh, pulling away from the microphone and saying, more clearly, this time, "It's called 'Smaller Town' and it's dedicated to all of you—all of you kids out there waiting and waiting and waiting to escape. It's about what happens when you finally do."

The room erupts into cheers and screams and foot-stomps as I move behind the drumkit and lean into the mic. I lift my sticks and count off.

Sarah tears into her guitar then, and I scan the crowd, my breath quickening, my hands clenching. Bethany's face shines back at me. And Steve's. And so many dark faces and flickering smiles and flashing eyes. And then I'm singing. I'm singing and the words are tearing at my throat. The words are pouring out of me and into the crowd and tightening their grip around all the bodies bobbing and rolling like waves.

Kids climb onto the stage and sail off, all tangled limbs and pulsating flesh and everything is bright, bright, bright as I scan the crowd. Bright and singing and beautiful until my eye snags on something there among the frenzy and fray—a white, white face. A face that's so white it's unnatural. A face that stands stoic and still before disappearing behind the bobbing masses and spinning into darkness. Back into the shadows. Into black.

THANK YOU

I don't know why writing the acknowledgements to this book scares me so much—like, more than writing this book did. Probably because I have to be real, you know? This has been a... what's a less clichéd word for "journey"? It's been one of those. Over the years I've spent writing *Placid Girl* I have lived in more than one apartment with more than a few roommates, made and lost amazing friends, changed jobs, fallen in and out of love too many times to count: and all of that (ALL OF IT) played some part in writing this book. I've left notes to myself in each sentence. It's like listening to a specific song that reminds you of a certain time: Every time I read this book all the memories will come flooding back whenever I turn a page. Jesus. That's a terrifying thought, right? Moving on...

Let's just get right into thanking those who helped me DIY this thing: and those who helped inspire it. First, I have endless gratitude for my family: Pamela and Brian Ehrlich, Lara Ehrlich and Doug Riggs. Mom, thanks for telling me I COULD write a book all those years ago and helping me edit this one. Lara, thanks for the many edits and reads and wonderful insight you provided. Dad, thanks for listening to me whine. Doug, thanks for being an awesome, supportive bro-in-law. The only fault my family has is that they did not provide me with an adequate model when writing the less-than-awesome families in *Placid Girl*. Seriously, how can NONE of you be addicted to drugs or the least bit absentee?

On to the un-related editors. Kathleen Howard, thanks so much for agreeing to take on this edit. You did a glorious job and asked questions that needed to be asked. Stephanie Feuer, I am so glad I found my birthday twin in that MediaBistro writing class. Thanks for all the notes and margaritas at Otto's Shrunken Head. Tonya Kuper, thanks for being the best crit partner (and friend) I've never met (hopefully we'll fix that soon). Radhika Marya, Rae Paoletta, Eleane Paguaga, Robert Perlick-Molinari, Russ Marshalek and Jolie O'Dell—thanks for your feedback and the time you took to read my book in its various stages. You are all amazing. And owe you edits, song feedback and whiskey. Thanks also to Heather Gross, for your expert and amazing copyedits—I owe YOU big-time.

Thanks also to Annabel Gat for teaching me about astrology, Nimai Larson for all the roadtrips, Alexandra Comito and Randy Reiser for karaoking my pain away, Hanady Kader for letting me bitch, Meg Prossnitz for also letting me bitch, Heather Gross for ... you see where this is going, Annie Joya for more of the same and more, and Edie, my cat, for not much at all because she's kind of an asshole.

Ashley Halsey, thanks for being a friend since we were born and designing this whole book—you did a beautiful job. I'm glad our moms met in Mommy and Me otherwise I'd be screwed. Barbara Geoghegan, another childhood friend, thank you for helping me launch *All Ages Press*'s first zine, *Smaller Town*, and for being hilarious in general. Dave Otto, thanks for letting me put out your debut solo tape, *MOTEL TV*, and for making "Placid Girl" a real-life song. Brian Orth, thanks for helping me—even though you don't know me—make that whole scene with the police and the teeth make sense. You gave me the final piece that made this whole thing click.

Thanks also to the team at All The Write Notes for the support, MTV News for letting me write about YA whenever I please, the Binders Ladies, Valerie Tejeda for being interested and, of course, Caryn Rose for all the invaluable advice on doing this DIY. You are kind of my hero.

I'm likely missing someone so please write your name here if you feel left out: Thank you, _____.

I would be remiss, also, if I didn't thank some bands and music folks. Thanks to Shea Stadium for hosting my launch party and inspiring Hallie's hometown venue. Thanks also to Mystic Disc and Rich Freitas for inspiring Picture Disc—and providing me with all the music that helped me survive my teens. Thanks to all the bands I listened to while writing, including but not limited to: The So So Glos, Nobunny, Man Man, Portugal. The Man, Gap Dream, White Fence, Together Pangea, The Ramones, The Slits, FIDLAR, The Black Lips, King Tuff, The Aquadolls, Diarrhea Planet, Shark?, Big Ups, Handjob Academy, High Pop, Ty Segall, Strange Kids, Atlantic Thrills, The Lemons, Ariel Pink, Lorde, Tacocat, The Growlers, Mrs. Magician, Hunx & His Punx, Shannon & The Clams, The Unicorns, Slothrust, Father John Misty, Mac Demarco, Sky Ferreira, Le Butch-erettes, The Okmoniks, The Julie Ruin, The Donnas, Helium, PUJOL and the Yeah Yeah Yeahs. Yes, I like more bands than people. Whatever, look them all up and buy their merch. Don't ask to be on the list because you can totally afford $8.

Finally, thank YOU, whoever you are. You read this far. You haven't burned this book—yet. We are now best friends. Hit me up on Twitter if you don't want to yell at me and maybe we can make something someday, too: @BrennaEhrlich